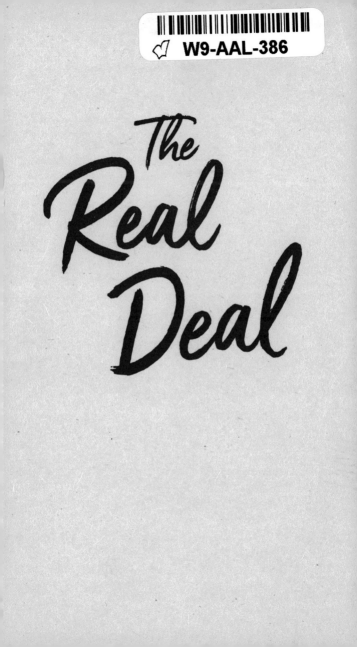

The
Real
Deal

The Real Deal

LAUREN BLAKELY

St. Martin's Paperbacks

This is a work of fiction. All of the characters, organizations, and events portrayed in this novel are either products of the author's imagination or are used fictitiously.

THE REAL DEAL

For information address St. Martin's Press, 175 Fifth Avenue, New York, NY 10010.

ISBN: 978-1-250-30961-7

Our books may be purchased in bulk for promotional, educational, or business use. Please contact your local bookseller or the Macmillan Corporate and Premium Sales Department at 1-800-221-7945, ext. 5442, or by e-mail at MacmillanSpecialMarkets@macmillan.com.

Printed in the United States of America

St. Martin's Griffin edition / July 2018
St. Martin's Paperbacks edition / April 2019

St. Martin's Paperbacks are published by St. Martin's Press, 175 Fifth Avenue, New York, NY 10010.

10 9 8 7 6 5 4 3 2 1

Thank you to Michelle and Eileen for believing
in this story from the start.

Prologue *Theo*

I can be anyone you want.

I can transform into the boss you're banging, your hot nerdy coworker who's *only* a friend, your best friend's brother you've had it bad for since he danced with you at prom way back when, the guy next door everyone adores since he mows your lawn, fixes your car, and repairs the sink. I can also pull off a fireman, a soldier, a cop, a billionaire, a rogue, an athlete, a pirate—yes, some women like to play with buried treasure—and the bad boy who will drive your family bananas.

How would you reach me if you needed me?

It's not that hard. You just have to know what you're looking for and plug the right terms into that trusty old search engine. You might even find me the next time you're hawking a Cuisinart or hunting for a used exercise bike on GigsForHire. There, you'll discover a menagerie of roles I can take on, characters I can play for you. The assignments rotate depending on the season, the needs, and what's in demand for weddings, reunions, Christmas parties, barbecues, and any other occasion where you might need a date.

I'm not an escort, a gigolo, or a stripper. This isn't about fluid exchange. My job is to become your arm candy, and you can pick the flavor you want. I've played them all.

And there's one role that outsells all the others. By far, the most popular part has been the bad boy.

Trust me when I say I wasn't your average bad boy. I was the goddamn dictionary definition, and this ad was my golden ticket:

☆ Heading Home and Need a Buffer? I'm Your Man

I'm a good-looking, 28-year-old ex-con. But I swear the time I got nabbed, it wasn't my fault. I was framed. I can play anywhere from 19 to 31, depending on if I shave or act like I love Ed Sheeran music. My most valuable possession is a scratched-up motorcycle one year younger than me that's painted like a snarling leopard. I'm a bartender and work till 2 a.m. at a dive bar. If you'd like to have me as your date for a wedding, reunion, or work soirée, I can pretend you picked me up when my shift ended and I banged you in the bathroom or that we're in a serious and committed relationship. Your choice.

I can do the following things at your request. . . .

1. Openly hit on other female guests, including your sister, any girlfriends, wives, or great-aunts. Moms aren't off-limits either.

2. Start provocative and/or incendiary discussions about politics and religion. Preferably both, and ideally on the most inflammatory topics of the day.

3. Propose to you in front of everyone. I'll even do it over the cake course and call you my sweet buttercream frosting girl.

4. Break up with you and then engage in a huge makeup lovefest involving (a) a ladder, (b) a megaphone, or (c) an announcement during a parade in your hometown. (Note: Public scenes aren't new to me. I know the drill.)

5. Start a fistfight with any of the other guests, including but not limited to your mom, your dad, your sister, your brother, and/or any of the guys. (Don't worry about me, sweetheart. That stint at County taught me excellent fight skills.)

6. Tell wild and risqué stories in front of everyone about our hot-as-sin sex life.

7. Leave in a huff with you over my shoulder in a fireman's carry, shouting, "It's time for me to go full caveman and take my woman home!"

If any of these skills meets your needs, please respond and book me for the event. A wide range of accents is available. My services are strictly platonic. Fee is negotiable and based on whether you opt for all the items or an à la carte offering. Also, payment is due upon completion, and only if you're thoroughly happy with my work. This is a 100% Satisfaction Guaranteed offer.

That's what the carefree city girl with the offbeat sense of humor and the big small-town heart hired me for. Since we hit it off from the start, it should have been the easiest gig in my life. Instead, it was the hardest job I ever had, once she pulled the big con on me.

Chapter One *April*

If the phone rings, it's bad news.

Why else would someone call?

Texts are for topics both easy and emotional, from *I'll meet you at Jane's at 7* to *I got the new gig* to *Don't let that jerk get you down.*

An email means a friend snagged a great deal on makeup, a massage, or a flight out of town, so she's forwarding it to you. It might also mean one of your crazy relatives is trying to pitch you on a blind date with her butcher.

But a ring-a-ling-ling? That means someone died, or someone's going to disappoint you so badly, it'll feel like death.

Fine, perhaps I'm being dramatic. Some might say I have a penchant for theatrics. But let's get real—who the hell uses the phone function anymore besides telemarketers or the insurance company? And, for the record, insurance companies don't call with good news.

Point proved.

When Xavier's high-cheekboned, so-pretty-I-covet-it face flashes on my phone, my Spidey-senses flare.

I adjust the strap on my fifty-ton bag of paint, makeup, and brushes. It's digging into my shoulder, but that's what it does. It dents me daily as I walk around Manhattan. I slide a finger across the screen and answer. "You're in prison and you need me to post bail?"

Xavier's laughter rings bright in my ear. "Love, you know *you'd* be the last person I'd call. You never have enough cash on hand for that."

"Not true. I always carry at least two hundred dollars." I lower my sunglasses over my eyes and weave through the afternoon crowds on Seventh Avenue. "Usually in small bills, though. In case I need to slip any in the G-strings of hot men at strip clubs. Oh, look. There's the *Magic Mike* bar. Gotta go make it rain for some hotties. But seriously. What's up, handsome? Are you all right? You never call unless you're bemoaning the loss of a hot date."

Okay, fine. I've spoken to my good friend a few times on the phone, but we always make arrangements for a call via text first. See? My point still stands.

A loudspeaker crackles from his side of the call. "Attention in the boarding area. We're about to begin boarding for Flight 405 to London."

All the air leaks out of me as I stop in my tracks outside a wig shop in the Village. A mannequin sporting a purple bob stares at me.

"April, I have good news and bad news." Xavier's tone is cheery. It's the official tone one adopts when delivering news that will feel terribly devastating to the recipient. Three, two, one, go: "The good news is I landed a last-minute opportunity and I'm heading to London for a photo shoot for the new Timeless Watch."

His news is devastating to me, but even so, I shriek. A

woman in a sharp gray suit raises an eyebrow as she marches past. "That's amazing!" I can't mask my excitement even if I would like to swat him with a makeup brush for leaving me high and dry at the worst possible time.

"The bad news—"

"You can't be my date at the family reunion," I say because, yes, this is horrible. But even if I'm out the hottest piece of arm candy, I'd be a total doucheberry if I wasn't excited for this huge opportunity. Generally, I strive to avoid being a doucheberry, a douchecanoe, or douchenozzle. And honestly, if there are other types of douches one can be, I don't want to be them either. "This is amazing for you. You're on the cusp of breaking into the big time."

"Do you really think this could be my big break?"

I nod resolutely. "Of course. The Timeless shoot is huge. It's only the hottest watchmaker in the world. Have you ever seen a guy wear one of those watches? They basically send all women into heat."

He laughs. "Some men, too."

"There's just something ridiculously sexy about a man wearing a big fancy wristwatch."

I resume my path to the subway, staring longingly at the cabs, Lyfts, and Ubers zipping by. I want to hail a taxi or order up a car stat, but I remind myself that all this damn walking with my makeup and paint is akin to a CrossFit workout. Those people who toss tires in parking lots in suburbia? *Pssh.* I'll show them. Try trudging through Manhattan with a bag full of body paint and hordes of harried New Yorkers to battle your way through. I'm the baddest badass in all of Fitnesslandia. I don't need a stinking gym membership.

"And now I'll be the man wearing the big fancy

wristwatch in the ads. I'm so excited about this." Xavier lets out a small scream of his own, then reins it in. "My group is about to board. Listen, you have to know I was so looking forward to playing your new boyfriend in front of Aunt Jeanie, Cousin Katie, and—who's the other one who fancies herself a matchmaker?"

"My sister, Xavier. My sister, Tess."

"Right. Her. I was looking forward to pretending to be your man. It would have been a true and challenging test for me."

"Thanks," I say dryly.

"You know what I mean, love."

"I do, and now I just have to find someone else," I say, letting some of my frustration trickle into my voice.

The thing is, I can't just suck this up and go dateless to the Hamilton Family Reunion, which comes complete with a day at the amusement park, a Hula-Hooping contest, lawn bowling, and Lord only knows what additional activities my parents have planned. Probably rock climbing, rope swinging, necklace beading, strawberry picking, and T-shirt tie-dyeing.

I'd rather take a cruise in the Arctic with ten thousand time-share salesmen than go solo to this extravaganza. My sister is already chomping at the bit to set me up.

"Are you seeing someone?" she asked in an email last week. "If not, I can ask Mark to be your scavenger hunt partner at the reunion. He's fabulous, and guess what? He's added tri-tip steak to the menu. It tastes absolutely amazing with pesto sauce. You must try it. Mark can tell you all about how the pesto is made."

Mark runs the local sandwich shop in my hometown. He's nice, and exceedingly boring.

"I'm not going to leave you in the lurch," Xavier says as the tinny speaker crackles once more in the background, alerting everyone in the terminal—and possibly the entire five-mile radius of Kennedy Airport, judging from the decibels—that Boarding Group B needs to get its collective ass on the plane.

"Did you put out a casting call for me?" I joke as I near the subway entrance. This is the toughest obstacle course portion of today's Manhattan CrossFit workout—successfully navigating the steps at the Christopher Street entrance. But I've mastered it. Just try to swing a dumbbell over your head as well as I can *Frogger* it down these steps, CrossFitters.

"No. *Better.* A good friend of mine can do it. He's available, and interested. He works next door. He tends bar."

"Code for 'he acts'?"

"Aren't we all acting all the time?"

Except for me. I might run with the same crowd as actors and models, but I don't pretend to be someone else. Instead, I paint them so *they* can become someone else—a leopard, a goddess, a swan, a woman in gold, a playing card, a nest with a baby bird in it. My hands are slicked with peach-orange and midnight-black from the cheetah I painted this afternoon on a fit, toned track star for a magazine spread advertising sneakers.

"Yes, he's an actor, and wait till you hear his voice," Xavier tells me amid the hustle and bustle of the boarding. "You might want to mate with it. I know I do, but lucky for you, he's straight, so he won't have to act as much as I would. You'll have to pay, though."

I don't bat an eye.

What choice do I have at this point? I need a date for the reunion like a bowl of cereal needs milk. Besides, a guy with a sexy voice could work as my reunion date if he can make it believable that we're a thing. Though, honestly,

what I really need is a big vial of Stop Trying to Set Me
Up with Men Who Are Wrong for Me formula to waft
under the noses of the wannabe matchmakers in my family. Which is pretty much every single person in my family.
But the apothecary I usually go to is fresh out of any
potions to calm the overactive matchmakers in the Hamilton clan. Hence, my quest for a man who can be my buffer.
If Mr. Phone Sex Operator is that guy, bring him on.
"Name and number, please."

"His name is Theo." He rattles off his phone number,
and I repeat it back instantly, since I'm good with remembering numbers. "But I'll text you his info in five minutes
just so you have it. I won't leave you hanging. Hanging is
for Christmas tree ornaments and other assorted unmen-
tionable items, not lovely girls with flawless skin."

I roll my eyes and laugh. "You have perfect skin, too,
since you're just as religious as I am about your lotions and
potions. Have fun in London. Wow them at Timeless. Make
them love you like a teenager loves her iPhone."

"When I'm through, it'll be more like how a teen wor-
ships selfies."

"I have no doubt."

I end the call and heave the sigh I've been holding in.
I'm beyond happy for him. Truly, I am. But we're all a little
selfish, aren't we? And the selfish part of me wishes my
friend were still playing the part of my date.

But really, my greatest wish is to *not* show up at my
parents' home without a plus-one. The women will smell
blood. They'll swarm me. I'm the fresh meat for the matchmaking grill. I'm one of the last single women left standing, and this single woman needs to stay standing.

I'm happy being single, and that seems to surprise
my family. They're not traditional or even old-fashioned.

They're just old-school. They're "small-town" and love it, and they want me to love that lifestyle, too.

Xavier would have been perfect as a temporary boyfriend. A true gentleman, he's the darling of parents, and mine would figure once and for all that I hadn't landed a dud. I can only hope his friend will be as good. I hoof it down the steps, and then I sprint ahead of a slinky gal in a pink halter top, swipe my subway card, push through the turnstile, and make it to the platform in two minutes flat, and without once knocking a single other person with my bag.

I peer down the tunnel to see if the train is coming, when my phone buzzes from my pocket.

I'm expecting Xavier to deliver a phone number.

But it's not a phone number that I get. It's a link, and a note:

> **Xman:** This is the first one I grabbed. His info is here. Gotta go. xoxo

Once I click and read, a strange little thrill zips through me. I don't think I want a gentleman anymore. No, I don't want a nice guy to take home to the parents at all.

I want *this* one.

Chapter Two *Theo*

"Please don't laugh."

Whenever someone says those three words, you're almost guaranteed to chuckle. Chances are the person is going to tell a ridiculous tale that makes him or her seem like a complete fool. You'll want to guffaw.

But I've mastered the art of giving people what they want, and the lady at the bar wants my straight face.

"I won't laugh, I promise," I tell the woman with red glasses and shoulder-length, TV-anchor-style black hair. Lori is dining solo today. She dines solo most days. She considers me a confidant.

"This is going to be a weird request," she warns.

I highly doubt her request will be weird to me. "I can handle it."

She takes a deep breath, then exhales. "Can you make sure—like, absolutely positive—that the nachos won't be steamed?"

Who the hell steams nachos? "You have my word the nachos you just ordered won't be steamed. And the gin and tonic won't be toasted either." My face is deadly serious, because I do know how to act.

She clasps her hand to her chest. "Thank God, Theo. Because that happened to me the other night. It was awful."

As I reach for the gin, I fix my gaze on her. "Tell me everything about the steamed-nacho debacle."

People tell me things. They always have. It's not just because I'm a bartender. It's that I have brown eyes, too. I've studied this phenomenon. People with brown eyes are more likely to be considered trustworthy.

Ironic, isn't it?

This trust has nothing to do with whether I'll spill a secret or not. Spoiler alert—I'm a vault. The trust issue has to do with the fact that having brown eyes also means you're more likely to have lips that turn up more frequently at the corners. Translation—the eyes come in a safe face, so you can trust me with your nacho secrets. Evidently, a smile is the number one social lubricant.

Lori drums her chipped peach fingernails along the edge of the bar. "I went to my favorite taco shop and I ordered the mini nachos, like I always do. Only, they brought me the full-size plate instead," she says as she eyes the drink longingly. She's on the fast track to becoming a regular here. "But do you know what the waitress did when I pointed it out?"

My phone vibrates in my jeans pocket. I grip the gin bottle tighter, because my fingers itch to check my messages. "What did she do?" I ask as I finish pouring the gin. I grab a napkin and set it in front of her, then place the glass on it. I can check the message later.

"They took the plate back, scraped off half the nachos, stuffed the plate in the microwave, and zapped it. *To rewarm it*," Lori says, taking her time with each awful word.

My nose crinkles. I swallow harshly. "And you not only had steamed and soggy nachos. You had hot sour cream as well." I shake my head, disgusted with how her food was treated.

"The guacamole was broiling. It had steam curling off it."

That actually sounds quite foul, especially because the image of a steaming pile of guacamole has now been planted in my brain. I shudder. She smiles so damn wide that her eyes crinkle behind her glasses. It's sweet, really. It makes me wonder if she has anyone to talk to besides the guy who fixes her drinks and takes her orders for apps. She usually doesn't even finish her drink when she comes here. I've often wondered if she wants me to join her on the other side, grab a stool, and chow down.

Sometimes I'm tempted. She seems like she needs someone, and she's nice enough. But I know what happens when you start opening up to someone. They let you down. Some of them stab you in the back. "Let me get you the best nachos you've ever had."

I head to the kitchen and turn in the order, and then I check my watch. I have a five-minute break, so I push open the heavy, rusted door that drops me into the alley behind the Two A.M. Club. It's six in the evening. One of the bus-boys leans against the wall, one foot parked behind him on the bricks, a cigarette dangling limply from his lips.

He gives me the barest of nods.

I do the same, then walk a few feet away. I unlock my screen with ten digits. Four digits are never enough. Once I click on my notification, my shoulders sag. Turns out the buzzing in my back pocket was the *sorry sucker* kind. You know how you'll get excited for an email, and then it's just a store with a sale, a news site with a new subscription offer, or a deal on Viagra. I don't need any little blue pills, thank you very much.

The buzz is for a notification that my credit card bill is due in three days. No shit, Visa. Tell me something I don't know.

I'd been hoping it was an email from GigsForHire, a notification that I'd been contacted by a potential customer.

I log into the site anyway. It's become an addiction. Most of the time it disappoints, because scoring a gig from here comes with the same odds as a slot machine payoff. You don't get three cherries terribly often, but when you do, man, they add up to a delicious treat.

Looks like someone viewed my ad, but there are no replies. On his way to the airport, Xavier called and told me he had a sure thing. What's odd, though, is he said I'd be a replacement for *him*. I love the dude, but we're hardly interchangeable, and I'd never peg my buddy as the bad boy. But that's what his friend needs, he told me when he asked if I could fill in for him at a family reunion.

"I can't let her down, but I can't let this job go. Any chance you could fill in for me for five days?"

"Five days," I'd said, surprised. Most gigs don't last that long. "I have the weekend off, and if the pay is right, I can swap shifts for the rest."

"Perfect. She's a darling, and you're the only one I know who can cover in a pinch."

"But she knows there's a fee?"

"Did you think I was going out of the goodness of my heart? April took a vow to tell me for the rest of my life if my jeans ever make me look fat. I'll be sure to let her know you require old-fashioned greenbacks."

"Tell me what she wants."

"If I know April, she'll go bananas for the ex-con ad. It's hilarious. Let me show her that one, 'kay?"

With a name like April, you'd figure she'd want the guy

next door. But hell, maybe she's the good girl who likes the black sheep.

I've slipped into that skin for Thanksgiving dinners, wedding dates, even bat mitzvahs. I've slipped into other roles, too. I've been a salesman, a pimp, a swindled fool, a beleaguered boyfriend. It's all in the eyes, and in the heart that you put into the role.

But the slot machine idles quietly as my break ends. No payouts come. Maybe April has cold feet. Perhaps she decided to try it solo rather than shell out for a rent-a-date.

I head inside as the busboy sucks the last ember of his cigarette. The nachos are ready. I grab the plate, spoon some extra guacamole on, and serve it to Lori.

She groans happily and dives in, her hand like a pelican swooping to pluck a fish from the sea.

"They're perfect," she declares, and I smile at her. It reaches my eyes. The eyes she trusts.

The thing is, I actually give a shit that she likes her nachos. People might be easy to read, and even easier to play, but I always cared too much.

Everyone has an Achilles' heel. That's mine.

That's why when my phone buzzes again a little later, I find a way to answer it immediately. I like what I see in my in-box.

Chapter Three *April*

From: Sweet Buttercream Frosting
To: Satisfaction Guaranteed
Re: Need a buffer?

Banged in a bathroom is how we met for sure. But do we tell that to everyone?

April

* * *

Every day, human behavior amazes me a little more.

I've just learned that a human hamster wheel is a thing, and it's for sale, used.

How is this possible? Who needs a human hamster wheel? I need it like I need an emu.

Scratch that. Emus are adorable. I want one someday. The vet around the corner from my building has a baby emu, and it's delightful to see the ostrich-like bird clucking around the office every time I walk by. He's always trying to flirt with the cats in the waiting room, to no avail.

As I twirl in the black leather barber chair, I peer more closely at the photo that accompanies the "Hamster Wheel for Sale" ad on GigsForHire. A man—dressed in strangely normal fashion, with a red Hawaiian shirt, jeans, sneakers, and glasses—climbs along the wheel, spinning it round and round.

Why? Why on earth is he doing this? I can't process this solo anymore.

"You have to put down your brush and come see this!" I shout across the empty salon to my friend Claire. She's in the back, sanitizing hairbrushes. If the looks she styles on anyone and everyone from moms to models to well-groomed men don't make her the best in Brooklyn, then her commitment to cleanliness certainly does. I swivel the chair at her booth, where I'm parked, waiting for her to finish for the evening.

What I'm really waiting for, though, is a reply.

My stomach has officially twisted in knots, so I'm entertaining myself with as many diversions as I can find. A couple hours after I saw the ad, I sent an inquiry to Xavier's friend. Now I'm in the limbo of waiting for a reply. Sometimes it sucks to want something.

Claire tromps over to me, her black knee-high boots *click-clack*ing like they're drilling holes in the floor.

I show her the man-size hamster wheel. "Can we get one, Mommy, someday, pretty please?"

As she peers at the image, her kohl-lined navy blue eyes widen to saucers. "That's a hamster wheel."

"I want one terribly."

"Let's put it on your birthday wish list, then."

I whisper conspiratorially, though it's only the two of

us. "I feel like there's probably some sordid sexual history to this wheel. Like, the dirtiest deeds must occur on this wheel."

She grabs the back of my chair and twirls me around so I face the mirror. It's the end of the day, and my hair is a little wild from the humidity. The sun has brought out the spray of freckles that travel across the bridge of my nose, but I'm not one of those freckles-hating girls. Better to embrace them than hide them. Claire arches an eyebrow at my reflection. "Why else would someone even have a hamster wheel?"

"Exactly. See? You get me. You understand the world. But why is he selling the fifty pounds of shredded newspaper, too?" I hover my finger over the screen, so she can't possibly miss the room full of ripped-up news headlines covering the floor by the wheel. The man truly is imitating a small rodent on that spinning wheel. "Even if I had a hamster wheel fetish, I'd completely say no to taking a spin on this one, on account of the shredded newspaper."

"How do you know that? If you had a hamster wheel fetish, you might very well like shredded newspaper."

I tap my chin, as though deeply considering the possibility. I shake my head back and forth, my blond curls going whip fast. "I don't think so. I'm not a fan of newsprint."

She moves to straighten the hair sprays on her booth counter. I pop up, joining her, because this passes the time. As I push an aerosol can against the wall, I glance up at the clock. As I rearrange some gel, I sneak a peek at my watch.

Claire gives me a sharp-eyed stare. "I know what you're doing."

"What am I doing?" I return her gaze with my best

doe-eyed look. It's a look I've mastered—big green eyes with brown flecks in them aid my efforts.

"You're worrying." She taps my temple. "You're wondering."

"And what am I wondering about?"

"If this is crazy. If you should do it. If it's the nuttiest thing you've ever done. Yet you want it badly."

"Shut up, mind reader."

She laughs. "Yes. I can see right into your skull. And he'll reply. Remember, he wants the gig."

"Do you think he'll reply *soon*?"

Strangely, nerves flutter in my chest, flapping dangerous wings against my rib cage. I'm not entirely sure why I'm the nervous one. I'm not the loon who posted the ad. No, I'm just the loon answering it, which I did about twenty minutes ago. Fine, I replied nineteen minutes and forty-seven seconds ago, but who's counting. Just me, the fidgety hummingbird jacked up on extra sugar water.

Claire pats my shoulder. "Xavier wouldn't hook you up with a flake. He's totally reliable. The guy is probably busy serving appletinis to socialites."

"At his dive bar? Doubtful." I sort the sprays and gels.

"Regardless, he'll respond. This is what he does. Kind of a cool little job, if you ask me."

I shrug noncommittally. "This would be so much easier if Tom would help me."

"You know I love you, but my boyfriend is not on loan."

I huff. "Please. I'm not stealing your man. I meant, if he would help me with a friend. Why doesn't he have any single men he can lend me? A Xavier replacement."

"No one gets that much time off work. Xavier was a rarity, and look what happened to him. He snagged a gig."

"It's either a gig or a significant other. I was going to ask Cole," I say, naming a talent agent friend of ours, "but he started dating someone a few weeks ago, so he's off the market. And Anders has a conference in Miami. I've combed through the list of last-minute replacements. Pickings are slim to nil."

Claire tucks a bottle of hair spray into a drawer. "See? It's better to hire someone than to ask for a favor." Her boyfriend is a world-class photographer, and he helped me get one of my biggest breaks. I, in turn, helped him with something even bigger: I introduced him to my best friend, and now they're madly in love, and they can't keep their hands off each other. Yep, it's love and sex, and sex and love, the lucky devils. Plus, he's not an emotional leech. Bonus points for that. "Besides, your Satisfaction Guaranteed man will totally work out." She taps her breastbone. "I can feel it."

Is it odd that I already want him to say yes? I don't even know this guy, but I swear his ad spoke to me. I don't mean in a cheesy, over-the-top romantic way. It spoke to my funny bone, and that's the biggest bone in my body.

I like to laugh. I like twisted, weird things. I like dares and wild days and nights. And I like men my family would never ever set me up with. That's all they seem to want to do, though I understand why. If I were them, I'd probably worry about my ability to attract a decent man, too. It's not exactly like I have a good track record.

Cough, cough, my ex-boyfriend Landon.

Be that as it may, I desperately need a perfect shield. Consider the emails they've sent in the last few days.

From: Aunt Jeanie
To: April

Can't wait to see you at the reunion! And I absolutely, positively can't wait to bring you to the town square to meet Linus. He's a mortgage banker, and he likes to find the best possible interest rate deals and steals and to go boating on weekends on the wide, open waters. Doesn't he sound perfect for you??? How about I set the two of you up on a morning coffee date? You can have cinnamon rolls at FlourChild!

Xoxo
Jeanie

Look, Linus might be perfectly decent. And who wouldn't want a great deal on an interest rate? That has to rank high on the list of things I'd need when adulting. But dating isn't the place for adulting, is it? Besides, if Aunt Jeanie's best sales pitch involves interest rates, I fear Linus would be dreadfully dull.

My mother is convinced, though, that *Calvin* is just who I need. Two days ago, she dropped this little hint.

From: Mom
To: April

Only a few more days! Can you hear the cat clock in the hallway ticking all the way in Manhattan? It's the sound of my excitement over seeing my little girl. I'm planning the most amazing scavenger hunt, and I need my scavenger hunt assistant. Plus, did you know Calvin likes scavenger hunts, too? You remember him. He runs the hardware store. The man knows his tools, if you know what I mean. What do you say about a little date? It's so much better to meet someone through a match than through those crazy online sites the kids today are using, DON'T YOU THINK?

(THAT WAS SHOUTY CAPS. Was that proper use of shouty caps? Regardless, love and hugs!)

Your mom

Meanwhile, Jeanie's daughter, my cousin Katie, who's a few years older than me, messaged me on Facebook to tell me the guy who walks her poodles has a great behind. I love a good ass as much as the next girl, but I worry a tad when the rear end is the only feature highlighted on his calling card. Then there's my sister. She texted me yesterday.

> **Tess:** Yoohoo! Cory and I found someone for you! He's one of our regular customers, and I keep telling Cory that this guy is perfect for you. He has a beard. Beards are in, right? That's what I hear, at least. Can't wait to see you. Please bring entertaining stories. Lord knows, I need them.

That's why I'm not going solo. I'll be poked and prodded and paraded around all week long. It's not that I don't want to date the guys from my hometown of Wistful. It's just that I don't want to date the guys from my hometown.

I don't want to move back there. And just because everyone in my family and their sister, cousin, aunt, uncle, friend, barber, butcher, and candlestick maker has met and married their significant other in Wistful doesn't mean I will want to.

Perhaps it's true that I haven't necessarily had better luck in Manhattan either, but sometimes it's really hard to tell that the sharp-dressed businessman you're dating still lives in his parents' basement. In *Jersey*. Fine, fine. We were always meeting suspiciously close to the Port Authority, and *maybe* that should have been the tip-off that he had zero ambition. But in my defense, Brody the Basement Dweller was a surprisingly excellent kisser, and that covers up all manner of sins.

Besides, ever since Landon the Liar, I've been living the dating-free life. Dating is a distraction I can't afford right now.

Claire twists the cord on her Dyson Supersonic hair dryer, coiling it up. "Maybe you should just skip the reunion."

I return to the barber chair. "They're actually strangely fun. Plus, it would just be wrong to bail."

She pats my shoulder again. "You have a conscience. They're not totally out of style yet."

"They will be someday."

My phone buzzes, and a flurry of hope wells up in me. I want the madness of a game of pretend. I want to hear from Xavier's replacement. I want the man who wrote that absolutely absurd ad to be my arm candy.

That's because my bigger wish is to remain focused on my career, and only my career. I have a huge chance in front of me to win the body-painting contract for the next *Sporting World* swimsuit issue. It's one of the most prestigious gigs in my unusual line of work, and if I get it, I can't risk bringing anything less than my A game to the table.

No strings attached to this girl.

But my family doesn't entirely understand my career. They can't comprehend why I like living in the city rather than a sleepy coastal town in Connecticut. I suspect they try to set me up, thinking they can lure me back home that way. If I show up single to the reunion, I'm grist for the local matchmaking mill. Telling them I'm on a dating diet won't fly. It'll raise too many questions about why that might be—questions I don't want to answer. A piece of arm candy is the easiest way for me to make it through the event unscathed, ready to zip back into Manhattan and—knock wood—land the big magazine gig.

When I slide open the screen, it's not an email about interest rates or scavenger hunts. It's *the* email I want.

From: Satisfaction Guaranteed
To: Sweet Buttercream Frosting
Re: My buffering skills are excellent.

Tell them we banged in a bathroom only if they seem insanely jealous of our fictional sex life. Wait. Better yet. Just wink, and leave the bathroom during the reunion with tousled hair. The JBF kind.

My stomach swoops at those three letters, knowing what they stand for: *just been fucked.* Sex isn't even on the table. His services are platonic. But damn, his role-playing is electric and unusually alluring. I reply quickly.

From: Sweet Buttercream Frosting
To: Satisfaction Guaranteed
Re: Hope your telling-a-tall-tale skills are top notch, too

If we're talking about nailing already, seems we should nail down our story. Meet up in person? Tomorrow? Prospect Park? My friends will be with me. One of them is roughly the size of a barge.

From: Satisfaction Guaranteed
To: Sweet Buttercream Frosting
Re: The Beauty and the Beast reference is
not lost on me

Message received loud and clear. Naturally, it makes
sense that you want to be sure I'm not going to whisk
you away forever on my snarling leopard.

From: Sweet Buttercream Frosting
To: Satisfaction Guaranteed
Re: And I thought snarling leopard was the
design of your motorcycle all this time

You do realize that sounds ridiculously dirty?

From: Satisfaction Guaranteed
To: Sweet Buttercream Frosting
Re: Yes

I do realize that.

We make a date. A strictly platonic one. . . .

Chapter Four *Theo*

We might be the Two A.M. Club, but plenty of patrons do their diving into liquor at ten in the morning, and that's why we open early.

The next day, before my make-sure-he's-not-a-serial-killer meeting, I head to the bar to punch in. A few hours gets me a few dollars closer. I clean and serve and pour and mix, and when I see a familiar profile in the doorway, I nearly duck, turn around, and try to sneak the hell out of here.

But running will get me nowhere. Addison has been here before. She'll find me because she wants something. Somebody always wants something, even when you think you're in the clear.

Addison slinks up to the bar, smooths a hand over her gray skirt, and arranges herself neatly on a cracked red barstool. I want to cut to the chase, to ask her what she wants. But she walked in. She can lay down her cards. I learned that lesson through no fault of my own: Don't be the first to reveal your hand. Always be the one willing to walk away.

I spin a coaster in front of her, then slap my hand on it. "What can I get you, miss?" I ask, treating her like anyone else. Don't let on she's a thorn in my side.

She hums. "Is your beer on tap good?"

"You can't go wrong with a pale ale," I tell her, and she flashes a grin that reaches her eyes. In the movies, she'd have ice blue irises and wintry blond hair slicked back and cinched tight. A black dress painted on. In real life, she's prettier now than when I knew her before. Round face, aqua eyes, brown hair.

"Well, doesn't that just sound delightful," she says in a southern accent.

C'mon, life. Throw some stereotypes at me. Give her a Russian accent and a guy with a scarred eye and broken nose as her heavy. What's the fun in this lack of caricature? But Addison's here solo. She does her own collecting.

"What about your wine, though? Any chance it can make up for a bad taste in your mouth?"

I grab a crinkled sheet of paper and hand the rudimentary wine list to her, ignoring her last comment. "We're not really known for wine. We have a few. Are you looking for white or red?"

She laughs. "I think you know that's not what I'm looking for, Theo."

Yeah, I know what she's looking for. It has a lot of zeros attached to it. She glides her finger down the list, clucking at each vintage like it's dog shit. Honestly, most are.

She lifts her face and stares at me, her gaze hard now, her lips a thin line. Gone is the camaraderie I knew when she was part of our crew. "I was hoping for one that's nine years old." She speaks tightly. "Is there any chance at all I'd find something like that in here?"

I stare right back at her. "I'm working on it. I'll get what you want."

She drops the list. It skids across the bar. She doesn't even watch it flutter to the floor. I bend to pick it up. When I meet her gaze again, her eyes radiate frustration. A part of me understands this woman deeply—she feels like she was screwed over, and she wants what's hers. "How long is this little cat-and-mouse game going to go on, Theo? It's not that complicated. I want what you owe me. Because it's mine. Do you think it's unreasonable for me to want what belongs to me?"

I scrub a hand over the back of my neck. "No," I answer truthfully. "It's not unreasonable."

"Of course it's not. I have bills to pay, too. Just like you do. And wouldn't you like to stop seeing me show up around here?"

I snort. "Hell yeah."

She makes a rolling gesture with her hands. "Then let's try to move this along."

I curl my hands around the bar, lean closer to her. "I'm working on it. Like I told you last time. And a minute ago. I'll take care of it."

"I'm running out of patience." She points to her watch. "You don't want me to contact your brother, do you?"

My spine straightens. That's precisely what I don't want. I'm about to answer her, but her voice rises. "After all, he has what he wants in his new woman. So I should get what I want, don't you think?"

"Addison," I say, softening, because I *get* that she feels burned, "I promise you'll get it soon."

A huge grin crosses her face. "Good. That's what I like

to hear. Let's be friends again. How about that delightful pale ale?"

"Coming right up." I pour and slide it to her. She takes a thirsty gulp, smacks her lips, and pronounces it "delicious."

A few minutes later, she tosses some bills my way. "I look forward to you honoring your side of the deal. Then we can put the past behind us. Wouldn't that be great?"

"Sure would," I say in the understatement of the year. It would be the best thing ever.

She leaves, and once the door swings shut, I flip her the bird. No one sees me do it, and it does absolutely nothing to change the situation, but it lets me blow off much-needed steam.

Another customer waltzes in, so I say hello, and before he even sits down, I pour a glass for the grizzled old dude who brings his e-reader here every day so he can read and drink, and drink and read. He thanks me, clicks open his book, and begins filling the gas tank.

I drag a hand through my hair, push on the door to the kitchen, and look at the clock. One more hour, and then maybe I'll be that much closer to getting the past off my back.

When I clock out and head for the park, anticipation runs through my veins like a good buzz on a night out. A reunion booking could be my way out of trouble. A five-day gig might bring me very close to the finish line.

Along the way, I stop in front of a dry cleaner, check my reflection in the plateglass shop window, and reckon that I look the part April wants: dark jeans, motorcycle boots, and well-worn T-shirt that shows off the ink on my arms. Tribal bands, a sunburst, and a compass. I haven't shaved in two days, and my stubble is rough. If she wanted clean-cut and business attire, I'd have covered up the tats with a crisp white shirt and a fine silk tie, then slid a blade across my jaw in the A.M. If she wanted sophisticated, I'd have given her the smooth, James Bond voice to boot. She could have me as a country boy, even, in a pair of steel-toed cowboy boots and with the drawl to match.

But April wants the guy who might have screwed her in the restroom of a bar.

She wants gravel and sandpaper, ink and danger, shades and leather.

The more you give someone what they want, the more you get in return.

When I reach the park, I head to the Terrace Bridge. She's not here, but I'm early, since I like to get a read on any and every situation. I scan the surrounding area, noting the benches, the nearby tables, the cool placid water gurgling under the bridge. June in New York City can seduce you or it can trick you.

What it has in store today is anyone's guess. I lean my hip against the stone railing, and I wait.

Two minutes later, I spot a threesome walking in my direction. My heart thumps, and I groan quietly.

Why does the universe do this to me?

Blond curls, lips like a bow, a tight trim waist. Even from several yards away, I can tell she wears little makeup—she has that fresh-faced, rosy glow about her, and something innocent yet knowing in her expression. Like Lily James, whom I developed a wicked crush on when I watched her in her latest movie.

April's not tiny, but she's not towering either. Maybe five-three, five-four. A delicious dream. Which translates roughly to "just my type." She wears tight jeans, a long black shirt that clings to her figure, and a huge silver necklace with a heart charm that dangles between her breasts.

As if I wouldn't already be checking them out without the pendant between them.

I've had many clients. Keeping it platonic has never been an issue since I've never been attracted to a customer.

Until now.

Looks like I'll be getting familiar with how to resist temptation.

Chapter Five *April*

Look, I'm keenly aware that if I answered his ad under any other circumstances, I'd be insane.

I might be known to get a little wild, to try crazy things—that hot sauce–eating contest was a doozy, though I swear cliff diving naked was actually quite fun, and I would do any upside-down roller coaster twenty times in a row, thank you very much.

But I don't have a death wish. If I were simply trawling the web for a used exercise bike or a place to pawn off my collection of Barry Manilow LPs—I won them years ago in a drunken bet in college, and I've held on to them because I'm convinced in my heart of hearts that someone will give them a good home someday—I wouldn't need to bring reinforcements for the transaction.

Actually, on second thought, I would definitely take a friend when handing off my albums. I bet there are horror stories of people getting snuffed for Manilow LPs. That dude can sing.

But this is different because Xavier vouched for Theo.

He's not some random guy I found online. He's a referral. A recommendation who simply happens to run a business off the somewhat outdated site.

Even so, a woman needs to be careful. As we enter Prospect Park, we make an interesting tableau. Tom is broad and shaped like a backboard of a tennis court. He's made of concrete, and accessorized with muscle. Claire in her killer boots and midnight-black hair is like a femme fatale superhero. They flank me, the innocent waif between them. We could be in a slow-mo frame of a film right now, as we walk *Reservoir Dogs* style. Damn, I wish it were winter and I had a trench coat flowing behind me in the breeze.

June in the city is humid as an armpit, and my shirt sticks to me. We head to the bridge, looking for a man with a compass tattoo on his right biceps and a well-worn navy blue shirt. My eyes swing around the park, hunting for my "new boyfriend."

I spot a silhouette on the bridge, and the movie sequence freezes.

This is the zoom shot.

A man with the most perfect arms I've ever seen leans casually against the stone railing, a thumb in his pocket, looking cool, dark, and badass.

He grins. The most deliciously endearing lopsided smile I've ever seen. As I get closer, I see his T-shirt: LOVE SUCKS. TRUE LOVE SWALLOWS.

I extend a hand. It's not tingles at first clasp, but he does have a large hand, and that makes me think about other things. *If you know what I mean.*

Good thing I'm in a *look but don't touch* phase of my twentysomething life. The view is indeed lovely. I quickly introduce Tom and Claire, and after quick nods and hellos, they linger a few steps behind us.

"The shirt is a keeper," I say to Theo, cutting straight to the chase. No need for formalities or *how was your day*s?

"It's perfect for us, isn't it, cupcake?" he says, already whipping out a term of endearment. "I can't think of a better way to signify our true and deep connection at your family reunion."

Whoa.

Xavier does not lie. I'm buying him the new bath and body wash he's been coveting. I'm buying him a whole crate.

Because . . . that voice.

It's deep and gravelly and sexy as hell. His voice might get me pregnant. I better take birth control so I don't conceive aurally.

"It was instant, wasn't it?" I let go of his hand as I pick up the thread. "The night I met you at the bar."

He segues without missing a beat. "When you ordered the Slippery Nipple, you gave me that smoldering, sexy look. The one in your eyes right now."

"I have a smoldering look in my eyes?" I think my voice might have just squeaked.

He raises his hand, and nearly touches my cheek. It's like he leaves the imprint of his fingers on the air. He gazes into my eyes. I might be tipsy from the way he looks at me. "Yeah, that one. Those eyes across the bar. It was fucking irresistible."

"Was it?" I suddenly feel wobbly. I feel like this made-up tale could be true.

"I never get it on with patrons. It's a rule. But then you walked into the bar. What could I do?" The man doesn't look away. He's so damn good, I'm convinced this is how we met.

I swallow. My throat is dry. Am I out of my league?

"And I told you about the terrible day I was having before I walked into your bar."

He nods thoughtfully, as though he's remembering that exact moment. The one we're crafting right now, in real time, live on the bridge. "The rude Uber driver who dropped you off. The way you just couldn't catch a break or a cab. You asked if you had to show some leg to catch a cab in this town. Your hair was soaked from the rain."

I run my hand down my curls. "So wet. I was like a dog caught in a downpour."

Tom and Claire move farther away, standing on the other side of the bridge, hands probably in each other's back pockets.

"You were the cutest poodle I'd ever seen. I wanted to take a towel and dry you off. Make sure you were never caught in the rain again. But all I could do was give you a vodka tonic on the house."

I love vodka tonic. I wonder if Xavier told him. "It was the best drink I'd ever had."

He wiggles an eyebrow. "It did crazy things to you that night."

I think he's doing crazy things to me now. My heart hammers, and my skin is hot, and I'm spinning a web with this stranger. A web of tales and stories and made-up moments that feel oddly true.

Tom clears his throat, and I see he's now by my side, one big hand parked on my shoulder. "Okay, now that we've established you, too, can pretend you've met, maybe we should sit and chat."

Theo laughs. "Just trying to get in character." His tone is smoother, less raspy. His smile is broader, more innocent. "Did you like it, April? Would that work for you?"

"I think it's perfect," I say, and my voice is ridiculously

breathy. Thank God, he's only going to be a fake boyfriend. "You're amazing. How are you not starring in movies?"

Claire jumps in. "We're all shocked. Let's go to the bench before you leap into his arms."

"My friends worry about me," I say, by way of explanation.

"That means they're good friends, then."

We walk to the bench on the other side of the bridge. I sit next to Theo, and Claire and Tom take spots by my side. Tom drapes an arm around Claire. He's rarely not touching her. She slides her fingers down his denim-clad thigh. They're such PDA'ers.

I rub my palms on my jeans and turn to my potential five-day beau. "So this is what you do as an actor? In between parts?"

"It's sort of like acting class," Theo explains. "A little live-action role-playing, so to speak. It's how I keep my skills sharp. Others do it by talking to birds."

I raise a brow in question.

"Earlier this week, I spotted a woman in the park, having a conversation with a pigeon. She was yelling at the bird. Telling the pigeon he'd let her down. I asked if she was okay, and she shot me a sharp stare and said, 'I'm practicing for my improv.'"

"Do you think being a fake date at my family reunion will be more fun than yelling at pigeons?"

A grin tugs at his lips. "Seems to be that way already."

"Making a living as an actor has to be tough," Tom chimes in. He does well as a photographer, but he knows how hard it is for those in front of the camera, whether models or actors. "Kudos to you for figuring out a clever side gig."

"Beats dog-food testing." Theo's tone is offhand, as if it's not a big deal that he might have eaten dog food.

I flinch. "You were a dog-food tester?"

"Someone has to make sure the right mix of lamb, chicken, and potatoes is in those fancy organic foods."

He can't be serious. "You really tested dog food?"

He barks, sounding just like a, well, a dog. *Arf, arf.* "I did, actually. For a month. I paid off some of my college loans with the extra money. I didn't swallow, though."

"So it wasn't true love?"

His smile spreads across his face. "No. And trust me, when people say something tastes like dog food, it does."

"How the heck do you find a job like that?" Claire asks the question, but Theo looks at me when he answers with, "Same place April found me. *Online.*"

"What else have you done?"

"You mean like the nerdy coworker or the best friend's brother you crushed on for years?" he asks, and those must be other personas in his repertoire. He reminds me of my favorite character on the cartoon *American Dad!*—the alien, Roger, who adopts the most insane personalities, from dangerous bounty hunters to drunk school principals.

"I mean the actual roles. Like TV or film or stage. Or is that rude to ask? I'm just curious more than anything," I say, since I don't have a problem asking questions. Some might say I talk too much, but I say screw them.

For a flicker of a second, Theo looks nervous. Then I realize he's embarrassed. Crap. I don't want to make him feel bad, but I suspect he hasn't done much on camera or onstage. It's insanely hard to land a gig as an actor, and roles are few and far between.

"I've done a few things," he says. "*The Badger. The Apartment.* A couple others. Nothing huge. Mostly in Jersey."

I nod several times, even though I wasn't aware Jersey

had a thriving scene for aspiring actors. "Ah, got it. So mostly stage and stuff?"

"Stage work. Student work. Hopefully, I'll get a big break someday."

Briefly, I meet Tom's eyes. We know too well what it's like to be an artist chasing a big break. Tom landed his. I snagged mine. Claire is an artist of sorts, too, and she's moved up from working at a salon to operating her own booth at a popular one, complete with a loyal client list.

"You will," I say to Theo, warmth in my tone. "It just takes time and persistence. And being in the right place at the right time."

"That's the truth, for sure," he says, scratching his jaw.

I consider his stubble. Why is the unshaven look so sexy? Why does it make a man seem like a rogue? And why are roguish men hot? I don't know the answers, but I like asking the questions as I stare at his handsome face, his square jaw, his full lips, and his utterly fantastic smile.

I picture him by my side at the barbecue, laughing while playing lawn Twister, killing it in the paper-airplane competition. My eyes drift to his hands. His fingers are long, and I bet he makes great paper airplanes with them.

I blink. "What do you usually charge?"

The question feels strange to ask. I know it's necessary, but it's a reminder that whatever chemistry we might have just concocted is fictional. This is a job. I'm the client and he's the contractor. While I'm not rolling in endless piles of dough, I've had a good year, I've saved well and wisely, and I consider this an investment in my mental health. If I stay the course and avoid dating, I have a better chance at landing the *Sporting World* gig, and cementing my rep in the business. Besides, I actually love the honesty of this sort of transactional date. Everything is on the table. Terms are arranged up front. This sure beats having the wool

pulled over my eyes by Landon, those three long months
with him.

Theo is straightforward and businesslike when he
answers. "I try to base it off the actors' union rates for
daywork," he says, then gives me some figures. All very
reasonable. All less than I imagine an escort would charge.
More important, his fee is worth the price to me—it'll save
me from hurting my parents' feelings by telling them I
don't want to come home to Wistful permanently. They
love the town I grew up in, and I do, too. But not enough
to live there again, and when you're the one in the family
who moves away, you're the one they try to lure home.

I glance at Claire, wanting to be sure, and she nods, her
way of saying the rate sounds good.

"That'll be fine," I say. "And you're able to take the time
off from the bar and the dog-food testing?"

"I've already turned down Alpo's request for me to give
a full and thorough report on its new food that makes
puppy coats extra soft. I'm sad because I was hoping it
would make my hair even softer," he says, raking a hand
through his thick hair that I bet is already soft and silky.
"But this seemed worth it."

A laugh bursts forth from deep within my belly. "Yes,
I believe it's safe to say the food will be better than kib-
ble, and you won't have to spit it out."

"Excellent," he says, his voice low and rumbly. "My
schedule is clear if you want to hire me."

I'm dying to hire him. But I want to make sure I've
crossed all my t's. "You've done this before? You've played
all sorts of pretend boyfriend roles?"

He nods, and rattles off a cast of characters from the
boss to the best friend's brother to the recently betrothed.
"Everyone has a different need. So I try to meet them."

"Quite a repertoire."

. "Xavier thought you'd want the bad boy."

Claire rolls her eyes and squeezes my arm. "No one wants a bad boy more than this girl."

"How bad do you want it?" Theo says.

"Um," I say, but my voice goes dry.

He laughs lightly, catching his own innuendo. He shakes his head, amused. "Sorry if that came out dirty. How bad do you want me to play?"

"How bad can you be?" I lean closer, curious. I might also want to smell him. He smells like pine, and I never thought pine was sexy till now. It might be an aphrodisiac.

"Do you want me to go full asshole? Start fights, instigate shit?"

I furrow my brow. "*What?* Start fights?" Is he crazy? My family drives me nuts, but I don't want someone to pummel them. I realize why he's asking. I *ordered* this character from his menu.

"The ad. The à la carte options," he says, reminding me.

I wave him off. "That's not necessary. The ad just made me laugh. It was hilarious. That's why I wanted to meet you. And, truth be told, my mom would probably enjoy it if you debated the most hot-button topics of the day. She loves that stuff."

He nods, a serious look in his eyes, like he's taking mental notes.

"But no," I continue, "I don't want you to be an asshole."

Claire jumps in. "April is off the market, but her parents don't seem to understand what that means. She's the youngest of the family by far, so they all think they know what's best for her. She's far too sweet to say, 'Mom, I never ever want to date the men you set me up with.'"

I give her a look. "That's not true."

Claire laughs. "You are sweet, but so is candy, so don't take it as an insult."

"What do you mean 'off the market,' though? If you've got a boyfriend already, we don't need to go any further," Theo says, his meaning clear—he's ready to walk if I'm a cheater, even a pretend one.

"Oh, God no," I say quickly, shaking my head. "Claire just means I'm devotedly single, on account of being supremely disappointed in the dating scene, and suffering from a complete lack of interest in participating in yet another date or relationship that belly flops."

"You just need to be convincingly into April, to ward them off," Claire says.

"That shouldn't be hard." Theo's voice drips with innuendo as he shoots me the most smoldering look. "Clearly, I've got it bad for my woman."

A wave of goose bumps slides over my skin.

His voice shifts to a more straightforward tone. "Like that?"

I blink. I think Claire does, too.

"I'm a professional," he adds. "I can do the job you're hiring me for. And as I said in the ad, I have a strict platonic policy. But I might have to put an arm around you at some point. Or hold your hand. And I want it to feel natural, so everyone knows you're off-limits. So they know you belong to me."

His voice has gone smoky again, letting me know he's in character. He's playing the role of *mine*.

I slip into my part. I bump my shoulder against his. Hello, firm wall of shoulder. "Because I'm taken."

"You are absolutely taken." The corner of his lips quirk up.

"And you will be my—" I slow, roam my eyes up and down this man. "—my inked, scruffed ex-con. Though we'll keep that last part between you and me."

I say that like the joke that it is. Because it's a perfect

ruse. He's the polar opposite of interest rates and hardware stores. The character he's concocted for me is a little crazy, maybe even a little wild, even if I don't want him to play up the dangerous parts with my parents.

"Who banged you in the bathroom of the bar when my shift ended," he says, reminding me of our origin story, the naughty tale of a body painter in New York who needs a buffer in Connecticut.

"Yes. The bartender with the intense eyes. That's all I want."

"Then that's all you'll get."

And it's odd, but a part of me is a bit sad that I won't get more.

Chapter Six *Theo*

Switching shifts is easy. Two hours later, I'm in the clear for a five-day fiesta of faking it. But pretending to dig April will not be a problem at all.

The bigger issue, though, is the heated debate I'm engaged in with Jared. "Why does everyone pick invisibility?"

"Easy," he says in his high-pitched voice—it's high because he hasn't hit puberty yet. Ah, good times coming this thirteen-year-old's way any day now. "It means you can sneak into a store and grab some candy or—"

"Dude. Why do you want a superpower that will let you steal?"

"You didn't let me finish," he says as we walk toward our building.

"I already know your answer is unacceptable."

"You could also get out of math tests if you were invisible. Like the one I have next week," Jared points out, flicking his wrist back and forth, back and forth, practicing his Frisbee throw. I just schooled this seventh grader in

Frisbee in the park. He asked to learn. No one ever learns if you go easy on them.

"Let me get this straight: You want a superpower to skip fractions and steal M&M's?" I shake my head, amused. "I need to teach you to think bigger, my man."

"Like what? Mind-reading?"

I shudder. "There was a time I might have wanted that. But not anymore. No way do you want to know the cesspool of thoughts that humanity keeps up here." I tap the side of my head.

He furrows his brow. He might not yet be aware that thoughts are a cesspool. I move past mind-reading. "How about flying?" I stretch my arms high to the sky, like Superman, and purse my lips together to make the sound of a plane taking off. A long, low zooming buzz.

Jared smiles. "How do you do that?"

I smirk. "That's the superpower you really want, isn't it?"

He laughs. "Funny noises, yeah. I'd make fart sounds when my math teacher walks around the classroom, so it sounds like he's doing it." Then he arches a blond eyebrow. "Flying is what you'd pick?"

"What's cooler than flying?"

"Superstrength is cooler. That's a good one."

"Too late. You already picked funny noises. Now you can make your teacher flatulent. Meanwhile, I'll fly to your school and make sure you don't miss the math test next week."

"You won't be able to see me, since I'm invisible," he says, laughing as we reach the stoop of our building at the edge of Brooklyn.

"Curses," I mutter like a cartoon villain. "Is your mom home from work yet?"

Jared grabs his cell phone from his pocket and clicks

to his texts. He shows me one from his mother. "Home in twenty minutes."

I clap his shoulder. "I need to pack for my trip."

"Can we ride your motorcycle next time?"

I laugh, thinking of the snarling leopard bike I've had since I finished college. Last year, when I played the role of the hometown boyfriend for a sweet, shy lady at her office Christmas party, she paid me in parking space rentals. It was worth it. Her brother owns a motorcycle parking lot, so she scored a deal from him and passed it on to me in place of my fee. I use the bike around the city now and then, but it's good to have in case I ever need to just . . . take off.

I drop a hand to Jared's shoulder again and squeeze. "You know you can't ride the leopard."

He adopts a too-big smile. "But I can keep asking."

"You do your homework till your mom gets home, okay?"

He salutes me. "I will."

I hope he will. But I know too well that what kids do without adult supervision isn't always what they say they'll do. I've done my part, though. And really, that's all I *can* do. At least he has only a twenty-minute window to get into hot water. When I was little older than Jared, I had windows lasting days. Endless days.

I grab a key and unlock the top lock. The middle lock. The bottom lock. It groans open, moaning its abject pain and distinct need for WD-40. "Catch you next week."

He high-fives me. "See ya."

I wait till he unlocks the door to his tiny apartment. His mom is a single parent, and she works late hours, trying to make ends meet. I try to hang out with Jared once or twice a week. Who knows. Maybe it'll make a difference for him.

I head upstairs, hoping to avoid Mr. Boyle and his bologna.

I can pull off a lot of impressive tricks—I learned to eat fire one summer on the Atlantic City Boardwalk, and I can also make a compass out of a dead cell phone's battery. But the one thing I haven't quite mastered is walking up the rickety steps in this ten-apartment building where I rent a studio slightly bigger than a steamer trunk. Like Indiana Jones hopscotching his way to the treasure in the South America cave, I've nearly mastered how to make it up the steps without him hearing. But the last one is the doozy. It groans. Every single time.

When I turn the corner on the second-floor landing, Boyle is standing in the doorway of his place, the scent of fried bologna curling through the dusty air. Before I moved into this building, I wasn't aware that bologna was still a food item people eat. Now I know a few key facts about bologna: The smell is strong. It carries in air vents. It sticks to clothes. It'll flood my room in about two minutes.

Let me tell you how I feel about bologna—I'd rather eat dog food.

Boyle wears a wife-beater. It's in the creepy-landlord dress code. He glares at me. "You know it's Monday in six days."

"Huh." I give him a surprised look. "You don't say." I stare thoughtfully at the ceiling. "Would that make tomorrow Wednesday, then?"

He shakes his head. "Don't mess with me, Banks."

"I'll have the rent on time. I always do."

He snorts. "You're lucky I let you stay. I've got someone willing to pay me a hundo more than you pay a month for that studio."

"That so?"

He nods, scratches his jowly jaw. "Yeah," he grunts. "Tell me why I shouldn't rent your room."

I jut up my shoulders. "Got me. If I were you, I'd kick my ass out."

"What?" He tilts his head as if what I just said makes no sense.

He wants me to cower. He wants me to pay him early. He wants to use the cash to go down to the pharmacy a few blocks away that writes him scrips for OxyContin. He thinks I don't know this. But I do, because all it takes to figure shit out about people is to pay attention.

That's why I know he'll back down first. He doesn't have someone for my place. Even if he did, I'd come up with something. It's what I've done: life hacking. I've had to do it since I was fourteen years old.

"You think I should kick you out?" Boyle asks, because for some reason, this guy likes fighting, and he's deciding I'm the one in the building he should antagonize. Better me than Jared or Jared's mom, I say.

Because I know how to get him to back down.

I've paid attention.

I defuse the bomb.

I laugh, take a step closer, and clap him on the meaty arm. "Get some rest, Frank. You're tired. Your daughter comes tomorrow for lunch. You don't want to miss her visit, right?"

He blinks, as though he's just remembering. The pills mess with his memory. He draws a deep breath. His expression transforms. Gratitude now. "Yeah, shit. Thanks, kid."

See? It's not about me. It's something else. It usually is.

He leaves, and I head to my studio at the end of the hall. I shut the door behind me and lock it.

Time to pack. Can I set a new world record for speed? I

grab clothes from a drawer and toss some options onto my bed. As I stare at the pile on the mattress, I figure it's best to check with April. I'm not looking for an excuse to text her. I just want to make sure I'm playing the part she wants.

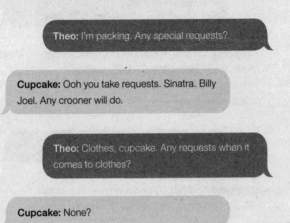

Theo: I'm packing. Any special requests?

Cupcake: Ooh you take requests. Sinatra. Billy Joel. Any crooner will do.

Theo: Clothes, cupcake. Any requests when it comes to clothes?

Cupcake: None?

Whoa. I wrench back when her one-word question appears on the screen. It surprises me, the return to the flirting. But it's not a bad surprise. Like the blast from the past knocking on your door to tell you, *Changed my mind, decided to collect on the ten-thousand-dollar debt after all. Plus the vig.*

Flirty April is a surprise I like.

Theo: So you want the exhibitionist? That's a new one for me, but hey, you placed the order. You should get what you want. I'll have the birthday suit on.

Cupcake: Why do I feel like you really would show up in the full monty?

Theo: Because I would.

Cupcake: Let's not shock the guests completely. How about: swim trunks, shorts, sandals, sneakers, shirts, satin pajamas, five pairs of black boxer briefs.

Theo: One of those things just doesn't belong.

Cupcake: I wanted to see if you'd notice the briefs. You're right. They don't belong. Commando is fine.

I run my hand through my hair and laugh. This girl has rapid-fire fingers and wit to match.

Cupcake: Actually, casual clothes are fine. Bring a polo shirt, but mostly T-shirts. I like how they show off your tattoos. By the way, your ink is perfection.

Theo: Got a favorite?

Cupcake: I'm not sure I've seen them all. You might have some hidden under that shirt. In fact, if I were a betting woman, I'd bet your chest is a canvas.

Theo: Got 'em in prison.

Cupcake: Ha. I call bullshit.

I flop down on the bed, a smile on my face.

Theo: You're an expert on tattoos from the joint?

Cupcake: No. But I have this thing known as common sense. And it tells me getting inked in the joint isn't as easy as it sounds. How does it work? Does a guy in an orange jumpsuit happen to have a needle, a tattoo gun, and all the colors of the rainbow? What does he charge? Did he smuggle in all the parts in a cake?

Theo: Yes. His name is GuardRail, and he's a traveling tattoo artist commissioned by the Bureau of Prisons to provide ink work for all the felons of the world.

Cupcake: GuardRail sounds fearsome.

Theo: He's a gentle giant.

Cupcake: Theo . . .

Theo: April . . .

Cupcake: You didn't really do time in prison, did you?

Theo: I've never been to prison.

Cupcake: OK, good. Are we pretending you were?

Theo: That's up to you. It's all up to you. I can be whoever you want.

She doesn't answer that one, and I toss some more T-shirts into a backpack, then roll up a pair of jeans and grab some shorts. I hate shorts. But the name of the gig is transformation, so I pack them and everything else April ordered.

Less than two minutes later, I'm done.

Yeah, I've won awards for my fast-packing ability. It's impressive, I know.

I grab my phone again, click over to Facebook, and out of habit, I visit my brother's profile, hoping he'll post a picture, since I haven't seen him in a while. He rarely posts pics on Facebook, though, so it's a futile mission.

I call him instead.

He answers on the first ring. He shouts above the noise in the background. It sounds like a celebration. He's been celebrating for a few months now. Glasses clink, voices rise, and music plays.

"Little dipshit!"

"Big shithead!"

"How the hell are you? I miss you, man. Come visit me," he says in his booming voice.

"I'm trying. It's hard to get away."

He scoffs. "Not that hard."

"Boston's almost five hours, and I've been working like crazy."

Another scoff. "Still, you'd think my little brother would come see me."

"I want to."

"Hey, don't worry. I can see you soon. I should be free to leave any day."

The tinkle of steel drums echoes, and my stomach drops. "Heath. Tell me you didn't skip town already. You're not in Jamaica, are you?"

He laughs, a deep, rich sound that was his calling card back when we did everything together. His laughter could seal any kind of deal we were working.

"Settle down. I'm just making up for lost time with Lacey. We're living it up. Listen, there's a band onstage, and Lacey is making those dirty eyes at me. She wants me to sidle up next to her on the dance floor."

I drop my forehead into my hand and sigh. "Are you still in Boston? You better be."

"Maybe I'm in a galaxy far, far away."

I groan and try again. "Are you in Boston?"

"Yes." His tone is as firm as mine. "Settle down. It's all good. You know I'd never leave without telling you. You know that, right?"

I sigh and nod. "I do know."

"You sure? Because you were talking to me like you weren't so sure. Like you don't know me."

"I know you. I just worry about you."

"It's my job to worry about you, not the other way around. Is everything okay with you? You got all the shit squared away now? Paid the final loans off?"

He's asking about school loans, so I tell him, "Yeah."

I don't tell him Addison came by. I don't tell him she wants money from me. I don't tell him those things, because I don't know what he'll do to get the money to get her off my back. Addison wasn't supposed to come collecting. But then Heath left Addison for Lacey, and Addison decided she wants her money back. All things being equal, I suppose I'd want it all back if I were Addison, too. She did things for us that went above and beyond, and when the going got tough, she was there.

But now? Now, she's all about Addison, and I get it. I understand where she's coming from even if I don't like it. She texted me this evening.

> Where is Heath? Do you want me to ask him for the money? Because I will.

My reply was swift and immediate as I told her I'd take care of it.

Love doesn't trump money.

Money trumps love.

And loyalty trumps everything, so I'll get the money for her.

"What about you? You good? Are you working?" I ask him, urgency in my voice.

"I'm great. I'm with my woman," he says, and I hear

Lacey whine, "C'mon, babe, dance with me like you used to."

And that's all she wrote. My brother is powerless before this woman. She's his Achilles' heel. My father suffered from the same condition. Too much love for one woman. That's what I need to shore up against.

"I gotta go, bro. Come see me soon." He hangs up.

I stare at the disconnected call as a familiar emptiness tunnels through me over money. There are so many romanticized notions claiming it's *not* what humans need. That money blackens your heart. But I dare anyone to say that money can't buy happiness. If you can say that and believe it, you're either poor or rich.

For the rest of us, money is everything.

It's life, it's food, it's freedom.

As I flop back on the bed, I wonder what it would be like to have enough money that you could siphon some off to hire someone to play your pretend suitor for a reunion.

I don't have a clue.

The things I want to do are shoved so far under the bed, in a corner, somewhere else, that sometimes it's hard to remember what I once wanted out of life. I never aspired to be an actor, and I'm one only in the broadest definition of the word, since I happen to be outrageously good at role-playing. Mostly, I'm a bartender. And I'm an occasional dog-food tester. I'm also a former teddy bear surgeon, a softball coach, an essay writer for hire, and for one glorious month last year, I was a professional sleeper. That was the best job ever, getting paid by a market researcher to test beds for "nappability." The trouble was, it ended far too soon. I was promised mystery shopping and mattress testing and all sorts of better-paying gigs by the chick who ran the market research firm.

Then she yanked those out from under me.

But acting? You won't find me auditioning for *CSI* or the next Broadway musical. Nothing I told April was technically a lie. I *do* act. Just not in traditional ways. I'm like the person in the park shouting at pigeons for improv, only being a boyfriend-for-hire pays better.

I realize I didn't even ask what April does for a living.

I curse out loud.

It's not like me to forget to get to know someone. I'll do better tomorrow on the train ride to Connecticut.

I have a woman to get to know and a job to do.

Chapter Seven *April*
The first night

I sink into the royal blue high-backed upholstered chair, groaning happily. "Oh my God, this chair is to die for," I say, wiggling around in it.

Theo grins as he tucks our suitcases in the overhead. "Glad you like the train, cupcake. I'm surprised you didn't want the motorcycle option, though."

"Two-plus hours on a bike?" I shake my head. "No thanks." I hold out my arms in front of me, mimicking gripping the handlebars. "After five minutes of that, I'd be like this." I flop my head to one side, shut my eyes, and pretend to snore.

Theo laughs, and when I open my eyes, he leans in close to me. "You got the position wrong. Your hands would be here." He reaches for my hands and sets them on his waist. My throat goes dry. I like the way he feels. I wonder if he likes my hands on him. I don't know the answer, so I let go, folding them in my lap.

"Well, then. That might make me miss the snarling

leopard a tiny bit more. Do you really have a bike with a snarling leopard on it?"

"As advertised."

I glance around, enjoying our digs. Bikes might be sexy in theory, but trains are sexy for real. "Train travel is so romantic, don't you think? Like in the movies." The reel plays. "I want to travel across Europe on a train someday. Wear a jewel-colored dress, long white gloves." I stretch my arms in front of me, threading on my imaginary gloves. "And my hair twisted in a silver clip." My hand goes to my hair, loosely coiling it. He watches me with avid interest. "I'll go down to the dining car, a waiter in a tuxedo will greet me and say 'Good Evening, Ms. Hamilton.' They'll serve champagne and caviar."

He laughs. "Do you actually like caviar?"

"Why do you ask?"

"I have a theory."

"I like theories. Tell me."

He parks a big hand on the back of his chair, looking down at me. "I don't think anyone actually likes caviar. It's turned into a word that signifies fancy shit. But who *likes* caviar?" He sits now, moving with a kind of graceful ease. His long legs stretch out in front of him, and he turns to face me. "Am I right? Do you actually like caviar?"

I feign shame as a pin-striped man takes the seat in front of us. "You know, maybe I don't. Maybe I've been tricked all these years by the movies. Maybe I have this whole elaborate fantasy of champagne and caviar when I actually detest it. Dear Lord, Watson. You've exposed all my truths."

A laugh bursts from his lips. It's rich and rumbly, and I like the sound. It's the sound of him enjoying this gig with me. It's reassuring to know I picked well, and that we'll be able to pull this off, return to New York, and continue on with our merry lives, no one the wiser. He quickly collects himself. "Here's another thing, cupcake," he says in that gritty voice of his as a mom scoots by in the aisle, her hands tucked into the paws of twin redheaded sprites in summer sundresses. "What are these romantic train movies you're watching?"

I arch a brow. "What do you mean?"

"Most train movies are about death and destruction. *Murder on the Orient Express*. Not entirely a romantic notion of train travel. *Throw Momma from the Train*. More murder. *Girl on the Train*. That movie is like Murphy's Law. Everything that could go wrong went wrong on a train."

I consider this, quirking my lips as I try to unearth a truly uplifting flick to fit the one in my mind's eye. Most of the movie train romances are also bittersweet, so those don't fit. "What about *The Polar Express*?"

"That movie's just creepy. Everyone looks like a talking mannequin."

I huff. "Fine, fine. You've just shattered all my illusions about trains being romantic. You're not going to push me from the train, are you?"

"You're not going to push me, are you?"

"I suppose I will refrain."

"Merci," he says in a deliciously French voice.

I wiggle an eyebrow. "Oh, that's right. You've got a whole closetful of accents available upon request. Tell me more."

"I can be British if you wish," he says, speaking like an Englishman. "Irish might be just your speed, too." My eyes widen because he says that in a perfect lilt. "If you want me go down under, Australian's an option," he says, sliding into the sexy twang of that country. He rattles off more, demonstrating each. "American South for you, darlin'. California surfer if you want to hang loose. French might be to your liking, mademoiselle."

"Wow."

"I'm not done." He pins me with an intense look. "I've also mastered Fake French."

I laugh. "What in the ever-loving hell is Fake French?"

"It entails a hell of a lot of Pepé Le Pew attitude when saying things like *'Zees ees deesgusting'* if a waiter served, say, soggy nachos. In a pinch, Fake French can also be achieved with a combination of words like *je de ne peu pas voulez vous avec ce soir bonjour.*"

I laugh even more. "I like your Fake French. I'm tempted to order up a serving of Theo Banks, the snooty Fake Frenchman."

"But that's not all," he says, and his voice goes deep and dark. So deep, in fact, that I shudder. It's familiar, and as fearsome as it was when it was first heard in movie theaters in 1977. "April, I am your boyfriend."

He says it in a dead-on Darth Vader tone.

I shove his shoulder. "Shut up."

He shifts once more, turning on Kermit the Frog's earnest nasal tone. "It's not easy being green."

"You're kind of a scary chameleon." The train doors swoosh shut.

He shrugs. "Yeah, that's true."

I give him the once-over. "Fine, your Darth and your Kermit are totally impressive. And so is the suitcase full of accents. Yet I do like that whole gravelly, phone sex, talk-dirty-to-me voice you've got going on."

It's his turn to raise an eyebrow. " 'Talk dirty to me'? That's how I sound to you?"

Yes, God yes. And some secret part of me is dying to hear your voice in the dark.

But I don't say that or anything more sanitized either,

since there's no point. We aren't going there. We aren't going anywhere. Plus, the conductor takes over, barking overhead. "Take your seats. The train is pulling out of the station."

Theo raises his right arm and yanks it down and up. "Toot toot."

He sounds exactly like a train whistle. He shoots me a sheepish look, and it's a new one for me. He's been all cocky confidence and irresistible charm. This new look is endearing, like he wants me to like his train noises. "Sound effects provided at no extra charge."

"A bonus? Lucky me." I cross my arms in mock indignation. "I suppose it's only fair that I get an extra service from you, seeing as how you've ruined caviar. You've ruined trains. I won't let you ruin my other train fantasy, though."

"What's that one?"

The car lurches forward, rolling out of the station.

Should I go here? Should I tell him my train fantasy? I've never shared it with another man, and looking back, I'm glad Landon the Liar doesn't know I have a thing for trains. I'm equally pleased that Brody the Basement Dweller never took me on the New Jersey PATH and tried to get it on.

But here with Theo? The guy I hired to play my lover, who's willing to "tell wild and risqué stories . . . about our hot-as-sin sex life?" Sure, I can tell him. Telling him is safe.

My voice drops in volume as I set the scene. "A quiet train at night. Nearing midnight. The car is almost empty. All the interior lights are dimmed, and there's just a flicker now and then from a passing town." I let my hand brush down my chest, the fantasy unfolding so vividly before my mind's eye. "And we're quiet, no one can hear us. But we have to be careful."

He breathes harder for a second, and I feel like I've
caught him off guard. Hell, I think I've caught myself off
guard. Here it is, more fantasy unspooled as the wheels
stroke against the rails and we move backwards.

"You'd like that?" His voice is deeper, rougher. And
that's saying something.

I turn to him. It's early evening, we're surrounded by
people, and the conductor is trundling up the aisle, a few
rows ahead.

"I would like that," I say, my voice barely a whisper;
then I latch on to the stories we tell. "Isn't that something
we did the other night?"

He slides so seamlessly into the way we played the other
afternoon. His eyes darken. The corner of his lips curves
up. "Yeah, you wore a black dress. The kind that wraps
around your waist," he says, ghosting his fingers over my
stomach, not quite touching. My back nearly arches. I will
myself to stay still. He hasn't even put his fingers on me,
but I can feel how he would.

"You like it when I wear those dresses."

His voice is like a growl, low and dirty. "Because I like
having access to you."

He tugs at the imaginary tie around my waist, and a
thrill races through me, like a pulse. I turn my face, even
closer, and we're inches away, spinning stories of our
imaginary love life. "Sometimes you can't keep your hands
off me."

He laughs, but it's a sexy sound, raspy and masculine.
"'Sometimes,' cupcake?" He raises a brow, then drags his
index finger from my shoulder down to my wrist, leaving
a trail of hot sparks in his wake. How I wish I'd already
taken off this little summer sweater. I'm dying to know
how he feels flesh to flesh. "Try all the time."

"All the time," I repeat, because it sounds too good, too intoxicating not to say it again.

I watch his throat move as he swallows, his Adam's apple bobbing. "Like the time on the train a few weeks ago."

"The car was nearly empty," I whisper as heat sweeps over my skin.

"Only another couple far up in the front. We took a chance." His eyes are on me the whole time, and I swear they're blazing.

"We like to take chances."

He dips his face closer to my neck. "I couldn't wait, April. I had to have you then." The way he says my name is dark and sensual.

The pulse beats faster. "You looked around, made sure no one was walking by. Then you pulled me onto your lap."

"And lifted your skirt," he says, his voice smoky and sending me into a tailspin of lust. I can see this all in my mind's eye. His pants undone. My knees on either side of his thighs. His hands wrapped around my hips. My face in the crook of his shoulder as I swallow all the sounds. Our moves as subtle as possible so no one knows.

No one but us.

"We were fast and quiet," I whisper, my voice like a feather.

A rumble sounds across his lips as he goes next. "But it was good. So fucking good."

"It always is."

"Every. Single. Time."

A man's voice interrupts. "Tickets, please."

I snap out of this dreamy state. Take a deep breath, center myself. I grab the tickets from my purse, handing them to the silver-haired man with the bushy mustache. His conductor hat perches low on his forehead, obscuring his eyes as he punches the tickets. When he raises his face, he studies my green eyes longer than I expect. "Everything okay? Your face is . . ."

I clasp my hand to my cheek. I'm flaming hot. I fan my face and point to the window. "It's from the sun," I say, even though we're heading into evening.

"Be sure to get some water." He turns, ambles to the next row, and says, "Tickets, please."

Theo laughs under his breath.

I swat him. "Thanks for not sticking up for me."

"What was I supposed to say? My pretend girlfriend gets hot from the stories of our fake sex life?"

He says it like it's the most ridiculous thing, but my eyes stray downward, and the shape of his jeans tells me it's not ridiculous at all. I'm not the only one aroused from stories of our make-believe midnight train ride.

"Finish the story," he demands, his voice husky again.

Yeah, I'm not the only one at all. But this sort of arousal hardly counts. We're like two actors getting turned on from a screen kiss. Surely, Emma Stone has gone weak in the knees from at least a couple of the times she's kissed Ryan Gosling on camera.

"Hmm." I tap my lip and hum. "I can't seem to remember now. Did it end well? Do you recall?"

He brings his mouth near my ear. Dangerously close. "I always get you there."

"Dangerously close" describes us perfectly. Dangerously close to trouble.

I smooth a hand down my shirt. "Now that we're clear on that fable, we should probably settle on the other details, don't you think?"

He nods. "Of course."

"You're going to be Theo, right?"

"It's just easier to use my name."

"We met at your bar. We've been together for a month and a half. We like to go bowling, play retro arcade games, and I regularly whip your ass in foosball."

"What? No way. I school you."

I stare down the bridge of my nose. "We'll see about that. If you want to take me on in foosball, go ahead and try."

"Fine. You're the foosball champ."

"Other details. Let's see. My family has no idea Xavier was going to be my original plus-one, so we're fine on that count. You've met Claire and Tom, so you can reference them, especially since the four of us sometimes go dancing at clubs. I've never met a cuisine I won't try. I drink coffee, tea, or soda. I'm completely caffeine omnivorous, and I can have it at any time of day. I love hot food and ice cream, and I'm waiting to find out if I'll win the gig painting the swimsuit edition of *Sporting World*."

"You're up for *that*?" There's genuine enthusiasm in his tone.

As the train slaloms out of Manhattan, rattling past concrete buildings, I answer. "I painted a few models last year, and I'm under consideration to be the lead painter."

"Holy shit. You paint people for a living. That's your actual job?"

I smile, proud of what I do. "Yes, it is."

"That's fascinating. You have to tell me when you land that gig. Promise me you'll tell me."

I laugh. "Sure."

"How did you get started?"

"You really want to know?"

"Yes. I've never met a body painter. I want to know it

all." His eyes are fixed on me, and he seems to listen intently.

"I started with my brother's kids. He's thirteen years older than I am."

"Does that mean you're an 'oops' baby?"

I shake my head. "No. Well, I suppose it's possible, but my parents made it pretty clear that I was their 'later in life' baby. My brother Mitch is forty-one, my sister is thirty-six, and I'm twenty-eight. Mitch's daughters are teenagers now, but they were grade schoolers when I was in high school, so I learned to paint faces on them. Then I moved on to the local farmers' market and painted there. I was quite good at it, so I started doing parties in college for fun. After college, I picked up random little gigs here and there. Halloween, then a mom would hire me for a kids' party, then her friend would hire me for a sexy nighttime party, an adults-only affair where I'd paint sensual images on the women in their low-cut dresses. Soon, I was invited to corporate events, and shows, and my friend Tom got me my first big gig for a magazine. That broke me out, and one thing led to another."

"And now what do you do?"

"Magazines, commercials, photo spreads, even some movies from time to time. Music videos. I painted all these slinky tall women silver in a music video last year for Jane Black," I say, mentioning a ridiculously popular singer.

"That was *you*?"

"That was me," I say, and I whip out my phone and flip through some pictures I've taken of my work through the years. He points to the shot of the cheetah I painted this week. "That's awesome. Can you send it to me?"

"Sure," I say. "Why do you want it, though?"

"Because it's cool. Because *that*—" He stabs his finger at the phone. "—that is crazy talent."

I beam as though a ray of light glows inside my chest. This is what I long for. Not the praise per se. But the understanding.

I fire it off to his phone; then we look at some more pictures. He whistles appreciatively, a look of wonderment in his eyes that makes me happy. "Your family must be so proud of you."

"Actually," I say, wincing, "not entirely."

"How could they not be?"

"They don't think it's real."

He knits his brow. "Real? How could they not think it's real?"

"They don't really understand it. Everyone in my family has more straightforward jobs. Boatbuilders and bakery owners and such. They think I'm cobbling together a living painting faces at farmers' markets and Renaissance festivals."

He laughs. "Not that there's anything wrong with that either."

"Exactly. That's good work, too. And I've tried to explain that I'm one of the lucky ones in my field—I've moved up, I've nabbed fantastic gigs for commercials, magazines, and catalogs. I've shown them the pictures, but some are too risqué for their tastes. They still think I'm painting butterflies on faces."

"I bet they loved that."

"They did, and I'm sure they'll demand more at the reunion. I'm quite skilled at painting pretty much anything you can imagine on a person."

"What would you paint on me? If you could pick anything?"

I use this chance to let my eyes take a tour of his body. I have more than free rein. I have express permission to stare. He's fit and toned, and I could turn him to a chrome-plated man, I could transform his back into a cello, change his chest into a sky about to storm. "Ask me in a few days. I'll have a better answer then."

"It's on my to-do list for a few days from now." He mimes writing an item on a pad of paper. He asks me more questions as the towns slide past the windows, showing off lush hills and verdant trees that tower over white colonials and redbrick mansions.

But all these questions are about me, and I need to know the man I'm bringing home. My buffer. My new lover.

"My turn," I say. "What about your family? I want the real Theo truth now. We can pretend with other people, but we should be honest with each other, don't you think?"

He blinks, then meets my eyes. "Everything I've told you has been the truth."

I arch a brow. "Really?"

"Yes. Really."

"Do you have brothers and sisters?"

"One brother."

"Are you close?"

"Yes. No. Sometimes. Very."

"Okay. That covers just about everything."

A sad smile crosses his mouth, then meets his eyes. "Yep. It sure does."

"Where is he now?"

His voice is strained when he says, "Boston."

"What about—?"

He cuts me off before I can say *parents.* "They passed away."

My heart hurts. It pounds achingly, and I want to run a hand through his hair. "I'm sorry, Theo."

"Me, too."

"How old were you?"

He licks his lips. Closes his eyes. I would paint sparrows

on him now, with folded wings and sad eyes, because that's what would suit him. "It's okay, you don't have to answer."

"Fourteen. I was fourteen."

My chest collapses, like a Coke can stepped on by a giant. I can't even imagine. Here I am, bringing him home to ward off efforts by my family simply to pair me with a man. He doesn't have a family. Then it hits me again, like a double whammy. He was fourteen when he lost *them*—they must have died in a car crash or some other terrible tragedy.

"Is it easier for you to pretend you have parents or are you comfortable when someone asks about them? Because they will ask." I shrug sheepishly. "It's only a natural question, and my family will want to know you."

He raises his face. "It's easier for me to speak truthfully on this one. Maybe that means I'm not so good an actor as I thought, but if I make up a story about them, it'll feel real and I don't want to go there."

"I understand," I say softly, then segue to his profession. "Have you always wanted to be an actor?"

He angles away from me. "I've wanted to be different things at different times."

"But do you like what you do now? Acting requires so much passion and dedication. Even to do this kind of acting."

He stares straight ahead. "Yeah. I like it."

He doesn't seem to want to talk more about it, though, so I move on to other areas.

We settle on a few more key details of our backstory as the train rattles along the Long Island Sound, the ribbon of water framing our journey. The sun slips down the sky in a fiery ball of orange and pink fury. Houses shimmer and whole hillsides are swallowed up by the speed of the train as twilight flirts with the sky. The story of us feels so believable, from the night I met him to our tryst on the train to the foosball matches, and I wonder if it's because we already have this fictional intimacy or because he's truly a star at pretending.

Then I remind myself—he's good at pretending.

Snap out of it. It feels true because you hired an actor, dumbass.

The conductor announces the next stop.

"That's one stop away from Wistful," I say, amused. "That means we talked the whole ride."

"Yeah, we did. You're a chatty one."

I act shocked. "So are you. Also, you and I don't do what's known as," I say, stopping to sketch air quotes, " 'companionable silence.' "

He gives me a quizzical look. "That's a thing?"

"In some books it is. I was reading a romance novel the other day, and the couple had met and slept together at some chichi event, and now it was into the getting-to-know-you part. So at the start of chapter ten or whatever, Jane and Dave were sitting in 'companionable silence' in his Range Rover as they drove to the next town over for dinner."

Theo's nose crinkles. "That sounds as unpleasant as hot guacamole."

I chuckle. "Yes. It does."

"Companionable silence sounds like something married people do."

"Right? And the funniest part is that it was their third date. By the end of the car ride, during which they've said all of, I dunno, three things—want the heat on, I love heat, want some music, I love George Strait, you look pretty tonight, thank you—she says she feels like she knows him well and she's falling for him."

He laughs loudly, tossing his head back as if this is the most absurd idea ever to him, and I like that he feels the same as I do. He shakes his head vigorously. "You can't fall for someone in companionable silence."

"My point exactly. How else would you know you like someone if not through talking to them?"

"Personally, I don't think you can truly know a person unless you know if she'd rather be invisible or able to fly."

I quirk up a corner of my lips. "Ah, but here's the thing about that question. There's a big loophole, and no one ever remembers to qualify it properly."

"How so?"

"Consider this: If you were invisible, would your clothes be invisible, too?" I gesture to his dark jeans and the black T-shirt with the words THE PROBLEM WITH QUOTES ON THE INTERNET IS YOU NEVER KNOW WHICH ONES ARE REAL—ABRAHAM LINCOLN. "Or would they remain completely visible?"

He brings his fingers to his temple, and mimes an explosion. "Mind. Blown."

I point at him. "See? That's what I mean. The clothing issue changes the game completely."

His eyes are intense as he stares at me. "It changes everything." Theo brings his face closer to mine, and for a brief moment I feel as though we're marooned on a little train island of these two dark blue seats. "Especially since I'm now thinking about how you'd look with invisible clothes on."

A pulse beats low in my body, and I nearly squirm because he's looking at me like my clothes are already off. Like he's removed them, and they're puddled on the floor in a pile of invisible fabric.

"Yeah," he says in a dirty whisper. "You'd look fantastic with invisible clothes on."

I can't take it. I can't handle this haze of heat. I feel naked, and absolutely unsure what's real and fake. All I know is this arousal is too real, and I have to squash it. "Do you like George Strait?"

He pushes his head back into the headrest, laughing. "I'm not playing the companionable silence game, April. Also, speaking of talking, there's something we haven't discussed," he says as the train glides into Wistful's station a few minutes early.

"What's that?"

"What are the sleeping arrangements for the reunion?"

Chapter Eight *Theo*

The sign dangling above the doors of the station proudly boasts WISTFUL, CONNECTICUT. HOME OF THE WILD THUN-DERCOASTER, BELUGA WHALES, THE MARITIME MUSEUM, AND THE BEST TOWN EVER. POPULATION, 8,233.

April popped into a restroom, so I wander through the tiny station though there's not much to see. A tired woman with a dark black braid stands at the ticket window, her chin in her hand. A long wooden bench spreads across half the station, and behind me, the sound of the train pulling away ripples through the summer evening air. I stare at the open wooden doors that spill out into the small town, and there are probably a thousand million more questions I should have asked April on the train.

I don't mean favorite-color shit. The stuff that matters: life, liberty, the pursuit of happiness.

But winging it is sometimes the name of the game.

A minute later, her high-heeled sandals smack against the tiled floor. I turn around and decide that "high-heeled" really isn't the best description. They're more like chunky heels.

Wedges, I think they're called.

Focusing on her shoes helps me to avoid focusing on other parts of her.

Like *every* other part of her.

Her curvy body looks fantastic in her dark red summer dress with spaghetti straps. She has on one of those half sweaters, a white number that hits right at the side of the breasts. I'm convinced those sweaters were designed by someone who wanted to screw with boob aficionados like myself.

But she's screwing with other parts too because it's difficult not to like her. She's a pistol, with a sharp, silver-tongued wit, and the quickest mouth I've ever known.

As I let my eyes play tour guide, roaming over her body, I force myself to remember—*she's not my girlfriend.* Liking her would be a colossal mistake. My brother once liked Addison, and look what happened there. His ex is a goddamn bounty hunter, Boba Fett chasing Han Solo's debt.

April gestures to the suitcases at my feet. "Thanks for getting the bags."

"Want to catch a cab to your parents' place?" I ask.

She didn't tell me the sleeping arrangements yet. The conductor barked our arrival after I asked, and then she said she needed to text her mom that we were a few minutes early.

"My mother will pick us up any second. My father is probably in bed. He's a grizzly bear if he doesn't go to sleep by nine." She takes a breath and nibbles on a corner of her lip. "But I've failed to give you a full and proper warning about my mom."

I raise an eyebrow. "What sort of warning do I need?

Does she collect garden gnomes?" April shakes her head, her pretty curls hitting her cheeks. "Brew moonshine in the backyard in an underground bootlegging ring?" Another shake. "She knows Krav Maga and uses it regularly on all her children's significant others when they least expect it?"

She laughs and answers as she shrugs off that little white wrap, displaying bare arms. But I lose track of what she says because her arms are sexier than I ever imagined a woman's arms could be. They're fit and toned, and just the tiniest bit muscular. I stifle a groan. Maybe it's a rumble. Because my traitorous brain had the brilliant but very bad idea to imagine how she'd look with those arms above her head, grasping the headboard. All long, and stretched out, and ready.

Nice work, brain.

"So you won't mind?"

I blink, trying to shoo away the thoughts of her without any clothes, invisible or not. I have no idea what I won't mind. "No, that won't be a problem."

"Good." April nods several times, draws a sharp breath, rocks on those wedge heels. "Because she's a recovering attorney," April spits out, like it's a confession on par with, *She's got one glass eye and hates when you stare at it, so please don't.*

"Recovering?"

"You can never truly be fully recovered from being an attorney. We really had to be there for her to support her as she broke the addiction to lawyering."

"I trust she's happier now?"

"Yes, but the attorney in her is never far from the surface. She was a former prosecutor. She sometimes can't help herself. She likes to ask questions."

I nod and give her a reassuring grin. "I can handle that."

"A *lot* of questions, Theo." She's emphatic, and clearly she's prepping me for the Mom Inquisition. "She tries really hard to be nonargumentative, but that's sort of like asking a banana to be round."

"Have you done that before? Asked a banana to be round?" I ask in complete seriousness.

"No, because I've heard it's quite difficult."

I drop a hand to her shoulder so I can reassure her.

Bad mistake.

Her skin is soft. Incredibly soft. My brain goes haywire, and I picture the inside of my head like a robot's circuit board, frying from contact. I should let go. I've never gotten physical with a client. I've never wanted to before, and I don't intend to this time either. It's the worst kind of mistake, as it'd blow my reputation as a boyfriend-for-hire to smithereens.

But this shoulder is insanely enticing.

And something is definitely wrong with me if I'm getting turned on by her shoulder. I let go. "I'm ready."

"Ready for what?"

That was not April.

That was the crisp, curious voice of a former attorney. I can tell in seconds. I turn to the voice.

"Mom," April says, throwing her arms around a woman in navy pants and a white blouse, with silvery blond hair pulled back in a low ponytail. Wrinkles line her blue eyes, but she looks more weatherworn than old. She looks experienced and wise.

"My little puppy," her mother says, practically tackle-hugging her daughter.

As April is consumed by motherly arms, I mouth *little puppy* behind her and smirk. She narrows her eyes in a *do not ever repeat that* way.

"Good to see you, Mom."

"How are you? How is everything? How is work? Are you getting by? Do you need us to help?"

And I see what April means about her parents and her job.

"Work is great, Mom. I finished a commercial earlier this week."

"A commercial! How exciting. I had no idea you could paint a commercial."

"I paint people in commercials, Mom," she says, clarifying.

"Right, of course. Be sure to tuck that money away, since you never know when you'll get another job like that."

April nods at me. Her mom jumps in. "And who do we have here? I'm Pamela Hamilton. And you are?"

She extends a hand and I shake. It's showtime. "Theo Banks. Pleasure to meet you."

"Pleasure to meet you, too."

April straightens her shoulders, raises her chin. It's like she's filling herself up with self-confidence. "He's my boyfriend," April chimes in, loud and chipper.

Pamela keeps her eyes on me. "So I surmised."

"We've been together for a little over one fabulous month," April adds brightly, nearly stammering on the lie.

"One month, you say?" Pamela asks, like she's cross-examining her and wondering why her daughter's boyfriend hasn't come up yet in conversation. But one month is a reasonable time for a new relationship to fly under the radar. A blush creeps across April's cheeks, and I can see the wheels turning in her head—they're saying, *Oh shit, I need to act totally cool and casual and not try to sell the jury on him, because if I sell too hard, Mom will sniff out the truth like a bloodhound.*

So I slide in to save her. I wrap an arm around her, tug

her close, and drop a quick kiss on her cheek. "Six fantastic weeks, to be precise. I was ready to shout it from the rooftop the week we met, but April wanted to play it safe."

Her mother clucks her tongue. "A month and a half is a solid start. Let's see what happens after another month."

I run my fingers through April's hair possessively. It feels amazing, soft and silky. April trembles the slightest bit. "And I convinced April that now would be a good time to let everyone know we're a thing."

April nods several times, recovering. "We're totally a thing."

Pamela gives me a quick once-over, then seems content enough to segue. "Are you tired? Are you hungry? Do you need anything?"

Those hardly seem like the kinds of questions one needs to be warned about. They're standard hostess inquiries. "I'm all good."

"Me, too," April says, then takes a step toward the door.

Pamela doesn't move. Her heels dig into the floor, and she stares at me. "Theo, where did you go to college?"

April sighs. "Seriously?"

"This is an important question," her mother says, leveling me with an intense *I'm waiting* stare.

Ah, that's more like it, the old college question. But it's answerable, too. I give my practiced reply. "School of Hard Knocks."

"Ha ha."

Yes, her mother actually says *ha ha*. It's cute. Not in an *I'm attracted to her mother* way, because that would be the type of creepiness that sets off alarm bells. But in an *I can see where April gets her sense of humor* way.

"I went there, too. And then I got my graduate degree from the University of Learning the Hard Way," her mom says.

I adopt a more serious expression and give her a truthful answer. "I went to state school in New York," I say, naming the public university I put myself through.

Her mom nods, satisfied, it seems. "That's a good school. I'm pleased to hear. And did you have a good train ride?"

A wild idea occurs to me. April doesn't want her family to set her up with anyone who would tie her to her hometown. Maybe I need to give her mom exactly what she wants, and maybe that'll help April, too. Perhaps April doesn't need the bad boy. Maybe she needs someone they'll like, and who'll get them off her case. I don't overthink my plan. I go for it. "It was great. April and I talked about politics, news, all the critical topics of the day. But that stuff probably bores you."

Pamela's eyes laser into me. "Are you kidding me? I love news and issues. Nobody ever wants to touch them, though."

I make a gesture with my index finger as if I've just touched something hot, then follow it with a sizzling noise. "Like legalized marijuana and minimum wage?"

Pamela's blue eyes shine, not just with happiness but possibly with glee. "I can chat all night about this. I firmly believe minimum wage should be higher, and I fully support legalizing marijuana, but only for medicinal reasons."

"I like your stance. How about the death penalty?"

"A part of me is completely in support of it, when it comes to the most heinous crimes. You won't see me batting an eye in those cases."

April's eyelids flutter, like she can't quite process this conversation. She gawks at me, then her mom, as Pamela launches into a discussion about murder convictions overturned, before we segue into a quick debate on gun control.

April nearly vibrates from shock. My fake girlfriend blinks, like she's trying to process what's going on before her very eyes as her mother discusses incendiary topics with her daughter's beau.

After a few minutes in the tiny train station, Pamela smiles and clasps my arm. "This was fun. I can't wait to chat even more with you." Then she seems to realize that she has more questions for me. Her eyes linger on my tats, and I bet she's thinking what most parents think—guys with ink are troublemakers. "Where do you see yourself in five years?"

"Mom!" April chides, having successfully reattached her jaw.

April wasn't kidding.

Her mom goes for it, so I do the same. I wrap an arm around April, yanking her close in my most possessive style. I don't give her mom the rebel attitude. I don't sling a question at her. I answer her in a way that a good attorney would, with something to keep her off-balance, and maybe with a little extra designed just to make a mother happy. "Married with two kids, and bringing them to visit their absolutely wonderful grandmother for the weekend."

Her mom's eyebrows knit. She's not sure what to make of me. April's expression morphs from shock to wonder to a strange sort of curiosity, like I'm not exactly what she expected either. Maybe Pamela thinks a guy like me can get April to move back home. Ha. Try again.

April squeezes her mom's arm. "Mom, why don't we head to the Sunnyside?"

"Let's go, and we can discuss these grandchildren another time." Her mother spins efficiently on her heel—I have a feeling her mother does everything efficiently, then nearly skips down the steps into the warm June night.

April nudges me, then playfully reprimands. "That was not a bad boy response."

I drop my nose to her neck and drag it up to her ear. "Forgive me." The sharp intake of air tells me I'm forgiven.

She swats me.

I laugh. "You said you wanted me because my ad was funny, not because you wanted me to do all those things."

"Fine. Fine. I just didn't expect she'd be eating out of the palm of your hand in ten seconds."

I lower my voice to a bare whisper. "But if she thought I was bad news, she might push you to marry the poodle man. I can be a jerk tomorrow, if you want?"

She shakes her head, then whispers once more. "I even told you to just smile and nod, but you had to go and win her over right away."

I laugh loudly. "Sorry, cupcake. I didn't hear that. I was distracted by you."

She arches one eyebrow. "What on earth were you distracted by?"

I roam my eyes along her arms. "You have nice arms. They're distracting."

April's lips twitch. She's fighting off a grin.

I touch her again, my fingers brushing along her triceps, my thumb on her biceps. She shivers the slightest bit. "I bet they're toned from work. From painting. You use your arms for everything. They're naturally strong."

A whoosh of breath comes from her lips. She blinks, breathes out hard again, then leans closer to me. "I have to tell you a secret."

"Tell me."

Her lips are near my ear. "Your arms are distracting, too."

Then she turns and gestures to the doorway. "Let's go."

"Whatever you say, little puppy."

She wheels on me and wags a finger. "Don't call me 'little puppy.'"

"It's going to be really hard for me not to call you that now." We walk down the steps to a waiting golf cart. I load our suitcases into the back.

"The Sunnyside is only a mile away," April explains, gesturing to the unusual mode of transport. "And my mom really likes to drive her golf cart around town when it's not too far."

Her mom pats the front seat, indicating I should join her. I do as she wishes. "A golf cart is better for the earth. It uses less gas. We can discuss global warming tomorrow, Theo."

April sighs from the backseat, but she sounds amused rather than annoyed. "At last, she's found someone who'll talk about the things no one else will discuss in polite company."

Pamela shrugs happily. "It's part of my twelve-step program. Find someone to debate issues with rather than practice law."

She turns the key in the ignition, and I ask, "So what's the Sunnyside?"

April leans forward. "It's what all recovering attorneys do. Take a guess."

I look at Pamela. "You've become a romance novelist?"

April's mom laughs and shakes her head as she pulls away from the station. "Do a lot of attorneys become romance writers?"

"Since attorneys are often unhappy, and romance writers seem to be happy, it seemed like you might jump from one to the other." I scrunch my brow for a few seconds, then snap my fingers. "I bet if you were once an attorney, you're now writing legal thrillers. Crazy jurors, dangerous attorneys, corrupt judges."

April's mom glances at her in the rearview mirror. "He has quite an active imagination."

April smirks. "You have no idea."

We roll along a quaint side street full of picturesque homes and cute bungalows. We aren't far from the water, and the scent of the sea wafts through the air. I look away briefly, toward the sound of the shore, and the lapping of the waves in the distance. The shore reminds me of some of our greatest hits—my brother and me. There's something about water, and the ocean, and sand. It does something to people. Opens them up. Makes them feel. Makes them want.

I snap my gaze away, and something clicks.

Golf cart. The Sunnyside. Recovering attorney. "Mrs. Hamilton, do you run a bed-and-breakfast?"

April's mom smiles as wide as the night sky, and she nods proudly. "I do indeed."

As we turn the corner onto a tree-lined block, the smell of salt air grows stronger, tickling my nostrils. Leaves flutter in the evening breeze, and streetlamps cast orange cones of light on the pavement. Up ahead, a wooden sign planted in the front lawn tells me we're approaching the B and B. It's a sprawling inn, three stories high and just as wide, perched at the end of a curving driveway. Pamela turns into the drive, and I can see a porch that wraps around the inn, with flowerpots adorning the railings, and a wooden swing swishing faintly. Even at night, the place looks both stately and full of warmth.

"All the Hamiltons will stay here," Pamela says proudly as she stops the cart and cuts the engine.

I carry our bags up the stone path, and a big, burly man waits on the porch.

"Dad!"

April races up the steps, and her father wraps her in the

very definition of a bear hug. "Hey, sweetie pie. I had to stay up to see my little girl." He closes his eyes as he hugs her, and the look on his face is pure contentment.

April's dad isn't a grizzly. He's a teddy bear.

He sports a beard that he's likely had since before beards were trendy. He's kept most of his brown hair on top of his head, too, and his face is lined with wrinkles and freckles, visible under the porch lights.

When he lets go of her, his smile is endless. "So good to see you."

"You, too."

His expression turns stern as he meets my eyes and extends a hand.

"I'm April's father. Josh Hamilton."

"Theo Banks. Pleasure to meet you, sir."

"You, too," he says gruffly, then gestures for us to go inside.

April heads in first, several feet ahead. As I step onto the polished hardwood past the entryway, I overhear her father whisper, "Did you give him the third degree?"

Pamela stammers for a moment with an "Um," before she recovers. "Of course. I kept him on his toes."

"Good. We need to give him a hard time," he says, leaving me wondering why her parents want me to feel unwelcome.

April swivels around. "Hey, Mom, what room are we in?" She turns to me. "Every room is named for a breakfast food."

Pamela's tone is that of a schoolteacher. "You can stay in the Crepe Room, April."

"Theo, you can stay in the Pancake Room," her dad adds quickly.

April shoots them a look that loosely translates to *Are*

you nuts? "Isn't every room going to be packed for the reunion?"

"Not until tomorrow," her mother says, and Operation Hard Time has begun.

I jump in, sensing a chance to let them know I'll play by their rules, even though I doubt April will accept them. "I'd be more than happy to sleep on the couch," I say with a smile, since I'll need to disarm their new attack with goodwill.

April's father nods, as if he likes that idea. "That's fine."

"Let me get you some blankets, then," April's mom says.

"And a pillow," Josh adds, and I smirk inside—if he wants me to have a soft landing for my head, his hard-ass routine is just a routine.

"Maybe we can give him a glass of milk and some cookies, too," April says, staring at her parents like they've each sprouted two heads.

"I can try to rustle some up," her mom offers.

I place my hands together, as in prayer. "I love cookies before bed."

"And I love cookies anytime," April says, frustration seeping into her tone. "But seriously, why do you want him to sleep in the living room?"

"Well," her father begins, but can't seem to finish the thought.

"Because . . . ," her mom tries.

April stares at her mom. "We're not some old-fashioned family. Tess and Cory lived together before they were married. So did Mitch and Candace."

"But the couch is so comfortable," her dad says, trying once more.

"There will be people coming and going the whole

time," April says. "That makes no sense to put him on the couch."

"You're right," April's dad says, tapping his lip. "I'll grab the old camping equipment and he can set up a tent on the lawn."

April slashes a hand through the air. "Mom! Dad! I'm not fifteen. Theo is sharing a room with me, and that's that."

"I forgot to warn you. Sometimes aliens inhabit my parents," April says as we walk up the stairs.

"I've heard that can happen after alien invasions, so no worries."

"No, seriously. I'm sorry about that couch episode," she says, flashing a contrite smile.

"Don't think twice about it. I suspect your mom realized she wasn't supposed to play so nice with me and is hoping to send me packing so you can date Merlin the Poodle. Or whoever they wanted to set you up with."

April laughs. "If dating a poodle brought me home, they'd set me up and find a way to kick you out."

"I'll be on the lookout for poodle suitors, then."

We reach a white door with an illustration of a crepe on it. When we enter the room, I see one bed.

That answers all my questions about the sleeping arrangements.

Chapter Nine *Theo*

Xman: Tell me stuff.

Theo: What sort of stuff do you want to know?

Xman: Oh gee. I don't know. I was mostly curious what kind of boxers you had on.

Theo: I'm wearing long johns.

Xman: Suits you, since you're an ugly bastard. Now tell me how you and April are getting on.

Theo: Wow. You pick up the Britishisms quickly.

Xman: I'm nimble like that. Extraordinarily flexible, too. Now, spill. Isn't she a total doll?

I look up from the screen. A mouthwatering image of blueberries folded inside a sugar-dusted crepe stares at me from the antique bureau. A mouthwatering woman is in the bathroom, getting ready for bed. I'm parked on a love seat wedged against the bay window that looks out over the spacious grounds. Briefly, I consider Xavier's question. Is April a doll? More like a babe. A fox.

Theo: She is. 100%.

Xman: Ooh. My phone just dropped due to shock.

Theo: Your phone is shocked?

Xman: *I'm* shocked. You responded without sarcasm.

Theo: Was I supposed to be sarcastic? She's great. It's that simple. I'm not sure if I should be thanking you or punching you when you return for connecting me with her.

Xman: Ooh! Every matchmaking bone in my body just tingled.

Theo: One, let's not discuss any bones in your body. Two, nothing will happen between us, so put your pretty little pom-poms away.

Xman: Why do you have to have that stupid don't-get-involved-with-clients rule?

Theo: Oh, you know. Just that crazy reason of wanting to keep my job.

Xman: And you truly think a little tryst would affect it?

Theo: Just imagine the next girl who hires me. I become a gigolo then.

Xman: Grrr. I'm so mad at you for being so principled. Besides, April could use it.

I sit up straighter. This information is getting interesting. I tap a quick reply—asking, *Yeah?*—as a spray of water grows louder, and strong. That's not the sink faucet. She's in the shower. Ah hell. She's in the shower, which means she's naked. Which means I now officially understand for the first time why people choose to be invisible. Yep. Because if I could, I absolutely would pick it now, open the door, slip into the bathroom, and watch her soap up her naked flesh. April could use *it;* so could I.

Part of me knows I should shut down this conversation. But another part is too curious to let it go.

> **Theo:** What do you mean?

> **Xman:** I might also have had a few drinks ☺

> **Xman:** Yes. The Guinness here is amazing.

> **Theo:** I meant about April.

> **Xman:** April's like the Guinness. She's amazing too. And she's on the wagon. Evidently, she's principled, just like you. But in her case, her last boyfriend was a lying cad, so she's sworn off men.

I stare at his message. *Lying cad.* But I'm not lying about anything important, I remind myself. *You're also not her boyfriend, idiot.*

> **Theo:** She deserves way better than that. She deserves someone who treats her well.

> **Xman:** I couldn't agree more. When I return to New York, I'll have to see if I can weave my magic and convince her to date again. I want to play fairy godmother and find her a fabulous man worthy of her.

A kernel of jealousy whips through me as I flop back on the love seat, reading the last note. But as the soundtrack of April's shower drums through the room, I tell myself I have no right to feel envy over men she might date down the road. April's a client, and that's all she is. The water in the bathroom slows to a trickle, so I need to shut down this exchange stat.

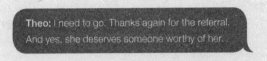

Theo: I need to go. Thanks again for the referral. And yes, she deserves someone worthy of her.

For the next few days, I need to convince her parents I'm that guy.

Chapter Ten *April*
Ten minutes earlier

Claire: Did he kill you on the train ride?

April: Yes, I'm dead. You're talking to my ghost.

Claire: Tell me every gory detail, and I will fight for justice for you. I hear ghost evidence is now admissible in court.

April: If you really thought he would kill me, why did you let me go?

Claire: Ah, so now it's my fault you're dead. Good to know.

April: It's your fault, but I'll still leave my yogurt shop frequent buyer card to you in my will, as well as the Manilow albums.

Claire: And you're close to a big cup yogurt with all the toppings, so that's pretty enticing. Also, since your date didn't snuff you, does that mean he survived meeting your parents?

April: The initial meeting, yes. My mom sort of fell for him immediately, then remembered he's the roadblock to all her hopes and desires.

Claire: Does that mean she'll be administering a secret intravenous drip of Benadryl to knock him out for four days, so she can implement her nefarious plan to convince you to move home?

April: Probably. Also, can you actually give someone a secret IV drip?

Claire: We sent a man to the moon and invented stain remover, so I don't see why not.

April: Let's not forget boyfriends-for-hire when it comes to useful inventions.

Claire: Speaking of, how's the hottie?

April: He's fun. Easy to talk to. We chatted the whole train ride.

Claire: Uh-oh.

April: Uh-oh what?

Claire: You know where talking leads.

April: To conversations?

Claire: To the end of a dating moratorium. Incidentally, Tom and I have a betting pool on how long it'll take you to cave.

April: You do not.

Claire: Tom has given you three days. And I decided it'll take you about 24 hours.

April: To what do I owe the utter lack of faith in my restraint?

Claire: How long has it been? A year?

April: I don't remember. I don't keep track. I'm not even thinking about that.

Claire: Lying liar who lies, with pants on fire.

April: Everything is fine, and there are no pants or parts on fire.

Claire: Somehow I doubt you. Are you sharing a room with him? I bet your mom put you in the Sausage Room!

April: There is no Sausage Room!

Claire: Yours is going to be the sausage room so very soon. So, are you sharing a room with him?

April: Yes.

Claire: I'm revising my wager. I'm going with 12 hours.

I toss the phone on the vanity across from the sink, and it clatters along the marble. Why did I get caught up in Claire's betting pool? In the reflection, I glance at the door behind me, leading into the bedroom. Behind that door is an antique bureau; a king-size bed covered in a pristine white comforter; a photo of ripe, red strawberries on the nightstand; and, most notable of all, an outrageously handsome man. With stubble, and wild dark eyes, and ink on his biceps, and a dirty grin on his face.

How am I going to get in that bed with that man? I cast a side-eye glance to the shower and heave a sigh.

A girl's got to do what a girl's got to do.

Personally, I find shower O's a bit challenging, and not always worth the effort. You have to find just the right angle, and then you have to diddle yourself standing up. That's just weird, right? If I had a showerhead with ten speeds, it might be a different story. But this bathroom doesn't have one, and if it did, you can bet I wouldn't slide something between my legs that might have been used by others.

I crank on the stream and give the fingers-only style the old college try. Maybe it's because Theo's in the room mere feet away, or perhaps it's because Theo is insanely hot in a criminally handsome way. Whatever the reason, my fingers slip-slide easily. Over, up, down. Heat rises in me, spreads over my skin, thrums through my body. I move faster, fly farther. And I'm on the cusp of getting there. Right there. A moan slips past my lips. A heavy ache pulses between my legs, and heat climbs up my thighs. I press my forehead to the tile while hot water streams down my back.

I shudder, then bite my lip, silencing the sounds I want to make, the name I want to moan into the steam.

When the release fades, I'm left with the stark awareness that I want my fake boyfriend more than I should.

More than is good for me. I wash up, turn off the water, and pull on a white T-shirt and sleep shorts, and towel-dry my hair.

When I yank open the bedroom door, Theo stuffs his phone into the pocket of his jeans like he's the fastest draw in the West. I half wonder what he's hiding, but then I'm not one to talk.

"It's all yours." I gesture grandly to the pleasure den. I mean, the bathroom. He heads in.

As I slip under the cool covers of the bed, the summer breeze lifting the white curtains in the window, I do feel a little better. A little relief.

But I also feel a little naughty.

Like when you have an unexpected dirty dream about a boss and have to go into work the next day.

When the click of the bathroom door unlocking hits my ears a few minutes later, I grip the top of the covers. Theo steps out of the bathroom, and I burn as I try not to stare at him. Every inch of my skin is sparking.

He gestures to his bare chest. "Do you care if I sleep without a shirt? I get hot at night."

"I get hot at night, too," I blurt out, and instantly, I want to reel those words back in.

His lips curve up, and he nods at me. "You look a little flushed, cupcake."

"The covers are hot," I say, pushing them to my stomach.

He tips his chin toward me. "And you've got that smoldering look in your eyes again. Like the night we met."

I take the small blue decorative pillow behind me and throw it at him.

Deftly, he catches it in one hand. He's grinning. "Nothing wrong with smoldering eyes. Especially wild green ones like you have."

He tosses the pillow back at me. I raise my arms and catch. "Yours are smoldering, too."

I know you are, but what am I?

I give myself a humongous mental eye roll. Why did I think hiring a hottie would be easy?

He pads across the wooden floor, the boards creaking gently. "Don't you remember?" He walks closer to the bed, leans down, parks his palms on the white covers. "Your smoldering eyes make you irresistible."

And I've officially melted. I'm a puddle of a woman. The circuit breakers have fried from the heat under my skin. I grab the wheel and swerve to the right. "I thought you'd have more ink." My words come out breathy, and that annoys me. "Your chest is bare."

The sky is blue.

Water is wet.

Can I say anything else that's patently obvious?

He looks down at his pecs, then back up at me. "I left that undone deliberately."

"Why?"

"So I'd have a blank canvas, in case I want that. Maybe someday I'll fill it in."

He lifts the cover and slides under. We are two logs. We are boards that frame the edge of a square. We lie there, noses pointed skyward, staring at the ceiling.

Silence descends. It's not companionable. It's necessary. But even so, I can't conceive of a world where he doesn't know what I did in the shower.

I roll to my side. "Good night, Theo."

"Good night, April."

But five minutes later, we're both restless and rustling. He props himself on his elbow. "Do you need a bedtime story?"

Chapter Eleven *Theo*

Her voice is soft, a hush against the night. "Do you have a good one to tell me?"

"Do you like fairy tales or real stories?" I ask her as the moonlight skates across her bare arm, tucked over the top of the cover.

"Real stories."

"Like the first time we stayed at a B and B?"

I can feel her smile. She shifts in the bed, the sheets rustling. Turning, she looks at me. "Remind me. When was that?"

"A couple weeks ago. We took a road trip. You hate my bike, so I rented a car."

"I don't hate your bike," she protests, but it's feeble. I know she hates it.

"You do, and it's okay if it bores you. That's why I rented a car. I know you like to talk when we drive, and you can't do that on a bike."

A small laugh flutters from her mouth. "I do like to talk."

"We sucked down Skittles and munched on Pringles

and stopped for dinner at an artichoke-themed diner and we talked the whole time, before we checked into an old-fashioned B and B with a ladybug theme."

"That's right. Our bedcovers were red with black polka dots."

I chuckle. This girl and her improv. "The bed was tiny. Not like this huge king-size bed," I say, sweeping my hand over the space between us. There is so much space between us. A shadow shimmies across the foot of the bed as the curtains drift in the breeze.

"We were stuffed in that tiny bed, and I woke with a terrible crick in my neck," she says, raising a hand over the sheets to rub against the back of her neck.

"Because I was a complete bed hog. And you were wedged along the side of the bed all night long."

She reaches to swat me. "You're so mean."

When she does that, the sheet slips low, down to her waist. Her little white shirt rides up, and my breath catches. I break character. "You have stars on your hips."

I point to the constellation on her skin. A swirl of midnight blue ink.

"Oh." She casts her eyes down, like she's just noticing the ink on her body. "Yeah, I do."

I hold my breath as I stare. It feels like a secret she kept from me, but I don't know why. All I know is it's beautiful, and never has a tattoo looked prettier on a girl than these five stars flying over her flesh. Maybe it's the location. There's nothing quite so seductive as the hip bone, and the promise of where it leads to.

Or maybe it's the surprise, since I didn't expect to see her skin marked.

"I love them," I say, and my voice is hoarse. Because what I want to say is that I'd like to kiss them. I'd like to touch them.

"You said that the night at the inn, even though you'd seen them so many times before," she speaks softly, reminding me of our bedtime tale.

"I say it a lot, don't I? Every time I see the stars, it feels like the first time."

"Maybe that's why you're always staring at them."

"I don't just stare at them."

"What else do you do?" she asks so softly, and it's an invitation. She's asking to play the train fantasy game again. I should turn her down, but instead I RSVP.

"Kiss them." My voice is rough. My answer is simple.

She says nothing, just shifts her hips almost imperceptibly.

"Lick them."

Her breath hitches, but she stays silent, because this is my fantasy, only I can tell from her reaction that it's hers, too. I lift my arm, moving closer, my fingers hovering near that hip bone, then I dust my thumb across it. "Touch them."

She closes her eyes as a slight tremble runs through her. It's so sexy, and it's so clear we need to stop this game.

I can't let the starlight on her body, or the silvery glow of the moon dancing on her pale skin erode my defenses. They exist for a reason. Nothing matters more than self-protection. I yank up the covers and flip her to her side, facing away from me. I pat the white cover, stuffing the downy material between us, so I'm not tempted to sidle up next to her. It's a barrier, and a necessary one. I lift my hand to her neck, and her breath catches once more as I push her blond curls off her neck. "No need for a crick in the neck. I'm good with my hands."

She lets out a soft sigh and seems to sink deeper into the mattress as I gently rub her neck. I push my thumb into the flesh. She moans her approval, so I keep going. A few minutes later, she whispers my name. "Theo?"

"Yeah?"

"You pulled off one of the items from your à la carte menu."

I laugh and recite the item: "Start provocative and/or incendiary discussion about politics and religion."

"Have your other clients wanted that, too?"

"Sometimes, but if someone hired me because she was truly mad at her parents, she'd usually want me to be a total dick. This one chick was so pissed at her dad for cheating on her mom that she wanted me to cause a huge scene at the Thanksgiving dinner table."

"Like throwing mashed potatoes?"

I laugh. "Green bean casserole, too."

"Did you do that?" Her tone drips with curiosity, and she shifts to her back, meeting my eyes.

"April, her dad was a dick for cheating on her mom. All I had to do was deliberately knock over a casserole to make my client feel the tiniest bit like she was getting even with her dad."

"Hmmm."

"Does that bother you? That I did that?"

I brace myself for her answer. If she's perturbed by the thought of me toppling a casserole, I can only imagine what she'd think if she learned about all the other shit I've pulled. But she won't learn, because I won't tell.

She shakes her head, and I'm relieved. I can feel the air flow more easily in my body. I wanted her green bean absolution. "No. I mean, it's odd to me to picture it, but only because I can't imagine truly wanting to do that. Sure, a part of me finds it amusing and entertaining, and I can understand the impulse to just strut into a family gathering and wreak havoc." She swings an arm back and forth, like a gal with attitude for miles. "But even though everyone is up in my business, I still don't want to flip a green bean casserole."

"If it's any consolation, it was a completely nasty casserole, and I saved everyone from having to eat that crap."

She laughs softly; then the sound fades into the inky night. She rests on her side again, and I resume massaging her neck. I highly doubt she has a crick in her neck, but I just like touching her.

"I love that you've found different ways to act. It reminds me of how I would paint faces on anyone willing. You have to do that when you're in this kind of creative field, don't you think?"

"Yes," I say, swallowing the lie. I wish she wasn't so fascinated with my "career." It's the one area where I can't be honest with her, but I have to perpetuate the tale. "You do have to find unique ways to exercise your artistic muscles."

"I love that analogy. I believe that."

Even though I have a poker face, I'm so glad she can't see mine right now. "Sorry I haven't won over your dad," I say, turning away from the topic of careers. "But I'll keep working on it. Your parents are cool, even though they're trying to hate me."

"They don't hate you at all. Is it weird that I mostly like my family?"

I swallow, unsure at first how to answer. "I'm not really the best expert on family. But I think it's a good weird."

She's quiet for a few more seconds; then she speaks softly. "Did your parents die in a car crash or a plane crash?"

I flinch.

"Sorry if that's too personal. But you said you were fourteen when they died. I figured they went together. I hope that's not too nosy, but I can't help but wonder. And

I hope it's not awful for you to be around my big crazy family tomorrow."

I heave a sigh. "Families are always complicated and crazy. It'll be fine."

She nods.

"And," I say, swallowing harshly, "you're right. It was a car crash."

I squeeze my eyes shut, tasting bile, tasting the acid of the lie.

She flips over, and runs a hand down my arm. It's not sexual. It's comforting. "I'm so sorry."

"Me, too." I look away, so she can't see that I'm sorry I'm lying to her. Sometimes the fable is better than the truth.

She lets out a long, lingering breath. "Thank you for telling me."

I mumble something incoherent. I don't know what to say. And I've no more words for a story either. There's no more make-believe to spin tonight, and I don't feel like being myself anymore either. I slip into Fake French. "Mademoiselle, let me feeneesh your mah-saj."

She rolls back over.

"Now, allow me to rub your shoulders, *s'il vous plaît*," I continue.

She laughs softly. *"Merci, monsieur."*

"De rien," I say in the accent that makes her chuckle. "I am only here to serve."

"The service is *très bien*."

"Oh là là. I see you know French, too."

"Un peu."

"Very nice, very nice. Then, we will have baguettes and croissants and sip *café*," I say, rattling off random French things as I rub her shoulders, and soon she drifts into slumber.

I let go of her, sink to my back, and recall my days as a professional sleeper. Those skills help me fall asleep quickly and keep my hands to myself all night, the cover a fortress keeping me from her.

In the morning I find I've slept like a log, the dreamless kind of sleep I like best. I wake up blinking to the sun blaring brightly through the open white curtains. April stands at the foot of the bed, wearing jeans shorts and holding a ceramic mug with an illustration of a big, blue whale shooting water out its blowhole. The caption? MORNINGS BLOW.

I give a faint wave and a raspy good morning. "Nice motto."

"I like mornings," she says with a shrug, her smile radiant, her freckles more noticeable in the bright sunlight.

"I like morning . . ." I trail off, not finishing the thought.

She leans her head back and laughs. "I bet you do."

I park my hands behind my head on the pillow. "You look like you want to make an announcement that has nothing to do with blowing and mornings."

She nods, and smiles wide. "It's the first full day, and I suppose this would be a good time to tell you the Hamiltons don't do regular family reunions."

"They don't?" I arch an eyebrow as she hands me her mug of steaming coffee. I sit up in bed and take a drink of the life-sustaining beverage.

She shakes her head. "Let's just say they're a little different."

I smirk. "You've been holding back. How are they different?"

She takes a deep breath. "Take a shower, join me for breakfast, and you'll learn what we do at the morning announcements."

Guess I'm not the only one who's been keeping secrets.

Chapter Twelve *April*
The second day

A year ago, I dated a man who told me he was divorced. Landon and I were together for three months, and during that time, he pulled off an astonishing lie. Or perhaps I'm just an astonishingly gullible girl.

Landon was a busy guy, a creative type working in the TV business, and I'd met him on a job promoting a new international-themed travel show. He'd stopped by the photo shoot and checked out the flags from the United States, the United Kingdom, and Australia that I'd been painting on the models for the promo. We hit it off and he asked me out. Landon took me out to fantastic dinners and on wonderful dates around the city—dates that were tailor-made for me. We went to art shows, and he'd grab my hand, tug me into a quiet alcove, and kiss the breath out of me, making my head hazy and my body vibrate with want for him. Then he'd take me to his Upper East Side place, the most pristine chrome-and-white man pad I'd ever seen.

"It looks like a show home," I'd said.

"I just moved into it, and I like to keep my place clean," he'd said with a chuckle, then he'd lift me up on the counter, and we'd make it dirty.

He never asked me to stay the night, and he didn't sleep at my place either. "I feel terrible, but I'm the lightest sleeper," he'd said. "The neighbor coming home and unlocking the door wakes me up, so I need to go full eye mask and earplugs. It's better if I sleep alone."

I'm all for quirks, but I could live without cuddling next to a masked man all night, so I didn't push.

He'd even met my friends. He'd gone out to drinks with Xavier, Claire, and me. A week later, Xavier spotted him at a Murray Hill restaurant with a brunette; then he slipped into the booth behind Landon's and actually recorded the conversation Landon was having with . . . *his wife.*

It was about their mortgage, the water bill, and if she'd picked up his dry cleaning.

I was shocked and hurt, but mostly I was flaming mad. I kept our date for that next evening, and over the shrimp course, I casually mentioned what I'd learned and showed him the photo. Landon backpedaled and told me his divorce just wasn't final yet. I hit Play on the recording.

"Babe, I need the pink-checked shirt for my meeting in L.A. later this week. Can you pick it up for me?"

He licked his lips, his eyes like a deer, but he wasn't a skilled liar for nothing. "We still help each other out. She happens to live closer to the cleaner."

"Right. I'm sure there's no cleaner next to your place." I smacked my forehead. "Oh, wait—it's not your new home. It's your screw pad for cheating."

"Let's talk about this. I swear we're not together, April."

I stood and parked my hands on the table, and boy, did I feel like a badass chick in a movie as I hissed, "And neither are we." I turned on my heel, then I stopped, looked over my shoulder, flicked my hair, and said, "By the way, the pink-checked shirt is hideous."

I'd walked out feeling like I was ten feet tall and wearing black stilettos.

But when I was home alone that night, the reality crashed down. Maybe I'd had the last word, and maybe it was silver screen worthy, but I was also the fool who'd believed him, who'd slept with him, who'd felt like she was falling in love with him.

To make matters worse, I'd risked something important. *My work.*

Fine. I hadn't known Landon was still married when I met him on the shoot. But what if I'd mentioned him to someone in the business? What if while out for drinks with work friends, I'd said I was involved with him? Then I'd be April the home-wrecker, and that wouldn't be so good for a woman rising up in her career.

It was pure, dumb luck that his name had never come up in my work circles. I was Indiana Jones grabbing his hat before the boulder crushed it. I'd escaped unscathed, and I needed to learn a lesson.

But what was the lesson? How would I have known Landon was lying? Maybe his pristine apartment was the tip-off, but I'd dated neat men before. Perhaps the "light sleeper" routine should have been the clue, but everyone has idiosyncrasies.

In the end, I exonerated myself because the truth was this: Landon was a world-class liar. The only way to protect myself was to avoid *any* Landons and, by extension, any men.

In my field, talent is all well and good, but no one wants to hire the contractor who'll sink claws into the married men.

I had to protect my reputation, and I made my choice.

Shut down romantic operations for a while till I developed better radar for separating the wheat from the chaff.

Landon is one of the reasons my family wants to find a man for me. My mom, my sister, and my aunt believe the Landons of the world are born and bred from online dating, from the world of Tinder. That's why the ladies have been sending me emails and notes and developing their plans to set me up with the men of Wistful. They want to save me from the men of the internet, and they want to bring me home.

After I leave the room so Theo can shower, I head outside, where Aunt Jeanie executes the first ambush.

She's stealthy as a pussycat. As I kneel in the gardens at the back of the Sunnyside, clipping sprigs of lavender for the table, her voice floats into my ear.

"There you are!"

I straighten and stand, the flowers in my hand. "Hey, Aunt Jeanie."

Jeanie, my father's sister, is spry and athletic and ready for action in her yoga pants and a formfitting raspberry sports top. Her short brown hair is tucked neatly behind each ear, a few strands of silver speckled throughout. She's younger than my father by a few years, making her sixty. An intensely athletic sixty. She gives me a warm hug.

"So good to see you. Why don't you come back more often?"

"I try to visit a couple times a year."

When we break the embrace, she waves a hand dismissively. "You were last here at Christmas, and that's simply not often enough." She drops her voice to a hushed whisper. *"You could live here, too, you know."*

I smile, the kind specifically designed to placate. "I know, but the work is in New York, for the most part."

"Pshh. We're only a train ride away. You can work here."

No, I can't.

I sidestep the age-old city versus country debate. "How are Gretchen and Fredericka? Still your best workers?"

Jeanie brings a hand to her heart and sighs contentedly. "Those ladies do me proud every day."

"Will we be enjoying any of their creations this morning?"

"Of course. Your father made the most amazing scrambled eggs, thanks to my top girls."

Aunt Jeanie and her husband, Greg, run an organic egg farm, the kind that devotes acres of leg room to the ladies, so they can lay as many eggs as they wish, all in chicken comfort. Aunt Jeanie's eggs are carried in several local farmers' markets, a handful of regional grocery stores, and nearly every farm-to-table restaurant in a hundred-mile radius.

My stomach growls. I pat it with my free hand. "I think it's safe to say I'm ready for some of Gretchen and Fredericka's output."

"Dear."

That one word is filled with meaning. It says, *Let's talk.* It's filled with *I must discuss something important with you.*

"Yes?"

"I sent you an email a few days ago, and I never heard back." She does her whisper thing again, as though it's a scandalous secret, what she's saying. "About the man I want you to meet."

"I was crazed with work and forgot to reply," I say as we walk across the soft grass to the back porch of the inn.

She pats me on the back. "I can only imagine how busy

you are, living in Manhattan and doing makeup for a living. Must be crazy."

"I paint," I say, correcting.

She nods. "Right. Painting. Painting makeup. So I took the liberty of setting up a morning coffee date with you and Linus."

"What?" I stop in my tracks.

"He's so sweet," she says, her pitch rising. "Linus is a lovely man with a solid, steady business. Greg and I both know him, and we can say that Linus is good, and kind, and smart," she says, speaking for her husband, since she always speaks for him. I've barely heard Uncle Greg utter a word my entire life—but hey, maybe that's what works for them. "Can you honestly tell me you're meeting anyone like that in the city?"

She says *city* like it's the far-distant capital in *The Hunger Games*, a strange and snooty land of otherness, bursting with pink-furred dogs and blue-haired women in pointy-toed heels who have no purpose other than to look pretty. There, I must spend my days whisking around in cool, smooth trams that speed efficiently above a mechanized metropolis.

"There are good men in the city," I say, insistent.

She arches a brow. "Really?"

"Yes. As a matter of fact—" I'm about to mention Theo when Jeanie interrupts.

"—If memory serves, your last boyfriend was a bit of an ass. Remember what you told us at Christmas?"

I cringe as we walk across the yard. "I tried to block that evening from my brain."

The memory of my one-too-many spiked eggnogs on Christmas Eve smashes back into me. That's when I word-vomited up all the sordid details of the married man I'd unknowingly fallen for. I suspect that's also when the Hamilton ladies went into full-on strategy mode, devising a plan to pair me up with a Wistful man. Kill two birds with one stone, they believe.

I meet Jeanie's inquisitive gaze. "Fine, fine. Landon was a mistake. But that doesn't mean every guy is like that. Theo's not," I say, feeling the need to defend my fake boyfriend. There's no way a guy like Theo could even be categorized the same way as a guy like Landon.

She shoots me a look, ignoring the mention of my plus-one as she launches into her next point. "It's so much better to find someone people know. Don't you want to know that a man comes from a good family, that he's truly single, that he's not trying to pull the wool over your eyes?"

"Of course, Aunt Jeanie," I say as we reach the steps at the back of the inn. The Hamiltons are the only ones here for the next four days. My mother doesn't rent the rooms in the Sunnyside during the reunion, so that we can all take over the inn, rather than crowd into my parents' home a mile away. "And I'm sure Linus is lovely. But I'm not interested in being set up."

Her face looks crestfallen. "He's so perfect for you, though, and you'd be nearby. Just give me a good reason."

"I'll give you three good reasons: I don't live here, so I don't want a long-distance relationship, I don't want to talk about mortgage rates, and three—"

"She's taken."

That voice is like a note being plucked on a guitar, held long and lasting, and spreading through my body.

It's possession. It's ownership.

Theo steps onto the porch, the ends of his hair still wet from the shower, his skin smelling fresh and completely lickable, his brown eyes dark and intense. He loops an arm around my waist, yanking me close; then he drops a kiss to my lips.

Stars.

I see stars.

The world winks off as his lips dust mine, soft and gentle and lasting barely more than a second or two.

He ends the kiss as tenderly as he began it, and I want to bring my fingers to my lips to reactivate the kiss, to imprint it on my memory. I'm wobbly and woozy, but he keeps a steady hand on my hip, then turns to my aunt and extends the other hand. "I'm Theo. Nice to meet you. I'm sure Linus is a great guy, but I'm a bit partial to keeping April all to myself. Hope you understand."

He shoots her that most delicious grin.

He's greeted with one in return. Then an arched brow. "Be good to our girl. No shenanigans."

If she only knew shenanigans are what we're up to.

But unlike with Landon, I know the score. There's no tricking me this time.

Chapter Thirteen Theo

The eggs come from Aunt Jeanie's organic egg farm two towns over. They're delicious, soft and fluffy. The breakfast biscuits are courtesy of Tess and her husband, Cory. They run the local bakery. The apricot jam I've spread on mine is the perfect mix of sweet and tarty, and the jam is their creation, too.

The white china with blue vine etching hails from the antiques and consignment shop owned and operated by April's auburn-haired cousin Katie, who is Jeanie's daughter. Katie's husband is in the coast guard, and has been called away on an assignment.

April's brother, Mitch, sits next to me and has been talking about sports, and how the Yankees are killing it this season, and so is his fantasy team. He's one of those guys who can talk about sports all the time, I suspect. Mitch looks like he plays sports, too. He has Popeye arms and an off-kilter nose that was probably broken more than once. He has two daughters, and his eldest already downed a cup of coffee, then excused herself. The younger one, wavy-haired Emma, stabs at her blueberries with the tines of her fork and makes idle chitchat with Jeanie about eggs. I suspect Emma knows the drill. What to say, what to do, how to manage the adults in the family.

I'm still waiting to find out what makes this gathering so unusual. So far this reunion seems 100 percent normal. I'm smothered in this family and all its quaint small-town-ness. I feel like I should break out in hives, but I don't. I've learned Tess thinks I'm cute, Cousin Katie might be naughty since she said my tats reminded her of the hero in a motor-cycle club romance that's been keeping her up at night. Oh, and Aunt Jeanie is off April's back, thanks to me.

I've never done that before—kissed a client on the lips. It's amazing how unnecessary it actually is to kiss on a fake date. Hand-holding, arms draped over shoulders, possessive hugs, tender cheek kisses, even slow dances—I've done all that, but have never crossed the "lip line."

Can't say I regret breaking my rule. As soon as I over-heard the tail end of the conversation, I knew two things: One, April could hold her own. Two, I had the perfect chance to stake my claim, and do the job she hired me to do.

Fine, there was a third thing, too. I wanted to know what her lips tasted like. The answer? Like oranges and sunshine.

I tell myself not to replay that two-second kiss over and over as we eat. It'll only get me aroused. And that's not a good state to be in in the midst of all this family.

Besides, the kiss was only two seconds. It was borderline chaste. Why the hell am I turned on by thinking of it again? Maybe because I slept next to her last night, because I saw those stars on her hip, because I touched her neck and that soft, silky hair. Maybe because we've been telling tales about our sex life, and for once I want life to imitate art.

"Cool T-shirt. Where'd you get it from?"

The question comes from Tess's husband, a balding dark-haired guy who seems to be trying to grow a goatee. My shirt is faded gray with an illustration of an office chair on it, and the words are printed in blocky letters. THE BEST THING ABOUT MY JOB IS THAT THE CHAIR SPINS.

"A store in Brooklyn. One of those places that sells Moleskine notebooks and LPs and T-shirts for hipsters," I say, since that seems to be what he wants to hear. The married guy in the suburbs is always endlessly fascinated by the life of singles in the city. Plus, it's the truth.

"It's awesome. Love it. I want one," he says as he bounces a baby on his shoulder.

Tess rolls her eyes as she tugs at her dark blond pony-tail. "You work at a bakery. You don't have a chair that spins. You don't even really have a chair."

"I don't either, but I still like the shirt," I say.

"See? He gets to have one," Cory says, following it with a hearty yawn.

That's my point exactly. Married dudes want what single guys have, even if it's just the duds. Judging from the bags under his eyes and the tone of voice, this guy might be on the exhausted end of married.

"Fine. I'll get you one," Tess says, but it doesn't sound flirty or affectionate. More resigned. Then, out of nowhere, a curly blond toddler climbs up from under the table and onto her lap. The kid smacks a small hand on his mom's cheek.

"Hi, Mom."

"Say hi with your words, not your hands," Tess admon-ishes.

He swats her again.

Tess sighs and gives her husband an exasperated look.

Cory speaks to his son in a sweet but teaching tone. "Davey, what did we say about hands on faces?"

As Davey answers, I'm about ready to tug off my T-shirt and hand it to Cory. Seems the dude could use a pick-me-up.

A fat orange cat named Mo lounges on a well-worn leather armchair in the sprawling living room adjacent to the dining area. He stares at me with big green eyes. He never blinks. On the wall, a black-and-white tuxedo cat clock ticks and winks, ticks and winks.

"Can I get you something else to eat?" April's mom asks me.

I set my fork down, having cleaned my plate. "No, thank you. That was as perfect as a breakfast can be."

I can't remember the last time anyone cooked breakfast for me. Oh, wait—I can. It was Richelle, the market researcher, who served me pancakes the morning she told me she wanted me to move in with her. The offer was tempting, considering she had a two-bedroom in the Village. She was loaded, and her closet full of Vuitton and Louboutin was like a billboard advertising the swell of her bank account. I didn't date her for money, though. I had no idea how well-off she was. I'd gotten involved with her after she hired me as a professional sleeper. She was impressed with my reports on the beds, and loved the touch of humor I included in my write-ups. Then she wanted me to show her my favorite uses for a bed. They were her favorite uses, too.

We grew closer, then close enough for me to share things I rarely shared with anyone. I told her things I don't tell anyone. Big mistake. A few days later, she rescinded the move-in-with-me offer, along with all her job offers, too. Kicked me out the door with barely a goodbye kiss.

Yeah, that gave me a bitter aftertaste when it comes to opening up my heart to someone.

I don't miss her. She showed her true colors early

enough. I do miss her pancakes, though. They were excellent with blueberries and syrup.

Before Richelle, breakfast was solely a do-it-yourself-dammit meal. My aunt didn't make us breakfast when we lived with her. She was, however, remarkably talented at leaving a box of Rice Krispies on the kitchen counter for Heath and me. Milk was a different story. We had to get that ourselves.

It's hard to fault her. She got stuck with the short end of a stick she never wanted when we were sent to live with her as two messed-up teenage boys, unexpectedly orphaned. But my brother and I figured out what we needed to survive on our own.

When we finish, and after I help Pamela clear the plates—hello, the newest guest *has* to help clear the plates—we take our seats again at the big breakfast table.

"It's time," April whispers with mischief in her tone.

"Good. Because I'm dying to know your little secret."

She laughs, tossing her head back. "It's so very scandalous."

"I'll be shocked, right?"

"Completely. Eyes bugging out of the head and everything."

"Good thing you didn't give me too much warning, then."

She sets her hand on my arm. "I find it's best to take snack-size bites when it comes to learning about my family."

She has no idea.

April's father stands, grabs a cowbell from the table and rings it. Loud and bright.

A boatbuilder, he's the kind of man who works in the sun. But his skin doesn't look like tree bark, so I bet his wife has kept him supplied with top-of-the-line sunscreen his whole life. She looks out for him. I can tell by the way she gazes at him adoringly. It's how my dad looked at my mom, once upon a time.

A lump has the audacity to form in my throat, and I swallow it away, looking at the timekeeping cat's tail switching mechanically back and forth until the feeling disappears.

"Everything okay?" April whispers.

Perceptive one. "Everything is perfect," I whisper, then brush another kiss on her cheek.

It's a harmless kiss, like the one I gave her last night in the train station. Cheeks are not verboten. Her eyelids flutter, though, and I catch a faint whiff of her shampoo. It's ridiculously sexy, and it smells like raspberries. Jesus Christ, I want to kiss her again. I want to move her hair off her neck and learn what the delicate skin there tastes like. I want to drag my nose through all those blond curls. The softest gasp had floated from her lips when I kissed her on the porch, and now I'm damn curious what sounds she'd make if I kissed her deeper, harder, all over.

I spread the napkin over my lap.

The conversations slow and still, and all eyes turn to the patriarch.

"Greetings and good morning to Hamiltons, in-laws of Hamiltons, and friends of Hamiltons, both old and new," he says, but doesn't look at me, and I sense it'll take some time to win him over.

"I couldn't be more delighted to welcome all of you to the Hamilton Family Reunion, to thank you for traveling to Wistful, and to let you know that this year, more than any other year, I want to bring *this* home."

He bends to his chair at the head of the table, grabs something square and silvery from the seat cushion, and holds it high above his head. I peer at the picture frame in his hands. The image inside is a trophy, Vince Lombardi style, with a replica of a wooden boat rather than a football.

"We'll do it, Josh! I know we can," Aunt Jeanie says with a fist pump and a festive cheer. Her husband, Greg, a skinny, quiet guy with a silver mustache, echoes her fist pump with one of his own.

Josh smiles, but it's rueful. "I hope so. It's been eight years since we claimed the trophy. Eight long, devastating years of my best friend and business partner besting me at the Quadrennial Hamilton and Moore Summer Lawn Olympics and Games."

Holy shit. It's a competitive reunion. It's not just picnics and barbecues. It's events, games, and contests.

April leans in to whisper. "Bob Moore is my dad's best friend, who lives down the street and runs the company with him."

"Real useful to give me the details now, cupcake," I tease.

She shrugs and shoots me a cute smile.

Her dad's voice booms across the breakfast room. "And this year, I know we can do it. I know we can beat him at cornhole, Frisbee, watermelon eating, scavenger hunt, egg toss, and even Junk in the Trunk."

I arch a brow at April, and she smirks. "That's a newer one, and it's so fun," she whispers, but I don't glean any more details since her father resumes his speech.

"There will be many more games and events, and over the next few days, I ask you to stand by my side so I can go out on top. As many of you know, at the amazingly young age of sixty-six, I'm retiring from Hamilton and Moore Boats this year, and I would love nothing more than to retire on top. Bob Moore is my best friend and my business partner, but every four years, he is the foe. And we must defeat him."

He thrusts an arm high in the air, and everyone cheers and claps.

April cups her hands around her mouth. "Go, Hamiltons!"

Not to be outdone, Mitch shouts, "Touchdown!"

Pamela takes her turn. "We'll show him who's boss!"

"Whoop whoop!" Cousin Katie calls out, since she seems to have inherited some of her mom's spirit. Or maybe she's just not worn down by young ones yet, like April's sister and her husband.

Because all Cory manages is a halfhearted "woohoo" as he offers a piece of toast to Davey, who swats it away. Tess is now breastfeeding the baby, and her eyes are falling closed.

Tess's eyes. Obviously, I'm not looking that closely at the baby while it's latched on to April's sister's boob.

Watching April's family is like staring at a Rube Goldberg machine, when a silver ball slides down a chute, then slaps a buzzer that sends another ball curling down a twisty coil. You can't look away from a Rube Goldberg machine—it's mesmerizing. So is watching the Hamiltons. If they only knew that family get-togethers when I was younger included strategy sessions for how to avoid my mom's opioid-addicted sister, who'd try to get other family members to nab prescriptions from their docs.

"I have complete faith in the Hamiltons." Josh stops, scratches his chin. His brown eyes twinkle with mischief. "After all, let us not forget what we have pulled off over the years." He gestures grandly to April, a proud look on his face. "Sixteen years ago, my youngest made the Hamilton win possible with her astonishing ability to eat watermelon and a whole pint of ice cream in under four minutes."

My eyebrows shoot into my hairline, and I mouth, *You've been holding out on me.*

She nudges my side with her elbow.

Her father then points to Mitch. "And my son led us to victory in cornhole twelve years ago. May he do it again."

"Hear! Hear!"

Josh Hamilton rattles off more victories over the years, giving everyone their due, it seems. "For those of you joining us for the first time, you might be wondering *why* we do this." He glances at me, meets my gaze. "The answer? Bragging rights, of course."

Everyone laughs. I join in, too, with a chuckle.

"And of course, the trophy itself would be a wonderful thing to gloat over and lord over Bob's head. But there's more at stake. The winning family will receive five thousand dollars from the losing family to donate to a favorite charity. I think we'd all agree that's the biggest prize of all."

"Absolutely," Pamela says as I reach for my coffee and take a drink. "I have a list of worthy causes we can donate to, and I've already researched each one to learn the charity's rating."

Of course she has.

"But because I want the prize badly this year, I'm upping the ante," Josh says. "If we win, I will award an additional five-thousand-dollar cash prize to the all-around winner, who earns the most points and individual victories to lead his or her team."

My mug of coffee nearly slips from my hand. I straighten. My ears perk up.

Cory drops his fork, and his eyes widen to pizza pie size.

Tess shoots him a stare. "Shhh."

He talks out of the corner of his mouth. "Babe, that's good money. We can use it for the college fund."

"The baby won't be going to college for eighteen years, Davey for sixteen. We have enough."

He huffs, and turns his focus back to Josh, and I want to jump in and say to Cory, *Dude, I understand. Believe me, I understand completely.*

Josh sweeps his arms out wide. "So this year, as the Moores descend on the other half of my darling bride's lovely B and B in a few minutes, may they enter with a spirit of camaraderie, but also with a quake in the boots because we will kick some summer reunion butt."

The crowd goes wild. Hoots, hollers, cheers, and yippee-ki-yays.

I'm still sitting here, slack-jawed, awestruck, and amazed that there's money on the table that wasn't here before. As the family scatters to the kitchen, yard, and sitting room, I pull April aside. "You were right. Your family reunion is indeed a little different. A cash prize is awesome."

She stares at me as if I've said something outlandish, like the earth is ending in 270 days, when an asteroid hits it. "It's not really a cash prize."

I wave my arm in the general direction of her dad. "But your dad said it was."

She laughs and rolls her eyes. "But it's really intended for charity. You're generally considered a doucheberry if you don't give it to charity. I mean, who would keep that?" she asks, and it's not a real question. It's a rhetorical one, because she laughs, shakes her head, and is so completely amused by the thought that someone would keep it.

I'm slack-jawed in a whole new way now.

Because she lives in a world where no one has any need to keep that kind of jack.

She drops a hand on my arm and tells me she's going

to see if her mom needs help. She strolls into the kitchen, and I stand alone.

From the doorway, I stare at the Hamiltons. A happy, successful, well-funded family.

An egg farmer, a baker, a boatbuilder, a B and B operator, a son working with his father, a body painter. They can all afford to laugh at five thousand dollars. It's nothing to them. It's funny money. It's money to win in a game, and toss at a charity. They can shrug it off.

I burn with frustration. It courses through my blood. I grit my teeth, then grind them. They play with their kids, and plan their games, and can do this all for what? For fun. For sport. For games.

To toss around five Gs like it's Monopoly money.

I could use five large to get out of debt. To be free. To start living life on my own terms for the first time in fourteen years. Or really, ever.

Does that make me a doucheberry? Maybe it does. April says that like it's the worst thing to be. If so, give me the Doucheberry Award. I can live with that. I'm a damn charity. A gal is chasing me down for money she gave my brother nine years ago. All I want is once and for all not to have to worry about money. To hop on my bike, ride away, and not think twice about who's chasing me.

Money has defined me since my parents died.

Money has been the thing Heath and I chased. We needed dough, and we figured out how to get it faster than by working the fry basket at a fast-food joint.

We were con artists. We were scammers. And, for a while, we were kings.

Looks like our very first scam is one of the events on the schedule for this afternoon.

Chapter Fourteen *Theo*

Bob has three sons and a truckload of grandchildren of all ages. They descend on the inn an hour after breakfast, and Pamela throws open one wing of the B and B to them. This place is spacious, more than twenty rooms, she'd told me.

When his tree-size sons stride out to the back lawn for the first event, I can see why they've dominated arm wrestling the last several years. Bob's got strength on his side. But even if you don't have cannonballs for arms, you can kick unholy ass at arm wrestling. A little speed, a little technique, and some brains are all you truly need.

Heath knew all that when we were kids, and so he started using me in arm wrestling competitions when I was fifteen and he was seventeen. Impromptu shit on the Jersey Shore boardwalks during the summers, when frat guys from the local colleges were drunk and daring.

I was his ringer. He'd hustle me, and set up bets with the Budweiser-swilling, swim-trunks-wearing, BMW-driving crowd. The college guys always took me on, thinking they could win.

I'd let them win the first time, of course. Sometimes the second, too. That's how we reeled them in. I'd take a couple for the team, putting up a short but valiant fight, grunting and groaning, and Heath would lay all the money down on me, then groan and curse when I lost.

That was the game. That's how the rest of them flocked to us like seagulls on french fries. Because all men suffer from the same affliction—they believe they can win at arm wrestling, and they love an easy target.

I wasn't easy, and we'd clean up after that. A few more rounds, and I'd win them all.

Stealth and skill beat brawn, and if you know a few moves, and use your head, you can slam their arms down on the picnic table. For a couple weeks the summer I turned fifteen, we made more than a thousand dollars from rich kids with twenty-dollar bills burning holes in their wet pockets.

Was it a scam? Not technically. But it was a hustle, and it taught us a key lesson—we could pull it off and make money on our own.

I'm not the skinny teen I was then. I'm tall and fit, and I have strong arms, but the guys in Bob's family are more like linemen.

I'm not worried. There's no hustle involved today. Just skill. The key is to take away their biceps power and turn it into a contest of hands. Move fast and first, and gain the leverage. I handle Bob easily, then a couple cousins. Next, Bob's big boys come at me, and under the heat of the high noon sun, I start taking them down.

Thing one, thing two, thing three. They all work on boats. They have names. Huey, Dewey, Louie. Something like that. The first two fall easily.

As the burly Louie parks his huge frame on the bench across from me with a grunty "Hey," I notice a new person wander across the lawn. He doesn't fit in with the others. He wears khaki shorts and a sky blue polo shirt, with a fat silver wristwatch. Dark hair, slicked back.

I grip Louie's hand and move like a speed demon.

Louie growls as I bring his log of an arm mere inches from the burgundy slatted wood, but then he recovers, pushing back, and for a minute or so, we're locked in a stalemate with his hand hovering two inches from the picnic table the whole time. My arm shakes; my muscles strain. But I keep him close to the wood. The trouble is, Louie won't concede, he won't give in. If this persists, we'll be locked like this for a long time.

New guy heads straight for April, who's chatting it up with some of the ladies.

I keep one eye on April, and the problem is her face. She's unbelievably happy. She's beaming, lit up like the Empire State Building on the Fourth of July when she sees the preppy dude.

A dose of envy spurs me on.

Time to finish Louie.

I rotate my shoulder so it's aligned with the table, and all my strength comes from that one part of my body as I slam Louie's hand down without breaking a sweat.

Boom. Done. See ya later.

"Nice match," I say as I stand.

He shakes his hand out, a dazed look in his eyes. As I walk away, I hear him mutter, "Is he a ringer or something?"

I have no interest in him, since the other guy has tugged my girlfriend—I mean, my pretend girlfriend—in his arms for a huge embrace. A flaming torch of jealousy ravages my body. I head straight for the two of them, and when April lets go, I butt in. "I'm Theo. Her boyfriend."

April smiles. "Theo, this is Dean. We went to high school together."

I shake his hand, but his light blue eyes are on her. "That's not the only thing we went to together."

The torch is a full-scale fire now, burning down trees.

April smiles sweetly as she drops a hand to his arm. "Dean was my prom date. You should see the photo. I had the worst dress ever."

"Hey, I don't think it was worse than my blue ruffled tux."

"You don't say," I deadpan.

"We did an '80s retro look. Big hair and all for me," April says, fluffing out her blond locks. "But it backfired. We kind of looked like dorks."

"But we did win prom king and queen—" Dean takes a beat, and mimes hitting the drums. "—with an asterisk."

April looks at me. "They gave us prom king and queen of the '80s."

"How cute." My tone is dry.

"Anyway. Dean lives in the city, too," April adds. "We get together every now and then. He keeps trying to convince me to train for a 10K with him."

Dean turns to April. "I know you can do it. And I promise you won't regret it."

"I'll consider it," April says.

Great. Just great. He's well-off, successful, and lives near her. He's exactly what her real boyfriend should be. He probably runs for charity, too. I bet he spends every free hour at the pediatric ward, entertaining sick children.

"That's fantastic," I say with a fake smile.

"Dean works in advertising. Creative stuff. We get along well, don't we?"

Dean smiles. "We absolutely do."

I want to punch him. "Want to arm wrestle?"

He holds up his hands and waves me off. "No thanks. I'll leave those macho games to my brothers. I don't need to break a hand that I need for work. I've got to create a concept for a new toothpaste commercial, where the toothbrush talks."

Ah, so he's Bob's other son. The one who's not a Mack truck. The creative one, the clever one, the one who left the hometown.

From across the lawn, April's mom lifts her face, and she notices us. When she sees Dean, she says something to Tess. Soon, all the matchmaking women are whispering, eyes shifting from April to Dean, Dean to April, and now to me, and I know there's history with this guy that goes well beyond prom.

I do the only thing that makes sense. I stand closer. Wrap an arm around her tighter. I even sniff her at some point. Eventually, he takes the hint and excuses himself to say hi to some of the others.

"What was that all about?" she asks, sounding just like a real girlfriend.

"You smell good. You always smell good. I'm always sniffing you, April. Don't you know?"

"Oh," she says, understanding dawning on her. "We're keeping up our backstory. Right. Got it."

But as I squeeze her shoulder, *backstory* doesn't entirely feel like the right word anymore.

Present story does.

I sniff her again. "Like raspberries," I whisper against her neck, and she shivers.

"It's my shampoo."

"It's delicious."

She turns to look at me, like she's trying to find an

answer to something in my eyes. I don't know if she finds it, but a few minutes later, April's mother grabs a megaphone.

Pamela's voice booms as she says, "And the first event goes to the Hamiltons! The leader in the individual competition is Theo Banks."

Her father strides over to me. His expression is stony, but he claps me on the shoulder. "Good job," he grumbles, like it costs him something.

I smile. "Happy to do my part."

Now his eyes peer closely at me. "Now, since you're so strong, do you think you could head around to the shed by the side of the inn and grab some bags of charcoal?"

"Of course."

"I need them all," he says, like a commanding officer. "Every single fifty-pound bag."

"Not a problem."

"There are six."

"I can handle it." Is he going to barbecue for the whole Eastern Seaboard?

"Bring them to the deck. Set them by the grill."

"Consider it done," I say with a smile.

He takes a step to leave, then swivels around. "We need more chairs, too."

"Tell me where they are, and I'll bring them out."

"Basement. The steps are a bit steep. And the light is poor in the cellar. You can find the door at the end of the first-floor hallway. But bring the chairs out the side entrance so you don't drag them through the main rooms of the inn," he says, never deviating from his gruff character. I need to give the man credit. He is working the "hard-ass dad" role like a pro.

"Where would you like them set up?" If he thinks carrying some furniture from a dank underground bunker is going to break me, he's challenging the wrong soldier. I've eaten dog food.

"The deck. We need two dozen chairs. Can you have them outside in twenty minutes?"

"I'll have them ready in fifteen, sir."

He gives a crisp nod, dismissing me.

A few seconds later, April walks across the lawn. She tips her forehead at her father. "What was that about?"

"The individual competition, evidently."

She arches a brow.

"Oh, let me elaborate: the one where he assigns me feats and challenges that he thinks I can't complete to break me down and send me home with my tail between my legs."

She laughs at the same time she rolls her eyes. "More 'sleep on the lawn in a tent' stuff?"

"Yep," I say, then explain my new assignments.

"You don't have to drag up two dozen chairs, Theo."

"Oh, but I do, April. I do, and I will."

"You do have great guns." She squeezes my right biceps. "Is this why you're so good at arm wrestling?"

I part my lips to speak, and I'm tempted to spin a tale, to tell her something false, as I did last night. But for some reason, I decide to opt for honesty. To test it out. I can say things to her that I can't say to anyone else since we aren't real. "I used to arm wrestle for money on the Jersey beaches when I was a teenager," I say, my eyes locked on hers as I answer. "My brother was like a coach. He'd place bets on me, too. He'd get the college guys to take me on, but I almost always won. I was fast, determined, and underestimated. We won a lot."

The words tumble out in an unformed pileup, and I check her reaction. The slow spread of her smile and the sparkle in her big green eyes tell me she's not judging me. "You were quite resourceful."

"Yeah, we were."

That's the best way to describe my brother and me. Resourceful. The arm wrestling hustle was only the beginning. The next three years we grew smarter, slicker, and more determined.

Our bank account swelled.

College wasn't free, and all the money that would have covered it was snatched away, thanks to my father's last decision.

We did what we had to do.

Chapter Fifteen *April*

"Left. Hand. Red."

Theo's hand reaches toward my boob.

Sadly, I can't enjoy the grazing of his knuckles against me, since I'm in a downward-facing dog as his left hand slides onto the red dot in the lawn under my breast. He brushes his fingers against me as he plants his hand on the grass. He shoots me a look that says he knows he's being a little risqué.

"You devil," I whisper.

His eyebrows waggle.

"You're trying to cop a feel amongst kids, you Lawn Twister perv," I whisper, loving the easy banter and teasing we've slid into so comfortably.

He laughs, and that knocks him off-balance, a hand skittering off the red spot. "Thanks. Now I'm out."

"Serves you right," I tease as he stands and walks off to the sidelines, and I smile inside. I'm a bit amazed that we play pretend boyfriend–girlfriend so well.

The game of Twister zooms on for another fifteen

minutes as my mother spins and calls out the combos while we turn and twist across the yard in a mélange of bizarre and laugh-inducing poses in the late afternoon sun.

Jeanie plops down on the grass when she has to stretch too far. Katie falls next when she's twisted up in Emma. One of Bob's big sons goes *kersplat* as he moves his big left foot up two dots. A handful of contestants remains.

It's my turn again.

Five years of three-times-a-week yoga come in handy when my mom shouts, "Left. Foot. Green!" and I have to slide into reverse tabletop to reach the green dot . . . right over there.

Foot goes down, and I'm a table now, my belly is the top.

Take that, all the limber little eleven- and twelve-year-old girls who are pretzeled across this huge patch of lawn spray-painted by yours truly with yellow, red, blue, and green dots. I stare upside down at my seventeen-year-old niece, Libby, who was ousted a few minutes ago. She's on the sidelines. "I'm a table. Come sit on me," I say.

She decides to take me up on my offer. "You're a good table, Aunt April," the towhead says, parking her butt on my stomach.

I crack up, but I remain strong. She hops off me.

Dean's still in, and when my mom barks his combo, he parks his hand underneath my rear and smacks a red circle. "Under the butt counts!"

My arm muscles strain as I hold the pose, but lugging that bag of paintbrushes and paint has paid off. Dean is half under me. I glance at Theo, on the sidelines, trying to get his attention so he can see what I'm pulling off. I kind of want him to be impressed, as I was when he told me about his arm wrestling prowess.

When I find him, his arms are crossed and his brown eyes are hard. He's not impressed with my skill at all. He's staring at me like he's pissed. What the hell? Then I realize he's not staring at *me*. He's staring at Dean's hand, so damn close to my butt.

He's staring at it like he wants to laser it off with his eyes.

Like he can ward it away from me in the strength of his white-hot glare.

Holy moly.

He's jealous of Dean.

I barely know what to make of his jealously except—I kind of love it. My heart springs into a silly jig. As though I've just been injected with a new dose of flirty confidence. It's a lovely drug. It spreads, floods into my veins, and lifts me up. A natural high.

It's the high of possibility—the possibility that maybe, just maybe, there's something more brewing.

My arms wobble.

What the hell? I don't want anything more, so why do I want him to feel jealousy? Or to feel anything at all? But when I steal a glance at Theo, something stirs inside me. Something makes my belly flip when those dark brown eyes of his stare intensely at me.

I have a game to win, though, and ten minutes later, I do just that, taking the Lawn Twister prize.

My father ambles over, clasping me in a huge hug. "I love you always, but I love you extra right now," he says as he embraces me.

"Thanks, Dad. I love you always, but I love you extra when you sneak chocolate chip cookies into my room instead of leaving mints on the pillow."

"That sounds more than reasonable. Want to help with the dinner prep?" he asks, nodding toward the kitchen.

My father's the cook of the family. My mom is, admittedly, a whiz at making toast. She can brown bread of all kinds like a world-class toaster operator. Her boiled water is top notch, too. Beyond that, she's rubbish in the kitchen. She's not the innkeeper who cooks—she hired a chef to handle the kitchen, and since the chef is off for the reunion weekend, my dad is on kitchen detail.

Which will mean grill detail.

I glance across the grass at Theo, and wave to him as he chats with Tess's husband. Cory's mouth is turned up in a smile, and his arms flap as he talks. Funny, I haven't seen Cory so animated in a long time. With two kids under the age of two, he's mostly been tending to babies and baked goods in a half-awake stupor for the last few years. As for Theo, his eyes are softer now, and the jealousy seems to have vanished. My heart sinks the tiniest bit. I should be glad he's no longer perturbed. But the traitorous heart flapping around in my chest found his jealousy wildly appealing.

Hearts are such dumb organs. That's why I'm glad whatever I'm feeling won't matter in the end—this is all pretend, and it's precisely what I ordered on GigsForHire.

My father drapes an arm around me. "What's his deal?"

I startle, and give him a look. "Cory?" I ask with a tilt of the head. Then, like a cartoon character slammed in the belly with a ten-ton bag of bricks—that's even been labeled TEN TONS O' BRICKS—I realize who he means.

"Theo. Your new beau," my father corrects, annoyance coming through loud and clear.

"What do you mean, 'what's his deal'?"

"Do you really like him?"

"Yes. I do." My answer is emphatic.

He harrumphs, and I decide to dive into the fray. We're living in close quarters for the next few days, so I'd rather know what I'm up against.

"I think the more important question is why don't you like him?"

My father grumbles something about "boys."

"Because he's a boy?" I ask, laughing.

He taps his nose. "Bingo."

I laugh again. "You're ridiculous, Dad."

"But I know how boys are."

"Is that why were you so difficult last night when we arrived?"

"Difficult?" He points at himself, his brow furrowed. "How was I difficult?"

"Dad," I sigh as I gesture to the chairs on the deck, "about the whole couch thing, and now having him do all the manual labor."

"Manual labor never hurt a soul."

"I know that, but it's interesting that you're singling out Theo."

"I don't know this guy from Adam," he says. "I can't help it if I'm a little protective of you."

"But Dad, I *do* know him," I say, and I'm keenly aware that my statement might seem at odds with the financial nature of my relationship with Theo—yet I feel as if I know him well.

"It's my job to look out for my kids. You're the youngest." He squeezes my shoulder. "That means I worry about you the most."

"But you don't need to. I'm fine."

He laughs. Then scoffs. Then scoff-laughs. "That's a losing battle, puppy. I worry about your job, and whether it's stable. I worry about you living in the city. I worry about the fact that men today are too busy swiping right or left or up or down or whatever it is, that you'll get hurt."

"There's nothing to worry about at all," I tell him with

a smile, and it's the truth, the complete truth, and nothing but the truth.

"But see, now you have yet another reason to like the city more than home," he says, and the note of sadness in his voice sounds like a father's lament. It's also his admission—Theo is a threat to my parents because he ties me to New York rather than Wistful. That's why they've been putting him through his paces.

"I'm okay. I swear."

He drops a rough kiss on my forehead. "I know. I just don't want you to be hurt."

My parents don't need to worry, since Theo can't hurt me. When it's not real, you can't get hurt. A real boyfriend comes with too many risks. Real heartbreak. Real drama. As I turn into the kitchen, I tell myself I've been a good egg, a good daughter, by ensuring my parents have zero cause for concern.

But as I help my father prep the meat for the grill, whatever sense of possibility I felt earlier morphs into an uncomfortable kernel, a small pebble wedged in the toe of a shoe. Only I don't know what to do about the small stone.

"Dad," I say, squeezing his arm, "you don't have to stress about Theo hurting me."

He shoots me a skeptical look.

"He's a good guy," I add.

"Is he good to you?"

I nod resolutely. "He is. I promise. Can you try to ease up on him?"

"Maybe," he says, but then he flashes a brief smile.

When my father heads outside to oversee the last batch of afternoon games—these are for the younger kids—I wander through the B and B front hallway to find Theo. I'm paying him good money to be mine. I ought to spend time with him, too. I find my sister first. She's curled up on the couch in the reading room, the baby sound asleep on her chest.

My sister holds an e-reader and swipes a page. "Hey, Tess," I say quietly.

She turns her face to me and puts her finger on her lips. I nod.

Quietly, I pad closer. "Do you want me to help with Andi?"

She smiles quickly; then it fades. "Mom asked earlier, too. But she won't sleep without me."

"You sure?"

"She's kind of clingy."

"That doesn't sound fun for you."

A quiet laugh falls from her lips. "I wouldn't exactly use the word 'fun' to describe my life right now."

"It'll get better soon," I say, then blow a kiss to the sleeping angel. "Let me know if I can help. The offer stands."

"Thanks. By the way, I think I was supposed to set you up with someone, but I can't remember who. And besides, Theo seems cool."

"He is," I say.

She returns to her book, and I head out of the reading room.

But I stop short before I step into the living room.

His voice lands in my ears first.

"You're sweet, smart, and kind," he says, and his tone reminds me of how he spoke to me on the train. It's got that rough, intense quality to it. Who the hell is he complimenting?

Doing my best imitation of a cat, I take a few quiet steps to the edge of the doorway. My eyes nearly pop out of their sockets when I peek into the living room.

Libby stands behind the couch, a hand resting on it. Theo stares intently at her.

"You think so?" she asks, her brows pulled in a frown.

"Yes," he says, banging the back of the couch with a fist. "You're a great girl. I mean that in every way."

I flinch. What in the ever-loving hell is he doing? Is he hitting on my niece? A seventeen-year-old? My blood boils, and I clench my fists.

"You're so sweet," Libby says. "April is so lucky to have you."

He shoots her a self-deprecating smile. "I'm the lucky one. And some guy will feel that way about you, Libby. But this guy is a dickhead. You deserve so much better."

She nods and wipes a tear from her cheek as I step into the living room. "Hey," I say.

Libby waves, and croaks out a hey. "Hi, April. Theo's so great."

"He sure is," I say, and who's the actor now? I have no clue what's going on, but when Libby turns on her heel and heads to the back door, I stare at Theo with narrowed eyes.

He crosses the distance to me, his expression quizzical. "You okay, cupcake?"

The term grates on me for the first time. I lick my lips, draw a breath and try to make sense of what I just heard. I can't, though, so I recite a line from his GigsForHire ad. " 'Openly hit on other female guests, including your sister and any girlfriends, wives, or great-aunts. Moms aren't off-limits either.' " I park my hands on my hips. "What about jailbait nieces?"

His eyes widen, and he goes completely still; then seconds later, a laugh moves through him. A full-body laugh that seems to shimmy up his legs, quake in his belly, and spread to his face. He cracks up completely. "Are you serious?" He points a thumb in the direction of the deck.

"You thought I was hitting on your brother's seventeen-year-old daughter?"

"Well? Why were you telling her she was sweet, smart, and kind?"

"Because she is. And because I bumped into her in the hallway, talking to a friend about some dickhead who dumped her. I told her he wasn't worth it, and someday she'd meet someone who treats her the way she deserves."

Ohhhhhh.

He was being nice. He was being thoughtful.

It seems I jumped to a massive conclusion—a massively unwarranted one. I breathe a huge sigh of relief. "By the way, I'm not sure if I told you this when we first met, but sometimes I can act like a world-class idiot. Just in case that wasn't evident, I wanted to state it for the record."

"Funny, you didn't mention that, but it's kind of adorable to see."

"Adorable or horrifying?"

"Sometimes they're one and the same." He reaches out to brush an errant curl from my face. "I just wanted her to feel better."

I smile, a burst of pride surging in my body. I picked well when it came to Theo. He did something kind for my niece, who needed it. "That's really sweet. You're too sweet. Stop being sweet, or they'll all like you too much."

He wraps an arm around me. "Cupcake, that ship has already sailed."

"Funny that I wanted you because of the bad boy mystique, but there's a good guy who's stealing the show," I say, tapping his breastbone.

He glances furtively around, and presses his finger to his lips. "Shhh. Don't tell anyone you think I'm a good guy."

I laugh and give his words right back to him. "Theo, that ship has sailed."

"Also, I can't believe you actually thought I'd hit on your niece."

I shake my head, embarrassed. "I guess I figured the 'start provocative conversations' part came true, and I thought this one was becoming real, too."

He laughs. "You made it clear you didn't want the à la carte options, and I'm all about giving you what you want," he says, and he drops a sweet but friendly kiss on my forehead.

It's a friendly peck. It's not romantic. It's the antidote to the porch kiss. It's a reminder that we aren't real. That he'll give me what I want because that's his job. I need the reminder. I need it badly. Because there's a part of me that's starting to think bits and pieces of us seem real. And the real thing is far too dangerous, so it's wise to remember the score.

It's only later, as I pour a lemonade and watch the younger kids play, that a new reality smashes into me. Libby likes Theo. My mom likes Theo, even though she tried valiantly to pretend she didn't. Tess's husband really likes Theo. Nearly everyone seems to like my fake boyfriend.

That's the pebble in the shoe.

That pride I felt a little while ago, when Theo gave Libby a pep talk? It's as misplaced as Theo's jealousy. I have nothing to be proud of, since he's not really mine. In a few more days, I'll count out some greenbacks, hand him his money, and thank him for a job well done. He'll return to the bar and his nascent acting career, and I'll return to painting bodies and avoiding men like Brody the Basement Dweller and Landon the Liar and, frankly, everyone else.

The trouble is, I won't truly be done with Theo when this is over. He's not a TV show I turn off, or a book I finish reading. He'll spill over beyond the reunion because my mom will ask about him. My father might wonder what happened to us. Libby could inquire about the guy I brought home for the long summer weekend. My sister surely will poke and prod and ask. And I'll have to invent a story for why we split. I had it all planned out perfectly with Xavier: I intended to say we realized we were better as friends, and we're still buddies. Isn't that grand? It was a no-harm, no-foul ending.

What will my breakup story be for Theo, this guy who helped my dad? The guy who gave my niece a pep talk? The guy who entertained my mom at the train station?

My heart plummets as I play out the disappointment my family will feel. I can already hear the sympathy in their voices. Maybe I should say he turned out to be a jerk, but somehow I know I won't be able to bring myself to utter that lie.

He's not a jerk at all, and even though it'll be a fake breakup, it will hurt in a way I never anticipated.

I down the rest of my lemonade, pretending it's a new amnesiac drink, and it makes me forget we have to break up in four days. I take the glass to the kitchen and set it in the sink, when someone taps my shoulder. I glance down and it's Libby's younger sister, Emma.

She's sixteen and still a sweetheart. She bats her big brown eyes, since she knows I'll do anything for her when she does that. "Can you paint my face before dinner? Something pretty."

Like I can say no. I learned how to paint on kids. These girls were my lab rats. "Of course."

Her brown eyes widen. "You brought your paint?"

"Do I look like the kind of aunt who's totally unprepared for you to make such a demand of me? I brought a travel kit for this very reason. Now, get me a chair and your face, and make some demands of me!"

The painting starts before dinner and continues once we're done feasting, too.

From my perch in an Adirondack chair on the big wraparound back deck, I work through my family and friends. Soon Emma sports an emerald green vine wrapped on her cheek. Bob's grandaughter Hannah begs for me to turn her mouth into a dog's, and now she looks like a cute little puppy. Bob's grandson Benny wants a football on his eye, so I paint that.

But Tess shakes her head when my mom suggests she take a turn. Tess holds up the baby in her arms to justify her no.

"You are aware I'm capable of holding the baby," my mom points out.

"I know, Mom. But she needs me," Tess says, running her hand down Andi's back.

"She needs her family, and we all fit that bill."

"I'm fine, really. I wasn't around when April was painting faces when she was younger, so I'm not really missing out."

I swivel around and point at her. "That's exactly why you need to take your turn. You were off in college while I was learning how to do this, and you need to know what you're missing out on this second."

I stand up, walk over to my sister, and pluck the baby from her grip. Tess tries to protest, but I drop a kiss on Andi's forehead. "You're the cutest baby ever," I say, and Andi coos at me; then I hand my littlest niece to my mom, who waits with outstretched arms.

"Does she ever let you watch the baby?"

"Yes, but not enough."

"I'm nursing and you're busy," Tess calls out.

"She's pigheaded and stubborn," my mom counters.

"I wonder where she got that from," I say to my mother.

Then I shoo her off. "Now, go enjoy your extra baby cuddles."

My mom mouths a thank you.

To Tess, I say, "You go get your big sister butt in the chair."

"If she needs anything . . . ," Tess says to our mom, but then trails off when she sees our mom is already in the house, singing to her granddaughter.

Tess takes her spot across from me.

"What would you like?"

She blinks her blue eyes at me. They're blank, as if she can't comprehend what she likes. My poor sister. Her baby-brain case is a bad one.

"I have an idea," I say.

"Sure, tell me."

"Cherry blossoms are feminine and beautiful, and the cherry tree is also strong. It's a symbol of spring and renewal," I say, thinking that's what my sister needs right now.

"Sounds lovely."

As I paint her, we chat. I don't ask her a single question about the baby. I ask her about the bakery, about new creations she's made, about crazy requests from customers. As I finish the pretty blush-pink lines on her face, she's told me a tale of a customer who said the coconut cupcakes remind her of her trip to Hawaii, and now that customer stops by once a week to feel like she's returned to paradise.

I haven't fixed my sister's tiredness. But maybe for a few minutes, I've taken her out of the routine she seems stuck in. As I finish, Cory wanders over.

"She's totally a babe. Right, Cory?" I say to her husband.

"She always is."

"I do look kind of strangely hot," Tess says as I hold up a phone mirror app to show her my handiwork.

"Then go take him upstairs and see if he rips off your clothes," I whisper as I nod to the inside of the inn.

Cory nods at the speed of light. He might even pant like a dog. "I'm game."

Tess rolls her eyes, as if I've suggested something ludicrous. "Yes, that's exactly what I want to do right now at the Sunnyside."

I speak the next words slowly, like I'm talking to a child. "Because there isn't bonking going on here at an inn?"

"Nope. Because the only action I want is at home with my California king," Tess says, like a naughty confession.

Cory's shoulders sag.

"Want me to paint a pillow on your husband's face, then?"

She rises from the chair. "Now, that's a brilliant idea. Right, hon?"

Cory heaves a dejected sigh, saying nothing.

I bend to my black leather bag of paints and stuff a few small jars back in their slots, when I sense someone walking near. I look up to see Dean. He holds a bottle of beer and tips it at me. I smile back and brandish a paintbrush. "Admit it. You want a butterfly."

Dean laughs, but before he can respond, someone slips into the hot seat in front of me.

Theo. "I want you to paint me."

The way he says those words makes my skin shiver. They all sound delicious dripping from his tongue. I want both halves to be true—he wants me, and he wants me to paint him.

For this sliver of time, I want real.

He pulls his chair closer, the wooden legs scratching noisily across the deck. His knees nearly touch mine. I consider whether it's possible to climax from knees knocking together.

Twilight dips across the sky, and even though we're surrounded by my family, the way Theo looks at me reminds me of our train ride—like we were all alone, shooting across the countryside, zipping through the night.

As my cousins scamper through the yard and my parents lounge in cushy chairs, sipping wine and drinking beer, I feel as though it's only us here in our little corner of the deck.

"What do you want me to paint?" I ask, my voice breathier than it should be. "Did you want a butterfly?"

He leans closer—so close, I could wrap my arms around him. I could curl my hand through his hair and bring those lips to mine in a second. So close, he could do the same. I swallow, and the air between us seems to vibrate.

"I don't care," he says, his voice gruff. It edges into me. Coils through me.

"You don't care what I paint? Why do you want me to paint you, then?"

"So you don't touch him."

There it is. The confirmation. The admission of what I knew already from Twister. Now it comes from his lips. His full lips that whispered over mine this morning. That dared to tease me with so much possibility. Goose bumps sweep over my skin as he holds my gaze.

This is the real risk.

Here on the porch, as night falls and my family mills about, telling jokes, playing in the huge yard, I raise a brush to his face.

Chapter Sixteen *Theo*

Willpower is my new best friend.

It's the only thing standing between me and kissing the hell out of her.

She dips a brush into a small red jar and raises it to my cheek. My gaze drifts to her arm, inches from me. She's as strong as I noticed last night.

"Distracting arm," I say in a low voice.

"Same for you," she whispers as she gently presses the brush to my cheek. It's soft, like a wet feather.

I tell her this.

"Why, yes, Theo, I'm painting you with a wet feather," she says as she roams across my skin with the bristles.

" 'Wet feather' sounds dirty."

She inches closer. "You think everything sounds dirty."

"Maybe I do," I murmur; then I take a beat, and add, "Maybe I do with you."

She stops midstroke as her breath hitches. "Do you?"

Her family is about twenty feet away, and I'm keenly aware that we're not alone. That I'm her fake boyfriend.

But that's why I'm allowed to be this close to her, I reckon. That's why I'm allowed to touch her in public. I've been given permission by the terms of this engagement. I inch forward and drop a hand to her knee. What surprises the hell out of me is how much that gesture turns me on. It's like a dart of lust straight to my groin. What the hell is it with this woman? Her hair gets me going, her arms turn me on, her knee gives me a semi. Briefly, it occurs to me that I might have regressed to a teenager when it comes to instant arousal around a chick. But I'm not about to stop. I curl my palm over her knee.

"You're touching me," she says in a soft gust of air.

"I am."

"Do you do that a lot?"

"I do," I say as she runs the bristles over my cheekbone. "I've told you. It's impossible not to."

I squeeze her knee. That little hitch comes again. Hell, if she makes that noise when I touch her knee, what would she do if I stripped off her clothes? What would she sound like if I ran my tongue down her soft flesh and pressed my lips to those stars on her hip?

I groan. Louder than I should.

"You okay?" April stops, the brush held midair.

Our eyes lock. Like a click. Like the movies. Tension vibrates between us. "Yeah, I'm okay. Just thinking."

"About what?"

My eyes close for a moment, and I clench my fists. *Don't say it. Don't let on.*

But when I open my lids, I see Dean at the end of the deck, kicking back with the crew, and jealousy flares once more. I don't know what's up between them, or what was once up between them, but at least for these few days, she's mine, and I want her to feel that way. That's what she ordered. That's what I tell myself to justify what I say next.

"Your stars."

She trembles. It's a visible thing. I see it in her shoulders. In the way she swallows. In her shaking hand. She quiets it with her other one.

"Theo," she whispers, and my name sounds like an admonishment.

"Yeah?"

Her voice is a low note against the night. "You can't say that stuff."

"Why?"

"Because. Everyone is around."

The clink of glasses and the chatter of conversation are close, but far enough away. "They can't hear me."

"I know, but I can."

"And it bothers you?" I ask, tensing.

She draws a breath, and I watch as she parts her lips, inhales, exhales. "No. It doesn't bother me. . . ." Her voice trails off, and the way the sentence is left hanging lets me fill in the dots about what my words do to her.

She lifts the brush again, works it over my jawline.

"So then I *can* tell you all the things I want to do to you." It's a statement, not a question.

She keeps her eyes fixed on my face, on the line of the brush against my skin, when she asks, "What do you want to do to me?"

I inch closer, cup both my hands over her knees. "Everything," I say, my voice raspy.

She stops, meets my gaze. Her wild green irises shine with desire. It's a look she wears extraordinarily well. *Lust.* I half want to talk dirty to her until she quivers and begs me to take her upstairs, and I half want to toss her on my shoulder, carry her to the bedroom, and show her.

But I slam on the brakes. I can't do any of the above. It's not because of her family. It's for all the other reasons:

Addison, Richelle, the money, the risks, the way people burn you when you get close to them. I've got to wrestle back some control around April. It's only the second night here, and I have to make it through two more after this one.

"But right now, I want you to finish painting me."

She nods, and resumes her work on my cheek. She moves to my eyelid and tells me to close my eyes. Bristles brush over me. "What are you painting on me?"

"It's a surprise."

"Does it mean something?" I ask when she tells me I can open my eyes.

Her lips quirk, and she reins in a laugh. "I think you'll know what it means, Theo."

A few minutes later, Libby pops over as April declares that she's done. She stands, pats my shoulder, and tells me to stand, too. She parks her hands on my shoulders and spins me around, showing me off to her niece.

Libby cracks up and points. "Oh my God. You look hilarious."

"What did you do to me?" I ask April.

She wiggles her eyebrows.

I dart out a hand and cup her cheek. I dip my head to her ear. "If you painted hairy balls on my face, you're in big trouble, cupcake."

She pats my other cheek. "Give me more credit than that, Theo. I painted a big, huge mushroom head schlong on you."

It's my turn to laugh deeply. She winks at me, and I deserve all the ribbing I'm getting from her. I welcome it, too, because there's something wildly entertaining about slipping from sexual tension so thick, it occupies its own zip code, to off-color jokes.

April's dad wanders over. His brow pinches, and I meet his eyes, waiting for his new marching orders. *Swab the*

deck. Mow the lawn. Run five miles doing cartwheels.
"Hey, Casanova. Want to help us set up for the obstacle course tomorrow?"

"Absolutely."

"It'll take a while," he adds.

"Not a problem."

"At least a few hours."

April rolls her eyes and mutters under her breath, *"So obvious."*

Yes, her father is indeed transparent. I suspect he's trying to send me to bed well past April's curfew, hoping we won't get so much alone time. He has no idea that he's saving me from temptation.

"I'm at your service," I tell him with a salute.

"Good," he says with a small smirk.

"Hey, Dad. Watch out. You might accidentally crack a smile now and then," April teases.

He turns to her. "I'm all grins for my girl."

"Good night, Dad," she says as she hoists the bag of paint on her shoulder and mouths *good luck* to me. I watch her head into the inn, thread her way through the living room, and turn out of sight.

Two hours of active obstacle course duty later, I'm tired and spent, but I've finished every task on his list. But this time, I didn't lug two dozen chairs alone. The other guys helped out, so perhaps April's dad is backing off a bit.

I go upstairs. I stop and look at the hallway mirror. I'm covered in lips. She painted kisses all over my cheek. Bright red kisses. Cherry red lipstick marks. Fire engine red lips pursed together in an O. Ruby red ones open wide. As I stare, all I see are her lips, covering my face. I imagine she left them all on me. Wet kisses, hard kisses, soft kisses. Openmouthed ones. Kisses with tongue. Kisses that steal your breath. Kisses that start slow and linger all night long.

You'll know what it means.

How the hell do I get in bed with her after that conversation on the deck? A conversation I pushed. I prodded it, led it along, made it happen. I heave a sigh.

I need an endless well of willpower.

When I creak open the door to the crepe room, I won't have to tap that well. April is curled on her side, fast asleep in the light of the moon.

It makes me sad and relieved at the same time.

Something tugs inside me, wishing she'd wake up, grab a towel, and wipe these marks off my face. I'd lean against the vanity, and she'd rise on tippy-toes, daubing the wet end of the towel across my cheek, her breath ghosting over my skin. I'd raise a hand, cup her cheek, and kiss her senseless.

I'd leave all the imprints on her.

But as I gently close the door, letting it click softly shut, I reason it's better this way.

Less risky. Less dangerous.

I head to the bathroom, shut the door, and strip out of my clothes. Under the hot stream, I scrub all the paint off my cheek, until it looks as though I've bled out in this pristine white shower. I look at the door, wishing I'd see it crack open, then she'd appear, slink around it, take off her clothes, and join me.

The room would steam up as I kiss her, touch her, taste her. We'd nearly slip in the tub, but I'd hold her steady, wash her hair, run my hands down her soft, wet skin. But the room remains just me. The water streams hot down my spine, and I'm alone with all these inappropriate thoughts. Eventually, I turn off the shower, brush my teeth, and slip into bed beside her, wondering what the hell I'm supposed to do with this jealousy, this want, this lust.

But there's something else at play, too.

Deep in the center of my gut is a seed of doubt that makes me question why I have any right to feel jealousy.

Not because we're playing a game, but because I could never be the guy April wants. April Hamilton was born and raised in an entirely different world than I. April comes from sunshine. She comes from pancakes and eggs for breakfast. She's from parents who meddle in her love life because they love her. Because they want her to come home and live near them. I don't have a family. Not really. Not like this.

I was born into normal, but then thrust into trouble. And I liked trouble. I caused trouble. I profited from it, once upon a time.

Now, I'm just a guy who's cobbling it together to make ends meet, and playing pretend to pay even the smallest bills. I can't be the guy that a girl like her needs, even if she's so damn hard to resist that I flirt with her on the deck of her mom's B and B.

She deserves better.

A guy like Dean.

But that thought burns black inside me.

Sometime later, in the middle of the night, when darkness streams through the open window, breath whispers on my neck. A quiet little rush of air rustles against my skin. I rouse from sleep to find she's still dozing, only she's wedged beside me. Her small frame is pushed up against my bigger one. Her face burrows into my neck. Her breasts are pressed to my back. Her quiet, even breathing tickles my naked shoulders.

I don't know if I'll ever fall back asleep, but this moment is when I call upon the reserves. I go completely still, because if I move one millimeter, I will leave lip marks all over her body.

Chapter Seventeen *April*

The third day

I yank my now-dry hair into a ponytail holder and slick on some lip gloss, then leave the bathroom. Theo is still sound asleep, the covers slipped down to his hips. His smooth, tanned skin shines golden in the early morning light.

I consider flying the full-on freak flag, by curling up in the corner chair and staring at him. Yeah, I could totally get into that. I'd earn my first-class weirdo stripes, for sure. But damn, he's worth it. From the morning scruff to the smooth expanse of skin to the hard planes of his abs, he's a sight to behold.

I sink into the cranberry-red armchair. I tuck my feet under me, prop my chin in my hand, and catalog the man in my bed. The compass on his biceps points north, and I wonder if there's a reason for it, or if the reason is simple—a compass points north. The sunburst is brilliant on his forearm, blazing with fiery shades. It speaks of possibilities and hope. Another day, another sunrise. His thick brown hair flops messily on his forehead, with a few strands sticking up. He breathes heavily, a small snore fluttering from his nose.

I laugh silently because even his snore is cute.

Evidently, I need to get out more. Claire is right. It's been too long. If I'm delighted by a snore, it might be time for me to either get my head checked out or try to date again. I grab my phone from my back pocket and tap out a quick message.

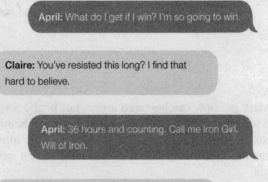

April: What do I get if I win? I'm so going to win.

Claire: You've resisted this long? I find that hard to believe.

April: 36 hours and counting. Call me Iron Girl. Will of Iron.

Claire: More like panties of iron. Are you human or cyborg?

April: Part cyborg, for sure.

Claire: Kudos to you. Maybe you're not attracted to him? That would be even better, right?

April: I wish I wasn't attracted to him. I think I'm suffering from an overdose of attraction.

Claire: What's the issue, then?

As I stare at her text, I repeat her question in my head. What is the issue? There are so many. Too many to enumerate.

April: You know . . .

Claire: Yes. Your sabbatical. It's been a year now, hon.

April: And I'm still waiting to see if I get the *Sporting World* gig.

Claire: I know it's wise to be cautious, but we aren't talking about shacking up or marriage. I'm just wondering why you don't try to, ya know, scratch that itch.

April: There's another issue.

Claire: Do tell.

This issue is the biggest one, and it's crystal clear to me at last. It's evident in the way we talked to each other on the deck, in how I reveled in his jealousy, in how I adore talking to him.

I take a deep, fueling breath and type the answer.

> **April:** I sort of like him.

> **Claire:** Well, that is a big issue indeed.

A soft rap on the door pulls me from my phone. Reflexively, I glance to the sleeping guy first, but he's still snoozing. I stand and head to the door, then quietly open it.

My father shoots me his signature *I need a favor* smile as I stand in the doorway, shielding the sleeping man.

"Hey, Dad."

"Hey, sweetie pie. Any chance you could do your dear old dad a favor and grab some Kleenex for today's event? I don't have enough. We need about ten boxes for Junk in the Trunk."

"Absolutely. I'll head out now."

"I can join you."

The masculine voice comes from down the hall. It's Dean, and he's dressed in gray workout shorts and a white T-shirt. Shades sit atop his head. "I'm about to go for a run. I can walk with you, and then I'll do my morning workout."

I turn to Dean, then my dad, and I'm about to say, *Sounds good,* when another voice cuts in.

"I'll be ready in two minutes."

It's Theo. I peer behind me. He's bolt upright, running a hand through his bed head.

Why does he look so sexy right now? Oh, wait. Because he's sleep-rumpled, and I bet he has morning wood.

Holy smokes. I did not just think about my pretend boyfriend's potential erection in front of my father.

Oops. I did it again.

Brain, shut down all dirty thoughts stat.

A blush the size of California spreads across my face. I try to slam the door shut, but my dad wedges his foot in it.

"Why don't you take your time? Show Theo downtown," my dad says; then a smile crosses his lips, and he glances past me at my pretend beau. "Sound like something you'd enjoy, Theo?"

That's the first time I've heard my dad use his name.

"Absolutely," he says, in his scratchy morning voice.

"Show him all the shops and cafés and the dock, too," my dad continues, and I understand him completely. He's switched tactics. He came up empty serving vinegar to Theo, so he's sweetening with sugar now. I suspect he and my mom hatched a new plot overnight—if they can't scare him off, they'll make him fall in love with Wistful, and woo me back through him.

They're relentless, my parents.

"I'll be the best tour guide ever," I say; then I slam the door shut and step back into my room, my heart racing as I turn around and look at the object of my deep thoughts.

Deep. He could totally go deep right now.

You don't know that. Hell, I don't even know if he has a morning boner.

Jesus. What's wrong with me? I'm thinking about his dick.

Must stop thinking about his dick.

Especially since he's walking across the room right now in those sleep pants hung low on his hips. The bathroom door closes, and before mortification sets in more deeply, I grab my bag, phone, and wallet and shout, "See you downstairs!"

As I race down the stairs, I vow to stop objectifying him.

It's my new project—get my mind out of the gutter.

Chapter Eighteen *April*

I wave at a young woman wearing a red bandanna over her hair inside FlourChild, my sister's bakery. The woman waves back. I've never met her, but she's Tess's employee.

We cross the street.

Sprays of ruby-red and fire-orange tulips line the windows in the florist shop. "That's Sally Linden's shop," I say, continuing my impression of a town docent. "When she's not arranging bouquets, she knits hats that she sells at the farmers' market every weekend in the winter."

Theo shakes his head, amused by the Wistful tales I've been telling. "That's too quaint."

I point to the diner at the end of the block. "Sam's Diner. Try to control yourself at the sheer originality of the name," I say, because talking so much helps smooth over the jitters inside me. I'm pretty sure I received an infestation of jumping beans of lust this morning, and now they're banging and jostling around inside me.

That's why I'm giving him a tour of my town, since it's a proven scientific phenomenon that little kills lust faster than a tour of too-charming shoppes. Yes, *shoppes,* with two *p*s and an *e.*

"But how are the fries at Sam's Diner?" Theo asks.

"To die for," I say emphatically. "And fries are the true measure of a diner's character."

"I'll second that." He holds up a fist. I knock mine to his.

See? We're buds now. All that *paint me* and *I want to do everything to you* yada yada yada from last night has gone sayonara. It's been brushed out the door or at least swept under the carpet. Thank God. It's far too difficult to maintain a fake relationship with someone you want to shag. The more I gab about flowers and fries and the nail salon that also offers massages and the adorable drugstore up the street that looks like something from the 1950s and the redbrick bank right next to it, the less I'll want to bang Theo, and the easier it'll be to pull this off.

At the end of the block, a ginger-haired man in a light blue polo shirt nurses a coffee alongside a woman dressed similarly.

"And there's a coffee shop, too. Truly, this town wants for nothing," I say with an exaggerated sigh.

"It is Bob's Coffee? Jane's Cup of Joe?"

"If only it were so original. It's called—wait for it—the Coffee Shoppe."

He stops in his tracks and holds up his hands. "Whoa. You're blowing my mind now."

"I know. But what it lacks in originality, it makes up for in awesome coffee. Plus, the owner donates one-quarter of the profits to the local animal rescue, so that's kind of awesome," I say as we reach the next block.

"That is actually incredibly awesome."

"That reminds me. You and I are neck and neck for first place. What charity would you give the money to? That is, if you beat me. Which you won't."

He laughs; then his expression turns more serious. He looks away from me, staring at the shops on the other side of the street. "Something with kids. Maybe an after-school community center that tries to keep kids off the street."

"Oh, I love that. Is that something you do in the city?" I ask, keeping up the one-two-three beat of the conversation. This safe banter is doing the trick.

"Sort of. There's a kid I hang out with, Jared. He lives in my building, and his mom works a lot, so I try to hang out with him a couple times a week. Play sports and stuff."

"That's amazing. And even better, in a way, that you do it on your own. Plus, that's amazing that you can fit it all in with your acting and the bartending and whatnot. Your schedule must be crazy when you're rehearsing."

"Yeah, it definitely is," he says, staring at the shops.

"What was the last thing you did? Would I have seen you in anything in New York?"

"Ha. I wish."

"What was the last GigsForHire job you did, then?"

"I did an office party a couple months ago."

"And was it challenging?"

He shakes his head. "It was a straightforward smile-and-wave type of gig."

"So pretty much the polar opposite of this assignment."

"Yes. What about you? What would you do with the prize money?" he asks, getting back to the subject.

"Probably an arts program for kids. I volunteer with one that tries to bring art classes to kids from all walks of life, so I'd do that."

The scent of salt water licks the air. We're so close to Wistful River here, and it connects to the Sound. The water's only a few blocks away, and I can practically taste it. I point to the end of the road, where pavement turns into dock. My father and Bob's corporate offices stand proudly at the end of the street, and the boats they build are moored to that dock.

"That's my dad's boat business."

"Show me."

We wander to the end of the street, and I show him the redbrick building that houses the offices; then we cross to the docks. The water laps the shore lazily with each pull of the morning tides.

I watch the marine life, from the gulls hunting for bread and other leftovers on the pier to the last of the fishermen prepping to head out to sea. They're likely fishing for fun rather than for a living. The commercial fishermen are long gone, weighing anchor well before the sun climbed over the horizon. They're off casting nets, hauling in their first catch of the day.

"Are any of those your dad's boats?" Theo asks.

I peer at the hundreds of boats bobbing in the water. Some are cruisers, some are cutters, and I explain that my dad and Bob make a handful of those types of boats every year. Those bigger ones bring in big paydays. "But they specialize in smaller, classic, handcrafted wooden boats. The kind a family of four or six and a dog might take out on the water for the day. Maybe to fish, maybe to lie in the sun, maybe to picnic."

"Just boats for fun?" he asks, as if it were an absurd concept.

Maybe it is if you're not used to it. "They're kind of a luxury. They cost fifty-two thousand dollars," I say, and admittedly, that does sound like quite a luxurious price tag.

Theo bursts out a cough. "Fifty grand? For a boat? For fun?" His brown eyes blink, rapid-fire.

"I know. It's nutty, right?"

"I can't even imagine." He swallows and shakes his head, breathing out hard. "Hey, whatever floats your boat, right?"

I laugh, and we turn around. "Our house is a mile or so from here, and it looks out over a small lake. My dad used to test his boats on that lake all the time. I guess boats are just normal to me. Boats, water, bridges, docks. There's a beautiful drawbridge about a mile away from here."

He groans. Playfully. "Don't tell me you spent your childhood wandering across the bridge, singing sad lullabies, and dropping flowers in the water."

Laughing, I swat his shoulder as we wander past the sandwich shop. I flash back briefly on the mention of tri-tip steak sandwiches, and I'm glad I'm not going on a date with Mark, the proprietor. I'm quite happy that I'm strolling past the shop with Theo. "And simply for suggesting I might have done that, I'll never ever take you to a bridge again."

He pouts. "You haven't even taken me to a bridge yet. So now you've taken away something you've never even given me."

"I'm terrible and cruel."

"If I'm good, will you take me to your drawbridge?" He bats his eyes playfully.

"Depends what 'good' is," I say, and then we turn and head back to the stores.

"So," Theo says, clucking his tongue as he changes the subject. "You and Dean."

Ah, there it is. My lips twitch in a grin that I try to hide. "Me and my prom date," I say playfully because I kind of can't resist teasing him on this front.

"You and your prom date," he echoes, his voice tight as we near the drugstore.

"We just had the best time that night eleven years ago,"

I say with a dreamy sigh. I sell it to the jury when I bring my hand to my heart. "I can remember every detail like it was yesterday."

He stops in his tracks, and I turn around and face him. The look in his eyes is priceless. He knows he's being played. I crack up.

"Fine. Fine. You win that one, but something is up with the two of you," he says, his gaze leveling mine.

We stand on the street corner, the brick of the bookshop nearly peach in the morning sun. "Does it bother you?"

He heaves a sigh and says no. "But I'd just rather know what the backstory is. Since I'm your—" He stops to sketch air quotes. "—'boyfriend.'"

My shoulders tense from the reminder of our fictional status. But then, why am I irritated? Of course, he's my pretend boyfriend. "Dean is just a friend."

"You sure?" Theo arches a skeptical eyebrow.

An image flickers before my eyes, and it's an answer to a question he posed on the train. I blurt it out. "Right now. I would paint you red."

"Yeah?" He slides a hand down his cheekbone, over his jawline. "My face?"

So much for the anti-lust zone. I've zipped back into Flirtville, and I can't say I regret it. I like Theo. A lot. It's coursing through me. My want is true and it's real, and in this moment, it's more powerful than my sabbatical.

I raise my hand and bring it near his neck. His Adam's apple bobs as he swallows. "I'd start here," I say with the gentlest touch on his throat. I hover my hand over him as I move with my words. "Then move down across your pecs. I'd make you a pot. Boiling over."

He laughs and drags a hand through his thick mess of hair. "It's that obvious? That I'm jealous?"

"Yes."

His expression softens, and he purses his lips, then whistles. But it's no ordinary whistle he makes. The sound from his lips is a teakettle boiling over.

I smile and clap. "Well done."

He shrugs and taps his chest with both hands. "Yes. Jealous. That's me."

"I shouldn't be surprised. You've always been the jealous type. The whole time we've been together," I say, sliding back into the stories. This time I go there because I like how they make me feel. I want the tingles all over. The burst of desire.

He tugs on my tank top strap and narrows his eyes. "I hate when other men even look at you."

"It drives you absolutely crazy, doesn't it?"

"Insane," he whispers in that hot dirty voice as he smooths the strap of my shirt, then fingers a curl of my blond hair. I fight back a tremble. My knees are wobbly. I want to fall into his arms. I want to swoon into him. I want to throw myself at him and smother him in kisses. He lets go of my hair, steps back, and drops the tale. "But you really don't have a thing for him?"

My stomach pirouettes. The realization that he's well and truly jealous—still, now, the morning after—is quite possibly the most awesome thing I've experienced in a while.

"Dean and I are friends. Yes, we went to prom together, but we went as friends. When I kissed him, I felt nothing."

Theo's eyes approximate saucers, and I hear a huff of breath through his nostrils. "You kissed him?" He bites out each word.

"It was prom. We were friends. It was nothing. We both looked at each other with this sense of 'that was like kissing your sister.'"

He takes a breath, which seems to be calming him down. "Fine. It was a sisterly kiss. Go on."

"Look, my mother was dying for me to marry him, but that's because she's best friends with Bob's wife, Carol, and I've no doubt the two of them plotted our nuptials many moons ago," I say as we resume our path to the drugstore, where he holds open the door. "I swear, whenever they see us talk, they hear Pachelbel's Canon play in their ears. Their minds latch on to calendar dates, and white dresses and cake tastings, and then to happily-ever-afters when both their city kids come home to roost."

His expression darkens for a moment as we head to the tissue aisle. "They want you to be with someone from here."

"Yes, they do. As you can see, they're ridiculously into this whole lifestyle. But they also don't want me to be hurt. They're convinced all the men from the big, scary city are liars and Slick Willies who'll break my heart," I say, and Theo flinches.

"We aren't all like that."

"I know that. But parents worry," I say; then I quickly correct myself. Theo doesn't have parents anymore, so he hasn't experienced the helicoptering even into one's twenties. "*My* parents worry."

"Because they love you. Because they want you to be happy."

"Yes, I suppose that's true. Sometimes I think it's because they don't know what to make of me or my job. It doesn't fit their construct of normal work. They think I paint faces at fairs, and I skip around the city, plucking petals off daisies without a care in the world. So they want me back here. They want me with someone from here. They want me near them. And my mom and Carol thought for the longest time that Dean and I were destined to be happy together," I say as I grab ten boxes of tissues and drop them into the big canvas bag I brought with me. "But Dean and I—we are only friends. We don't have that—" I stop to think about the words."—that butterflies-in-the-belly and crazy, madness feeling."

A corner of his lips quirks. "Butterflies are important to you?"

I look at him, wishing I didn't feel so many things this very second. "I like butterflies."

"Me, too," he says softly as we head to the checkout.

A curly-haired bottle redhead beams at me. "April! So good to see you."

"Hey, Ruth," I say to the cashier I've known my whole life. She owns the store, works the register and never has a bad day.

"Hey, sweet thing. How's the crazy reunion shindig going?"

"Crazy. Definitely crazy," I say, then briefly introduce her to Theo.

She tips her forehead to him and stage-whispers, "He's adorable. I'm so glad you met someone. Especially after—"

I shake my head and give her a knowing look, one that says *shhh*. Word spreads fast here. But then, I invited such gossip with my eggnog-fueled tell-all.

She blinks, and nods exaggeratedly. "Especially after how hard it is to meet someone. You both need to come back again soon. Promise me."

"Absolutely," Theo says as he takes the bag of tissues and slides it up his shoulder.

A stab of guilt hits me in the breastbone. Theo won't be coming back at the end of the summer. He won't be coming back for Christmas or New Year's or anything else.

I know that. Logically, I know that. But the words remind me that every single interaction we have is a fabrication. The awareness of that is like a stone in my gut. No matter how many stories we make up or how jealous he gets, this is a ruse.

I'd do best to remember that, rather than let myself be fooled by tingles or butterflies.

"Especially after what?" Theo asks once we leave.

I make light of the exchange. "Oh, you know how it goes."

"After what?" he pressed. "Or should I say after who."

"It's nothing."

"No, it's something. You had a douchey ex."

"Who doesn't have a douchey ex?" I say breezily.

"I have a douchey ex. She was the grade-A, top-choice, dictionary definition of 'douchey ex,'" he offers.

"Yeah? You think your douchey ex is more douchey than mine?"

"I'd be willing to bet."

"Okay, here goes: Mine said he was divorced, and it turned out he wasn't. The jerk was still married."

Theo nearly stumbles, and his eyes go wide as the sea. "You win."

"He had a bachelor pad that he took me back to. He had a whole believable storyline about not being able to spend the nights together due to a sleep disorder. For three months, I bought into it. Until Xavier spotted him out with his wife."

"The XMan busted him?"

I nod. "He sure did. I'm glad, but it also absolutely sucked to have all his lies shoved at me."

Theo's expression darkens, and his mouth turns into a thin line. "Yeah, that would suck. I'm sorry, April. You deserve so much better." He unleashes a deep sigh of frustration. "Like I said to your cousin—you're sweet, smart, and kind. What I didn't say to your cousin is this: You're feisty and fiery and funny and beautiful. You deserve the world. You deserve way better than a guy like that."

Hummingbirds dance in my chest. They take flight, and so do I. I'm floating, rising, and I don't want to come down ever. Each sweet word breaks down my resolve to stay away from men. Correction—I don't want to stay away from *this man*. I want to get closer, and that scares the hell out of me.

I cast the spotlight back on him. "Your story?"

"Let's see. It's not as bad. But I dated someone I worked with. She was a market researcher, and she promised me all sorts of work. Mystery shopping and such. And then we grew closer, and I shared some of the things I'd been through in my life." He swallows harshly. "The next day, she was done—and all the work was gone, too. It was a slap in the face, and a warning sign, too. People don't want to really know you."

I tilt my head to the side. "I don't think that's true. Some people do."

"Yeah?" he asks skeptically.

I nod, and those hummingbirds flap inside me again as I say, "I like getting to know you."

He offers a faint smile.

"Sounds more like she was a jerk," I add.

"I'd say the same for your ex."

Point taken. I've been lumping all men with Landon, but that's not entirely fair. "I suppose you're right. Let's start a club for horrible exes."

"We'll be charter members, and no wonder your family wants to set you up. It's kind of sweet," he says, his voice soft. "It's nice that they love you enough to worry about you."

"Yeah?"

"April, it's nice that you have a family to worry about you," he adds, and that's the true punch in the gut.

I wince. "Sorry if I sounded ungrateful."

"Not at all. I'm just pointing it out."

As we turn back toward the inn, the bag on his arm, I see the back of a sandy blond head and a pair of square shoulders outside the hardware shop. I squint for a second, trying to remember. "Calvin," I say out loud.

Theo asks, "Who's that?"

"Oh, just someone my mom wanted to set me up with."

Theo points to the man setting up a clapboard sign. "Him?"

"My mom was *dying* for me to have cinnamon rolls with him."

"Cinnamon rolls?" he asks as if it were a foul, dirty thing.

"She wanted me to have coffee and cinnamon rolls with him. She said he really wants to get to know me."

"Of course he does," Theo growls under his breath.

Calvin fusses with the sign, but then he's a blur, because Theo drops the bag, cups my cheek with one hand, and backs me up to the wall of the florist shop, which hasn't yet opened. My heart hammers. It's the loudest it's ever been in my whole life. He raises his other hand, holds my face, and brings his lips to mine.

Chapter Nineteen *April*

It's slow and soft and tender.

An exploration. As though I'm something curious he discovered, and he needs to turn the object over in his hands, consider it from all angles. Taste, touch, brush.

His lips are so gentle that for a moment, they're barely there. Then he kisses more.

More everything.

Closer. Firmer. More insistent.

This isn't the two-second kiss on the porch. But it *is* a kiss for the sake of an audience, and I fear I'm going to like it too much for my own good. I should stop it. I really should.

I raise my hands to his shoulders, and nearly push him away. I don't want all these pretend kisses that trick me. That feel too real. But when my hands make contact, my fingers curl over his shoulders instead of shove him away.

Stupid, stupid body wanting what's only a facade.

Dumb brain, too, because it goes haywire, like a TV station tuned in to a fuzzy channel as he kisses me harder and everything becomes a haze of static. Bodies and sensations, right and wrong, fake and real. It's all just one big gorgeous mess in my head right now.

This isn't real.

This isn't real.

This isn't real.

But the tingles everywhere tell me it is.

The flutter in my heart says this is no ordinary kiss.

The goose bumps that sweep over my skin are 100 percent genuine.

I'm dying to know if this is real, or just a show for him. I squint open one eye, scanning for Calvin. He's gone. It's just us and the sea breeze, and the sound of a car trundling down the street not far away.

There's no audience now, and that ought to reassure me.

But Theo's back is to Calvin, so he must not know the audience has left the cinema. Theo's probably just being thorough. He's playing the alpha, the *this is my woman* role.

Right now, I believe it. I buy in to it, and I'm ready to cast my Oscar ballot for him.

The winner for Most Convincing Fake Kiss is Theo Banks. For his performance in The GigsForHire Boyfriend, *the Academy proudly presents him with this top honor. Did you see how he kisses her into an amazing state of bliss?*

I sink into his kiss.

Floating takes on new meaning.

Turned on is the state of my soul.

If this is being kissed, nothing else has ever counted.

This is how women should demand to be kissed.

Someday, when I am old and brash and wear a red hat, I will tell young women the lesson I learned one fine summer morning on a street in my hometown: Don't settle for less than you deserve. Don't settle for second best at work or in life—or in kisses. I'll make speeches and deliver my rallying cry: "I've no patience for boring kisses after Theo Banks. Nor should you. Kiss like the world is on fire. Kiss like nothing else exists. Insist on it. Demand kisses that make the world disappear."

With his stubble and his ink and his edgy attitude, I expected rough. But he takes his time. A soft moan falls from his lips. I catch it in my mouth and swallow his sound. He slides a hand up my neck, and when he reaches my ear, he rubs his thumb over my earlobe.

My breath hitches.

My entire body lights up. I am a bright neon sign. I blaze in cherry red, in electric blue, in the hottest pink. Who knew his thumb on my earlobe would flip the switch in me from kiss to full-body swoon. It's like that moment when a violin solo shifts into a symphony, and I'm played everywhere. A tuning fork has been struck, and this is an all-over vibration. My senses go into overdrive, and I can hold only one thought in my brain.

Kiss me again.

He reads my mind.

He seamlessly slides into the role of a man who wants the same thing. Inching closer, he presses against me, ropes his hand through my hair, curls it around the back of my head.

I feel this kiss in my knees, in my bones, under my skin.

As his lips explore mine, the kiss takes on a new urgency. Lips press harder. Tongues slide. He demands more of me, and this fake kiss feels so real, so damn real, as he steals my breath.

He breaks the kiss. "This is how we kissed the first time," he says in my ear, his breath hot against my neck.

I try to devise something witty, something clever, but all I can manage is, "We didn't stop."

"We didn't want to stop," he murmurs as his lips return to me. They're sealed to my mouth, and he cages me against the brick wall. His hands are on my face, in my hair. He presses his body to mine, and that's not fake.

He's hard, thick, and I can feel the full length of him pressed into my belly. It's dizzyingly sexy. It's wildly arousing. All the dirty thoughts in my brain swirl together and combust as I imagine how it would feel to take him inside me. To wrap my legs around him. To draw him all the way in.

He pulls back, presses his forehead to mine, breathes hard. *"April."* My name sounds like champagne on his tongue.

"Yeah?" I sound like a dopey, drunk fool as I wait for him to speak.

Chapter Twenty *Theo*

I want to tell her *the* truth. A truth. Something. Anything. This fakery is eating me up. I don't want to be like her lying ex, but I don't want to get screwed over either.

"What? What is it?" April asks again.

Nerves prickle up my skin as I consider answering her. Telling her I'm into her. Telling her about my parents. Telling her what I did for a living years ago. I part my lips to speak because I want her to know me. Harboring secrets is too hard. They weigh you down. But as soon as I opened up to Richelle, she was done with me. No more boyfriend, and no more work. The jobs ended instantly.

I don't want to lose this gig.

I need this gig.

But I don't want to lose the chance to let April know that kiss was real.

I'm torn in two.

Make that three, because I also want to kiss her again. She's candy and sex appeal, and a little something different. She's left of center; she's right of center. She's not like anyone I've ever met. "I don't know what I was going to say. Kissing you fries my brain," I say, dodging the questions as I lean on humor.

She laughs softly, and that sound hums down my spine. How the hell is this possible? Her laughter turns me on. I dip my head to her neck. "Mmm. You taste like sunshine."

She murmurs.

"And oranges."

She sighs.

"And everything I shouldn't be attracted to," I say roughly. There it is. The admission that we're not a thing. We're a client and a contractor.

"I know," she whispers, her tone wistful. "But you're a great actor."

"So are you." And because I can't resist her, I press a kiss to her soft lips for one, two, three seconds. I inhale her. "Just because."

"That was a 'just because' kiss?" she asks with a lift of her eyebrow as we break apart.

"We do that a lot, don't we?" I ask, and though we're playing our game again, this moment feels more honest than anything with her so far. I've spent so much time pretending, playing, tricking, and right now, I want to ride close to the truth.

"We are the king and queen of 'just because' kisses," she says, and damn, if that doesn't make me want her more. We are like Mad Libs, filling in words to make the other laugh, to turn each other on.

I dust my lips along her jaw, to her ear. I nip her earlobe and murmur "Just because." She moans, looping her arms around my neck. I should stop. But as she melts in my arms and I tangle my tongue with hers, stopping seems impossible. Instead, I kiss her deeper. I slide my hand through her hair, and I steal yet another kiss. Then one more. She is soft, and she tastes fantastic, and I want to strip off her clothes and kiss her everywhere. Explore her body, lick her skin, taste the hollow of her throat.

I want to watch her back arch. To know what she looks like when she's coming. I kiss her like that. I kiss her so she knows I want to devour her. I want her wild little body under me, on me, bent over. I push my body to hers, making sure, making certain she can feel what she does to me, so she can know this is true. This is real. This is *just because*. I grind against her, and she moans into my mouth. I clasp her tighter, kiss her deeper, linger longer.

Somewhere in the back of my mind, there's a bell ringing. It clangs, the sound a warning. The more I do this, the more I'll *want* to do this. That's dangerous for a guy like me. Closeness means letting down your guard. Letting someone in means you can lose everything you're chasing. The finish line is in sight, and I need to run this race to the end.

I pull apart abruptly. I wipe my hand over my mouth. "I shouldn't have done that," I mutter.

I sound like a jackass. I am a jackass.

She blinks, then knits her brow. "Then why did you kiss me?"

I clench my teeth, grind out a lie. "That's why you wanted me here with you for the weekend. Right?"

"Right," she says with a nod, like she's recalling her own reasons. Her voice is sardonic. "To fight them all off."

I pretend I don't notice the sarcasm. "Well? Didn't you say everyone was trying to set you up and you wanted to appear taken?"

"Yes. But." She furrows her brow. "I . . ." She starts, then stops. "I don't get it."

"Get what?"

"*You.*"

"Me?"

She points. "Yeah. You. You kissed me because of Calvin, right?"

"Yes, that's what you wanted," I say, because self-preservation is stronger right now than admitting I wanted to kiss her.

"So Calvin knew we were kissing?"

I point behind me. "He was right over there."

She swivels around, then turns back to me and shoves a hand through those wild blond curls. Her hair is messy because of me. Her eyes are hard because of me. "Congratulations. You've successfully toyed with my head."

"How?"

She rolls her eyes. "Kissing me because of Calvin. Still kissing me. Saying 'just because.' Seriously. This is crazy," she says.

And even though I wanted to kiss her, that doesn't change the rules of engagement. I let myself get carried away. I need to be smarter and safer.

She grabs the bag of tissues and parks a hand on her hip. "I'm going back to the Sunnyside. It would be great if you return in a little bit, too, and maybe act like we didn't just have a fight, because I'm not in the mood for that."

She turns away, and I try to shout *Wait!*

But the word doesn't come.

I dig my heels into the ground, tuck my thumbs in my jeans, and let her go home.

Chapter Twenty-one *April*

I stab at the buttons on my phone as I text and walk. I huff and puff, tapping out note after frustrated note, my head bent over the screen as the stores and shops become a blur beside me.

> **April:** You were pretty much spot-on.

> **Claire:** You tackled him before lunch, then? Well done.

> **April:** Not exactly, and I'm not happy.

> **Claire:** Uh-oh. Talk to me.

> **April:** He kissed me like crazy this morning.

Claire: OK, so the moratorium ended. Got it. Also, yay for that! And yay for hot kisses.

April: Not exactly.

Claire: It wasn't hot? That's terribly sad. OK, tell him you're going back to your cold turkey lifestyle and you're sorry you went hot turkey on him for a minute there.

April: No, that's not it. The kiss was beyond hot. Beyond incredible. Like, a movie kiss. A book kiss. I could have been one of those girls who pops her leg up and melts into the kiss. It was head-to-toe shivers, and tingles everywhere.

Claire: I'm failing to see the problem. Perhaps you ought to be picking up some condoms and getting it on in the Pancake Room. You need to make pancakes with him. Or fritattas. That sounds vaguely naughty. Like, we made a frittatta today, wink wink.

I want to laugh. But I don't. I can't even acknowledge her attempt at humor. I'm so flaming frustrated. I'm so dang confused. I glance up from the screen as I stalk up the street. How did I wind up here? I was so careful. Cautious. When you hire someone to be your date, it's not

supposed to turn into a deeply passionate kiss that makes
your brain go hazy. At least, I don't think so. But inside
me is a tangle of emotions, a swirling mess.

> **April:** He went weird after the kiss.

> **Claire:** Ohhhhh.

> **April:** He acted all . . . guy strange . . . like, I
> want to kiss you, but we can't kiss, and I
> kissed you because I saw this other dude who
> wants you, and I kept kissing you, but now I
> can't because, you know. REASONS.

> **Claire:** I hate when guys go weird.

> **April:** It's literally my least favorite thing they do.

> **Claire:** Besides not being divorced?

> **April:** Fine. I hate that more.

> **Claire:** Besides not supporting himself financially?

> **April:** Whose side are you on?

Claire: The side of you and the side of kissing. Is it weirdness that can be solved with words? You know, talking. You like talking. You're a talker. Besides, what are these REASONS?

April: I'm groaning. Not the good groaning. I'm groaning in annoyance.

Claire: Let's just take it as a given that I don't hear you good-groan.

April: Perv. Anyway, what do I say TO HIM?

Claire: Say, "Hey, I know I hired you, but I'm hot for you, you're hot for me, what do you say we go horizontally?"

April: Ugh. This isn't supposed to be weird. It's supposed to be easy. Hiring someone makes things easier. Money changing hands makes it easier. Why is it harder?

Claire: Memo to April: It gets complicated when people like each other. If there's weirdness, maybe there's liking going on. Think about it. And deal with the REASONS.

I look up from the screen, breathe a big huge gulp of fresh sea air, and I hear shoes slapping the pavement. I march right into Cory.

"Oof!"

That's literally the sound that bursts from my lips when I smack into my sister's husband.

He removes his earbuds. "Hey! Sorry. I was so into this podcast, I didn't see you," he says with a smile. "Everything okay? I'm just heading to FlourChild to check on things before the games begin again."

"Perfect," I say as embarrassment churns through me. I'm not embarrassed that we bumped into each other. I'm embarrassed over why. I'm having a stupid fight with my unreal boyfriend, and now my sister's real husband is asking me if I'm okay. I'm not okay. I'm annoyed that my supposed boyfriend kissed the daylights out of me, then acted like it was . . . Well, an act. When it wasn't an act. But I can't say that to Cory or anyone here. Especially since my eyes drift to his phone and I see the name of the podcast. *Perking Up Your Marriage.*

My face flushes pink. I wish I hadn't peeked. I wish I didn't know what's on his mind. Are things that rough with Tess and Cory? Or is she just caught in the haze of an infant's needs?

"You sure?" he asks.

I blink, refocusing on his question. "I'm great!"

He glances around behind me, hunting for someone. "Where's Theo?" Cory seems eager for a glimpse of my plus-one.

I wave a hand through the air. "He had to take a phone call," I say, making something up on the spot. "Work thing."

"Got it. Want anything from the bakery? Does Theo

want something? We've got some badass seven-layer bars. I bet he'd like one."

I crack a smile. Oh my. My brother-in-law must think Theo is the cool guy he wants to be if he's trying to impress him through baked goods.

"That sounds great, and I'll take a cake the size of my head." *To drown my idiotic misplaced sorrows in. I hear your chocolate frosting is the new therapy.*

"Hey, cupcake. My work thing's over. I can get you a cake like that if you want. And a badass seven-layer bar sounds awesome, Cory."

I turn to the voice that sends shivers up my spine. But I'm still pissed at him. And I'm even angrier at myself.

Chapter Twenty-two *Theo*

With a happy salute and a promise to bring me a badass seven-layer bar, Cory leaves and it's just the two of us at the end of the last block in downtown Wistful.

Now I need to man up and say what I should have said before. "You're still mad at me."

She shrugs. "Not really."

"Liar," I tease. "You are."

She sighs, but shakes her head. "Doesn't matter. I have no right to be mad at you."

"You do," I say emphatically. "You have every right."

"Do you want me to be mad at you?" She resumes her pace to the inn.

Watching her walk away earlier this morning was a slap in the face. That was a dumbass move on my part to dance circles around her questions and to let her think stuff that wasn't true. It was a dumbass move to lie to her the other night. I rip off the Band-Aid: "My parents didn't die in a car crash," I say, the words spilling out, jagged and raw.

That stops April and she pivots around, standing in

front of me, the bright light of the sun haloing her face, illuminating her wild green eyes and those freckles that occasionally make her look even younger. "What do you mean?"

A ball of steel lodges in my chest. I hate talking about this. I hate that it happened. I hate how it was twisted and turned and used to define my future.

"It was easier than the truth," I scratch out.

"What happened, then?"

I bite off the bitter truth. "My mom had pancreatic cancer when I was thirteen. It was fast-moving and awful. She had very little time. Nine months from diagnosis to death."

"Oh, Theo," April says, her voice thick with emotion. "I'm so sorry."

"We had no idea why she had it. There was no family history, no indicators. She had a regular life. She was an English teacher, and so was my father. We were so ordinary. We had these ordinary, regular lives in Boston."

"There's nothing wrong with an ordinary life. Sometimes normal is good."

"All my parents wanted was for my brother and me to go to college. Even when my mom got sick. College was everything, and they'd just started saving for it, but they had very little. What they had they used for my mom's treatments."

She is crestfallen, those wide eyes brimming with sadness. "That's so sad about your mom."

I draw a deep breath. This is where the shit gets real. "I was fourteen when she died. Two weeks later, my father killed himself."

Her jaw unhinges, and she blinks. She clasps her hand to her mouth. Richelle reacted the same way when I told her. I brace myself because Richelle left me soon after she learned that Heath and I turned into con artists to survive.

Richelle wanted a boyfriend who fit her neat, orderly design for life, and she didn't handle it well when I told her what happened to my parents. When she found out I had a past and it wasn't pretty, she tensed. She tightened. She retreated.

April's the opposite.

The sweet, sarcastic goofball of a girl puts her hand on my shoulder and squeezes. "Theo," she says softly. Where Richelle recoiled, April moves closer. "I can't even imagine what you went through."

And because of that, right there, telling her feels different. I hope I'm not wrong.

"I'm sorry I pressured you to tell me by asking the first night," she says.

I close my eyes and shake my head. When I open them, I take the hand she's offering me. "I'm sorry I lied."

"Don't apologize. I understand. That's all just so hard to say. Infinitely harder to have gone through."

I swallow past the lump as she squeezes my fingers. "He was supposed to be there for us. Take care of us. But he couldn't live without her. He put a bullet in a gun and a gun in his mouth."

She winces. "That's terrible."

"That's why it's easier to say they died in a car crash."

With her free hand, she reaches for my hair, brushes a few strands off my forehead. I catalog that response, too. Also different. I like April's differences. "Thank you for telling me the truth, even when it's so hard to say. And especially when we hardly know each other. Is that why you told me? Because it's easier to tell someone you don't really know?"

I pause, considering her question. I shake my head. "I feel like I do know you."

She smiles softly. "I guess I feel that way, too. It's been

only a few days, but I do feel like I know you—or at least, that I want to."

With my fingers threaded through hers, I tug her closer and give her another true answer. "I don't want to mess with your head. I told you about my parents because when I say I don't get involved on a job, and when I say I've never kissed a client, I want you to know all those things are true." My eyes lock with hers, and what I say next is laced with import—it's important to me, to who I want to be. "I want you to know I'm not a liar. And it's the truth when I say I've never wanted to kiss someone as much as I wanted to kiss you. It's true, too, when I say I'm incredibly attracted to you."

Maybe I'm just testing gradations of truth. To see what works. I want to be free of who I was before. I want to move on. I want to head into whatever the future is beyond debts and payments and trouble that chases me around. Trying sections of honesty, like they're pieces of fruit served on a platter, seems to be the way to go.

"You might have figured out that I'm kind of attracted to you, too," she says with a little glint in her eyes as she tugs my hand and guides me to a nearby bench.

"Kind of?" I ask, toying with her.

"Hey, don't go fishing," she chides.

"I'll take 'kind of.'"

"What happened after they died?" she asks, returning to the topic at hand. "Where did you live? Where did you go?"

"I was fourteen. Heath was sixteen. We grew up in Boston, but after my dad killed himself, we were sent to my aunt in Jersey."

"Are you close with her?"

I shake my head. "If by 'close,' you mean she gave me a ride to my own high school graduation, then took off to see her friends, yes. Also, that was the first event she ever took us to."

"Wow," April says under her breath. "So, not close at all."

"Let's put it this way: I haven't seen her since she knocked on my door a few years ago and asked me for money for pills."

"She was that direct? She didn't even try to cover it up?"

"She's far gone. Desperate now. And it was the most ironic request, since I could barely rub two sticks together," I say, and brace myself for her response. She might not be a country club gal, but she's surrounded by a hell of a lot more than two sticks. She has logs for roaring fires. "Some days it's still that way."

Tension zooms through me. I've just confessed one of the basic truths of my existence. That every day can be a scramble. "I'm saying that as the guy who's attracted to you, not as the guy you hired," I add.

"I'm glad that's why you told me. And you do work hard. You juggle so many jobs now."

"I try."

"Thank you for sharing all that. I'm glad you were honest with me. And even though I'm on a man diet, I'm glad you're the one who broke it with that kiss," she says with a sweet lift of her lips.

"Me, too." I want to kiss her again, all day long. All of a sudden, all my reasons for not kissing her seem unimportant. They seem meaningless when I look at her, with her hair a wild tangle from my hands, her eyes inviting.

But then, a familiar ring sounds from my pocket. Force of habit kicks in, and I grab my phone. It's Heath.

I answer instantly. "Hey, there."

"Hey, little shit," he says, and I cover the mouthpiece and tell April, "My brother."

"You got a minute?" he says to me.

"Yeah, give me a second." I turn to April. "I'll be fast."

She shoos me along. "Talk to him. Meet me back at the house?"

"You sure?" I whisper.

She nods. "Absolutely. You can find it? It's only a couple blocks away."

I salute her. "I can find it."

She gives me a faint wave, and I turn the other way, pressing the phone to my ear. "Hey, what's up?"

"What's up with you, man?"

His voice is deep and rough. It's sandpaper and grit. "Just finished some work, and I took a break to play a new game on the Xbox, but it bored me."

"Ah, so I'm the recipient of your boredom? Or Lacey is out?"

He laughs as I wander slowly up the block. "Lacey's working, but I have some work, too."

"Yeah?"

"Yep. Your big brother isn't such a screw-up. I've picked up work here and there. I have some new clients."

"I never thought you were a screw-up."

He laughs dismissively. "You know better than anyone that I was. You don't go to prison for eighteen months without being one."

"It was ridiculous that you went."

"I deserved to be there. But I also deserve to be out."

"No doubt. What sort of work are you getting, Heath?" I ask, my throat crawling with nerves. It better not be the kind of work that put him behind bars in the first place.

Heath went to the pen for fraud. He ran some shady online scams, and the one that earned him a two-year felony conviction that was shortened to one year and six months was a pump-and-dump stock scam.

"I told you last time I'm expanding my computer work," he says.

I groan as I reach the end of the block. In the distance, a boat's horn bleats.

"Heath," I say, like a warning, "you're not doing that again, are you?"

"Straight and narrow, baby. Just like you, right?"

"You know I've been good since County."

"That was the real bullshit that you went. I wish I could have stopped you."

"Nothing could have, right? Besides, you were out of town with Addison."

"Don't mention her name."

My shoulders tighten. "Why? Has she called you?"

"No. Because I try to put her out of my mind." A door creaks open on his side of the call. "Ooh, Lacey's home."

Lacey was always the one for him. He'd give up everything for her. He'd run to her. He'd turn to her. I just wish I knew if he went straight for her, too. I want to believe him.

"Tell Lacey hi from me."

"Hey, handsome!" she says, shouting from nearby into the phone.

"Somehow I'll see you soon. Miss you, you little bastard," Heath says.

"Miss you, too, dickhead," I say with nothing but great affection for the person who, for all intents and purposes, raised me once our parents were gone. I love him like crazy.

He's my family. My only family. He stayed by my side. He didn't put a bullet in his head when our parents died.

Chapter Twenty-three *Theo*

Arm wrestling was only the start.

After Heath and I learned we could con college guys out of dough, we put our enterprising teenage brains together and tried to figure out whom to trick next.

We weren't targeting anyone in particular. We were targeting our pasts, we were aiming for our future. Heath was pissed we had to leave Boston to move in with our aunt. He was in love with his high school girlfriend, and he hated leaving Lacey behind to live with someone we barely knew. Our aunt didn't care what we did. She was so loopy on pain meds and chasing down more Vicodin that the two wayward charges sent to live with her meant little. We were nothing but trouble, and we had jack shit.

When someone kills himself, life insurance doesn't often pay out. I don't know if my father knew this little loophole or not. His policy was only a year old, so even if it would have paid off later, it didn't matter. It didn't pay then. We had no money for college. We had no money to live. It was sink or swim, do or die. In retrospect, we could have tried to win jobs at a grocery store, a gas station, a pizza place. Carved out a niche as upstanding young citizens, teenagers earning minimum wage.

We didn't want minimum wage. We wanted what our mom wanted for us.

"Go to college. Challenge your mind. Earn a degree," she'd said.

We chose the fastest path we could devise to get from point A to point B.

We were troubadours of the Jersey boardwalks, fashioning ourselves into modern-day *fraud-preneurs*.

First, we were quick-change artists, tricking gas station registers in a grift that we played all year long. It's simple, and like a magic trick, it relies on sleight of hand and confusing the mark. I'd pay for a pack of gum with a ten-dollar bill, get back nine ones and change, and then tell the clerk I had a one-dollar bill, and exchange ten ones for a ten. I'd make more change, and do it so quickly, the clerk would get flustered to the point where I'd swapped ten dollars for twenty. The key was having several change transactions running at once, and that's how we stayed ahead of the clerks.

We had speed and confidence on our side, and that was honestly all we needed to rack up a thousand a month going store to store with that grift. That doesn't pay for college, though, so Heath didn't start school when he turned eighteen.

But short cons lead to long cons.

And once you hustle money from frat guys and clerks, you get thirstier for more.

That's where Addison entered the scene. She's the same age as my brother. She became his girlfriend after he finished high school, and she started conning with us. She was our badger, and she was nineteen. I'd scope out the marks on the beach, men whom she'd then chat up. She'd get them to buy her a drink, then go back to our place.

Heath would play the part of her big brother, barging in, covered in tats, bulging with muscles, promising to rip the guy's lungs out. *Leave my sister alone!* Shake him down for all he's worth or we'd call the police.

That's why when I told April and her friends that my "acting credits" included *The Badger,* I wasn't really lying. It was like a nightly act we performed, and we cleaned up.

We were masters, too, at *The Rental.* We'd list an apartment online for rent at just below market value, asking for first and last months' rent up front. Payment would clear the bank, new tenants would arrive, ready to move in, but the same unit had been rented to others. We were nowhere to be found. Now you see us; now you don't.

That's how we made a living that was better than slinging fastfood. Better than any job.

There's a rush when you pull off a scam. It's a high, a thrill, a burst of adrenaline. We got ballsier and more daring, and you know what? We were never caught. Not once.

The irony is I went to county jail for two weeks for something else. I didn't lie in my GigsForHire ad. I've done time. I did a stint behind bars when I was nineteen. Heath was away on a trip with Addison. They'd traveled to South Carolina for a vacation and a little gambling grift. Addison fronted the dough for a gambling ring they were setting up. They were trying to make his college pot swell courtesy of poker. Meanwhile, I'd been working on my own side business, selling fake IDs to college students who wanted to get plastered more easily.

Until I was busted, and thrown in jail for fourteen days.

Besides my parents dying, those were the worst two weeks of my life. I shared a cell with a crackhead and a former felon nabbed for possessing a firearm. Fun times. They were scary as shit, while I was the budding white collar criminal. Perhaps the justice system figured if they stopped me then, they'd prevent the next Madoff.

Maybe they were right.

When I was released, I quit scams and cons cold turkey.

I stopped because I liked college a hell of a lot better than I liked being locked up. I spent the next five years at university, finally graduating at age twenty-four. We used our con money for my school and then for Heath's, taking out small loans for the amount we didn't have. In retrospect, we might have been able to qualify for financial aid for college, but we had no clue when we were younger. After our parents died, we were effectively raised by wolves—ourselves—and neither one of us had a guidance counselor who cared enough to mention aid, and once we applied, we didn't think about asking for a handout. But even if we'd known, the reality is conning was fast and quick and effective. We were good at it. We didn't have to fill out endless forms to see if we qualified. We found our marks and we went for it.

Every now and then, I'd think about our marks, the guys we conned out of dough. Some were confused cashiers. Some were drunk frat guys. Some were just average Joes on the beach. A ten-dollar bill here, a twenty there, in some cases a few hundred. I'd like to think my choices didn't break anyone's bank, but who was I to know what our tricks did and didn't do to the marks?

At the very least, I took some solace in knowing I hadn't scammed anyone out of a retirement, or a home, or a college fund. Like a twelve-stepper, I figured I should make amends in some broader sense of the word. I started donating to a pancreatic cancer research fund, and I still do. Every month, I write a check, and I've never missed a single payment. Maybe it's my small way of restoring order. Maybe it's my belief in karma. Or maybe it's just the right thing to do.

By the time I graduated from college, my con artist days were far in the rearview mirror, but Heath had started up again. He'd gotten a taste of big paydays, and he liked them too much. He'd studied computers, and that gave him enough skills to establish his stock-fraud scam when he finished school. He wanted to refill the till, he'd said one evening over drinks as we caught up. "The kitty's empty. Everything went to the registrar."

"Everything was supposed to go to the registrar. That's why we did it," I'd pointed out. "So we'd be done."

"And now we can replenish it," he'd told me.

"Mom wouldn't approve."

"Mom's lack of approval didn't stop you from cleaning up with me all along the boardwalk."

"That was different," I'd said. "We had nothing then. We had a reason and we had no choice."

"And I have a reason now. I need to get ahead. I need to have my act together when I look up Lacey again."

That name. A blast from the past. I wrenched back, surprised to hear him mention her. "Your high school girlfriend?"

"Yep. Some girls—you just can't get them out of your head."

"Is that so?"

"Sometimes you meet a girl, and she stays here." He'd tapped his temple. "But that's because she's here." He'd knocked his knuckles against his breastbone. "She's definitely right here in my heart. I need to see her again."

"What about Addison?"

He'd shook his head. "Addison is a businesswoman. We liked each other. Hell, maybe it was even love at one point. But it was always first and foremost business for her."

I wasn't sure if that meant they were through. I didn't ask. I didn't care that much about her. A tactical error on my part, but one I couldn't have anticipated. "Just be careful."

"That's my middle name."

And that's when Addison comes back into the story.

It's always about a girl, isn't it?

Men will move mountains for women. They'll burn cities. They'll rob banks. They'll live in cells.

Addison had stopped conning and had landed a job as a business consultant, so she was already pulling away from my brother. Someone else was trying to get close to him. Lacey had tracked him down, found out he was back in Boston. She'd missed him, always had, and had never gotten him out of her mind either.

He said see you later to the drifting-away Addison, and started up with the girl he'd probably always loved. Lacey stayed with him when he was cuffed for the stock scam, when he was sent away, and for the eighteen months he was locked up. She waited for him to get out. She vowed to me that she'd make sure he stayed clean. I paid his restitution with my meager savings, even though he chewed me out for doing so. "I was going to take care of that on my own. Don't do that again," he'd said one day when I'd visited him.

"Don't go to prison again, and I won't have to," I'd said.

Addison waited for something, too. While he was behind bars, she decided she wanted her money back from their poker games in South Carolina. Maybe she hadn't been the one drifting away. Maybe Heath had. Perhaps the return of Lacey to the scene meant Addison didn't feel so generous with her money anymore. That's my best guess, since soon after he was locked up, she found me, reminded me how our cons had helped the little brother the most. How they'd paid for my school. She'd told me she'd happily shake down Heath when he got out of prison.

"Would you like me to do that, sweetheart?" she'd said in her southern drawl.

That's where she had me over the barrel.

She knew me. Knew I wanted my brother to stay out of trouble. I don't know what he'd do to get the money back. That's what I worry about. That's why I took on the debt myself and never told him. I don't mind. My brother put me first when we were younger. Even though he's older, he made sure we had money for my school before his.

The least I could do was cover for him.

As I walk to the inn, a new text message flashes at me.

> **Addison:** Should I come find you? I got the feeling the other night that you didn't take me seriously. Would it be more helpful if I brought someone along you'd treat more seriously?

> **Theo:** You'll have it next week when I return to New York.

I stuff the phone into my jeans pocket and return to the Sunnyside.

Might as well call this place the Flip Side, because that's

what it is compared to my life. When I walk into the homey B and B, a passel of Hamiltons and Moores are drinking coffee and playing a riotous game of Monopoly.

April's mom calls out to me. "Join us."

My heart pinches and feels smaller, like it's caving in. This is the stuff I don't know how to do.

April is curled up in a roomy chair, her feet tucked under her. She pats the chair. I cut across the rug, squeeze in with her, and she wraps her arms around me, and kisses my cheek.

Liking her is dangerous. There's a text message on my phone that'll remind me just how dangerous it is.

I need the money a lot more than I need a distraction as delicious as her.

Chapter Twenty-four *April*

When my cousin Katie lands on Marvin Gardens, I wiggle my fingers and tell her to pay the piper.

"Don't cross her. She's one badass landlord," Theo says with a smile as Katie hands over some pink, yellow, and green bills.

Cory returns home midway through the game and dispenses baked goods like Santa Claus with his bag of toys. He seems to take special care to give Theo the badass seven-layer bar. Cory totally has a man crush on Theo, and it's adorable.

When Theo finishes, he gives Cory a thumbs-up. "This is indeed a heavenly bar."

Cory beams, and I bet he wishes his wife were praising him like that. But then, what do I know? Maybe it's not praise he wants. Maybe he just wants a private moment with her.

I'm not sure what's going on with my sister and her husband.

But as I watch Theo laugh and chitchat with Cory and

the others, something hits me: Theo's having fun. In fact, he's been having fun the whole time, and it occurs to me how much I want him to have a good time. Not just for me, but for him as well. I want him to know that family doesn't have to be painful.

I hired him for what felt like a most perfect reason at the time—to ward off the hometown matchmaking scheme my family has been hatching to get me to move back to Wistful. But in light of what Theo shared this morning, my concerns seem petty. As I glance around the cozy living room of a B and B that's stuffed full of family, my dilemma suddenly feels unimportant.

There's no doubt that I still need to focus on my long-term career. The dating diet is still my meal plan. But thanks to Theo, I can see that though my family meddles, they have my best interests at heart. From my mother and her wish to set me up with the hardware store owner to Jeanie and the mortgage banker, they all want the same thing—they want me to be happy. We might have different notions on how to get there, but the goal is the same. And while I have no more interest in their matchmaking than I did before, I no longer want Theo to serve as my shield. I no longer want to lie. I don't want to deceive people I love.

I want something else now. Something I never expected. After we call a halt to the game, I pop upstairs to brush my teeth, and I text Claire.

> **April:** I think we made up.

> **Claire:** Good. Now make up properly. Sex and all.

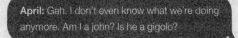

April: Gah. I don't even know what we're doing anymore. Am I a john? Is he a gigolo?

Claire: Are you turning tricks now? Are you on the merry path to seven magical O's?

April: I wish.

Claire: You'll get there. But the real question is, do you like him?

April: I do. I really do.

Claire: So then, what's next?

April: I don't know. . . . What do I do?

Claire: Sometimes you need to go after what you want.

What if we could be good together?

I don't mean forever, and I don't even mean when I return to New York. But maybe for now? Maybe for the next few days we won't have to pretend. Maybe we can be real for this sliver of time.

A small laugh bursts from my lips. I've got it bad for the guy I hired. This is like a movie, and as I set down my toothbrush, I wonder what the spunky, crazy heroine would do.

I stare at my shiny white teeth in the mirror and turn over the question in my mind until I find the answer.

"She'd show him what real is," I say to the girl staring back at me.

But I have to take care of one itty-bitty pressing matter first.

I check the time. I can't do it yet, but I will this afternoon. Right now, I have a game of Junk in the Trunk to win. I head outside and help Aunt Jeanie, Cousin Katie, Libby, Dean, and Theo fill the empty tissue boxes with plastic Ping-Pong balls.

Theo holds one up. *"Voilà,"* he says in his perfect French accent.

"Real French," I say, looking at him.

"Oui, mademoiselle, but only *pour vous."*

Dean arches a brow. "You can do accents?"

"I can," Theo answers.

"Do the others," I say proudly, and this time it's real pride. I don't feel phony anymore, because my feelings aren't fake. Maybe this started as a ruse, but it's turning into something else.

Theo waves them off deferentially. "Oh no, I surely can't do that at the moment, love." Full-on British, and the proper enunciation makes my toes tingle.

As we tie Kleenex boxes around our waists, so they're perched on our rears, Theo slips in and out of his accents, entertaining the whole crew. By the time he finishes with a "thanks, y'all" in delicious southern, he has everyone eating out of the palm of his hand.

My mother grabs the megaphone and calls the start to Junk in the Trunk. "You have one minute to get rid of all eight balls."

We shake and shimmy in a race to eject the Ping-Pong balls from our boxes. Bob's big sons get in on the action, and it cracks me up to see the guys that Theo privately told me he calls Huey, Dewey, and Louie shaking their big bodies. Aunt Jeanie is a master, her athleticism in full swing as she shows off how well she can wiggle her rear with a tissue box on it. Her husband, Greg, laughs when she laughs, shakes when she shakes, and kisses her on the cheek when one of the rounds ends. He adores her, even if he hardly speaks. He shows it in his actions, if not his words. Katie catcalls Theo when he tries to eject the Ping-Pong balls, shouting, "April thinks you look hot doing that!"

I laugh at my bawdy cousin.

For all his marathoning prowess, Dean is horrible at Junk in the Trunk, but he shrugs it off with a smile.

We all laugh.

Even my sister and her husband join in for a few rounds. I glance over at my mom, and see she's pried the baby away from my sister once more, and is clutching Andi tight as my dad takes over megaphone duties.

I give Tess a wave, and she manages a small smile, her ponytail whipping back and forth as she shakes.

We're playing a ridiculous game with people we love under the summer sun.

For the first time, Theo looks like a complete dork rather than a cool guy. But you're not supposed to look cool or athletic in Junk in the Trunk. You're supposed to look silly. We keep it up, going for round after round after round. When we collapse onto the grass, one of Bob's young granddaughters has dominated, winning three of five rounds as the first to empty her junk in the trunk. Jeanie wins one, and Emma wins another.

Once the event is over, I turn to my fake boyfriend, and my heart skips a beat because his smile looks genuine even though he lost. He loops an arm around my waist and tugs me close. He drops a soft kiss on the end of my nose.

Is it a kiss for the crowd? Or one just for me? I cross my fingers, wishing for the latter.

Chapter Twenty-five *Theo*

I'm losing. What the hell? I should be good at this stuff. Games are my bailiwick, but who the hell knew the teenager would own me in Junk in the Trunk? I splash water on my face in the bathroom of our room at the inn. I scrub a hand over my jaw.

Focus, I tell myself.

I *need* to win the individual prize. I need it to be fully free and clear. April's fee will get me most of the way out of Addison's debt, and the five thousand dollars would get me over the hump.

But it's hard to focus when the woman I'm with is so distracting. When I want her, and when I want her to have the time of her life, too. I ask myself if I'm good to April. I kissed her. I messed with her head. I unloaded my sob story. I kissed her again. But I'm doing what I was hired to do. I'm keeping the matchmakers at bay, and I'm operating as her arm candy, so she can stay on her dating diet. As an unexpected bonus, her family actually seems to like me.

I step out of the bathroom and stop in my tracks, since

she's in the room now. She's bent over her suitcase, rooting around for something in it. She startles and straightens. "Hey."

"Hey."

"I was just going to change for Hula-Hoop." She drops her voice to a whisper and glances around furtively. "I put Velcro on the back of my skirt so the Hula-Hoop will never fall off."

"You trickster," I say, though I know she's joking.

"Truth is, I'm kind of awesome at Hula-Hoop." She wiggles an eyebrow.

"Yeah?"

She holds up a palm like she's in court swearing on a Bible. "Truth. Whole truth."

"How'd you get so good at Hula-Hooping?"

"I lost horribly the last time, so I took a Hula-Hoop class, since I was determined to win."

"Damn, that's impressive."

She shoots me a *come and get me* look. "I'm gonna take you down."

"Yeah? You talking to me?" I say, sliding into De Niro mode.

"Oh yeah. I'm talking to you, and I'm going to school you."

"You think so?"

She showboats, miming the moves she'll do. "I can Hula-Hoop around my neck. Around my calves. I can jump in and out of the hoop. I can send it round and round my body in a crazy diagonal." She slams her palms to my chest. "So take that."

I grab her hands. "That so?"

"I'm going to Hula-Hoop circles around you."

I grip her hands harder. "What if I Hula-Hoop circles around you?"

"Can you even Hula-Hoop?" She arches a skeptical brow.

"No," I admit.

She grins. "Then I'll beat you," she says, taunting me as I rope my fingers through hers. She lets out a small gasp. The rush of air makes me want to do more to her. Hold her tighter.

"You're trying to best your boyfriend," I say, and those last two words nearly trip me up. They are precisely what I'm supposed to be, but they sound truer than they have before. How is that possible? How can I feel like her boyfriend in only a few days?

Her lips twitch in an evil grin. "All's fair."

"What if I kiss you senseless, darlin'? Would that knock you off your game?" I say, tossing that option into the ring as I slide into my southern accent.

"Oh, so is this your cowboy option, then? Maybe I should have ordered this one. And why would kissing knock me off my game, pardner?"

"If it doesn't, I'm not doing it right, sweet thing," I say, my drawl going low, rough.

"Do you think you're doing it right?"

I grip even tighter, pull her a little closer. Everything we do is suddenly foreplay, even our role play. *Especially* our role play. "Pretty sure I've been doin' it right."

"You think so?"

I nod, nice and slow, watching her expression soften more as I stare at her with desire in my eyes. "Damn sure."

She breathes my name softly. *"Theo."*

Something in me snaps.

I cup her cheeks. I kiss her again. There's no gentleness this time. It's only heat. Roughness. Desire.

She claws at my shirt, and I grab her face harder. I walk her to the edge of the bed, till the backs of her knees hit the mattress. I seal my mouth to hers and swallow her sighs, kiss her breath.

Taste her.

I run my tongue over hers, and her mouth intoxicates me. It fries my brain. She's the sweetest, most sensual thing I've ever tasted. Like a sun-kissed peach, a honey apricot. Hell, thinking of summer fruit makes me leap twenty steps ahead to how she'd taste everywhere. I want to wrap my arms around her thighs and bury my face between her legs, and devour her. I want to know the noises she makes when she comes.

When I pull apart, a sound rips from my throat like an animal. It's the sound of how much I want her.

"What are you thinking?" she asks.

I groan. "You don't want to know."

She grabs my face, stares into my eyes. "I painted lips all over this face. You think I don't want to know? I do want to know."

I bring my mouth to her ear. "I'm thinking of things I can do to you with my lips."

She shudders. "Tell me what you want to do."

"April." I try to put on the brakes. But I have no luck, since I lick the shell of her ear instead. She trembles as my tongue roams her flesh, traveling to her neck.

"What are we doing?" she says, her voice sounding as hazy as my head.

I don't know anymore. I don't know a thing. I felt certain a few minutes ago when I gave myself a pep talk. Now all I want is to have her under me.

"Tell me," she says again. "Tell me what we're doing."

I reach for her hands and lay her body on the bed, pressing against her. Grinding against her. "You're demanding with all your questions."

"Maybe I am."

"I'll tell you what I'm thinking about doing. Kissing you everywhere. Wondering how you taste. What you sound like."

Her eyes float closed and she arches into me. "Can we just make out the rest of the afternoon?"

I laugh and push against her once more. "I can't say I'd object. But I think the cavalry would come looking for us."

She groans in frustration, but pushes her hips up against me, rubbing against the full length of my hard-on.

"Evidently, thinking of you Hula-Hooping turns me on," I say, going for humor, and she laughs.

"Apparently, thinking of you watching me Hula-Hoop gets me going, too."

"That's why we're a perfect pair of fakers, huh?"

Her expression darkens. "Yes. Yes, we are," she says, but her tone is crisper, and she pushes gently back on me. "We should get out of here." Her tone is cool again.

I furrow my brow. "Why do I feel like I've said the wrong thing again?"

She shakes her head. "You said nothing wrong."

"Are you sure?"

She sighs as I tug her up from the bed and let go of her hands. "You're just so good at what you do that I have to remind myself you're an actor."

My shoulders sag. "April."

She shakes her head. "It's okay. I hired you to act."

I run the back of my fingers down her cheek. "It's not acting with you. I swear."

A small smile seems to tug at her lips. "Yeah?"

I nod. "I swear."

I dust my lips over hers, whispering each word: "Not. An. Act."

She trembles, then pulls back to look at me. "It's not for

me either. I know I'm pretending with my parents about us, but being with you hardly feels like an act."

A megaphone sounds from the yard, blaring across the air. "Time for the next round."

I stand up, run my hand through my hair.

She points her thumb to the door. "I should go."

I point mine to my pants. "I should wait a minute."

"I should apologize for causing your tardiness, but I can't seem to find it in me to do that," she says with a wicked grin.

She leaves, and as the door shuts, I smile like a fool. She makes me laugh. She keeps me on my toes.

And as I stand here, killing time, I've got a new problem. A bigger one. I want this woman more than I want to stay away from her.

I don't know what the hell to do about that little predicament.

A few minutes later, the flagpole in my pants fades, so I make my way to the yard and I try to keep my eye on the prize. I can still win the individual prize. I can still nab that "charity money." And if I do that, then maybe I can get out from under the weight of money problems.

Outside, I catch April executing some of the most badass Hula-Hoop moves I never knew existed. Water-balloon baseball comes next, and I destroy all comers in that. I kick ass in the paper-airplane competition, but Emma is pretty awesome, too, at making gliders from paper. A little later, I take third place in the ring toss, and then when it comes to the obstacle course, April is a master, jumping through tires, swinging on ropes, until the end, where I swear she slows down.

For a second, it feels as though she lets me win.

But that's crazy.

Chapter Twenty-six *April*

I'm not saying all my ideas are bright ones. Some could be classified as zany. Others as positively harebrained. Some might be labeled just plain batty, even though I swear that washing my hands with the wooden air freshener sticks in the fancy bathroom of the Michelin three-star restaurant I went to seemed like a good idea at the time. The sticks looked like some new kind of elegant soap.

But the idea that landed in my brain just now feels right. I'm not referring to the idea to let him win the obstacle course, which I did since I have the impression he wants to win the individual prize for charity.

I mean the new plan I hatched. I should have just enough time to pull it off this afternoon, since we split up into boys and girls. Games are fine and good, but sometimes a woman likes to be pampered. As the men take off for an afternoon fishing expedition, the ladies head into town. The first order of business is the nail salon, and we pile inside, snagging all the big cushy leather chairs for pedicures and the swivel seats for manicures. My toes could use some attention, so I opt for a pedicure. As I lounge in the massage chair—with Emma operating the remote control on my back and taking a particular mischievous delight in turning the setting all the way to high—a dose of jitters courses through me.

When my silver-polished toes are nearly dry, I slide my feet into my flip-flops and stand. I've finished first, since I'm not getting a manicure. When you work with your hands, manicures are as pointless as a man's nipples.

"I need to run a quick errand," I say to my mom as a manicurist cuts her cuticles. "To grab coffee," I add, since the open-ended nature of *an errand* might invite too many questions. It's best to have a simple and airtight alibi, like caffeine.

The trouble is, everyone proceeds to give me their coffee orders.

"Hold on," I say, and grab my phone to enter their preferences, from the "Can you please see if they have a pink drink like a Unicorn Frappuccino?" per Emma to the French roast, 127 degrees, from Jeanie to the mocha chai latte for Tess, who holds the baby as she gets a pedicure. Only my mother has an easy request—coffee, black.

I leave the salon, drop my shades on my eyes, and imagine I'm a secret agent. I don't want anyone to recognize me. That probably sounds more furtive than need be. But my errand is personal and private. I pick up the pace, my flip-flops slapping against the sidewalk, my heart sprinting as I race-walk to the redbrick building near the drugstore. I go inside and march to the counter. Ten minutes later, my transaction is complete, and I stuff all the evidence inside my bra, then dart to the coffee shop.

If anyone asks why the coffee mission took a little more time than usual, I'll say the line was long for caffeine.

Unfortunately, it is.

I tap my heel and watch the clock, and soon I make it to the front, where I place the order. As the teenage barista whips up a collection of beverages, I fire off a text to Theo.

> **April:** Any chance I could make up for that horrible egregious omission and take you to the drawbridge later?

He doesn't respond instantly, though I suspect that's because he's on the open water, those strong muscled arms rippling under the bright afternoon sun as he reels in a huge fish. My stomach flips at the image. I don't even like fish, but rampant lust is making me think dirty thoughts about Theo as a fisherman. Go figure. Two days with him, and I've got it bad. I'm so going to break my diet. I'm going to chocolate-cake my way through the next few days.

"Here you go, and our best attempt at a Unicorn Frappuccino, but we have to call it a Unicorn Frapperino for trademark reasons," the barista explains.

"As long as it tastes pink and glittery, you can call it a sock, for all I care," I say with a laugh.

She knits her pimpled brow. "I don't think a sock would sell well."

"Good point," I say, then slide my shades back on and gather the cardboard trays. With one in each arm, I head to the door, pushing it with my butt. Once I'm outside, my gaze drifts to the docks. I wonder if Theo has returned. I wonder if he caught anything. I wonder if he even enjoyed this afternoon with the guys. Fishing doesn't seem like his jam, but I hope he had fun.

When I return to the nail salon, a wave of nervousness washes over me as I think of my plan. My stomach flips and flutters with trepidation. I drop my hand to my belly to try to settle the worries. My mother waves her copper-colored nails in front of a small fan and roams her eyes over me, narrowing them when she sees my hand on my belly. I frown and turn away from her.

As I dole out the drinks, handing the Frapperino thingie to Emma, who's now listening to Katy Perry in her earbuds, judging from the words she's singing along, I take a thirsty gulp of my iced vanilla latte. When I hand a black coffee to my mother, she arches a well-groomed eyebrow and says in a clear voice, "Are you pregnant, my little puppy?"

I nearly cough all my iced beverage on her. "Are you kidding me?"

"For a moment, you looked like you just rode a Tilt-A-Whirl. You set your hand on your belly as if you had morning sickness."

I roll my eyes. "That'd be kind of impossible, Mom," I say sarcastically, because—hello?—I haven't had sex in a year. "You need to have—"

I stop talking before I slip up.

My mom arches a brow once again, hunting for the hole in my words. "The only way that would be impossible is if you're not sleeping with someone. Are you having sex with your boyfriend? You've been together for six weeks. That seems a reasonable time frame for sexual relations, doesn't it?" she asks, like the prosecutor she once was. Yep, this is my mother. She's never met a question she's afraid to ask.

I groan as the red heat of embarrassment spreads across my cheeks. "You're really asking me if I'm sleeping with Theo?"

Tess cracks up from her pedicure perch, and the sound of her laughter surprises me. So do her words. "Mom, have you seen him? He's the hottest thing ever to show up in this town. He's also about ten thousand times hotter than any guy April has ever dated. Of course she's tapping that man. I bet she's tapping him all night long."

Yep. It's official. The red color in my cheeks has entered the beet zone.

"And, yes, that's why I asked. You've never brought a man home before, so I thought perhaps you might be pregnant. Plus, things seemed a bit intense between the two of you," my mom says, as if this were now a simple, logical conversation. "And you were quite insistent on sharing a room with him."

"And you'd be fine with this?" I ask, incredulous. "You'd be fine with me being pregnant?"

"I'm an open-minded woman, and you're twenty-eight. Why on earth would I be upset? But does that mean you're pregnant?" she asks, her voice dripping with hope.

Oh my. My mother wants this. She's champing at the bit for a bun in my oven.

And I'm going to enjoy bursting her bubble. "What I was going to say before is that to be pregnant, you'd need to have *unprotected* sex," I say, staring pointedly at my mom. "And obviously, I'm not going to have unprotected sex, since I don't want to be pregnant."

Katie chimes in, all redheaded bawdiness in full force. "Protected or unprotected, tell us more. I've always suspected guys with ink are great in bed." The woman painting sapphire blue on Katie's toes stifles a laugh. "Am I right?"

Silvery-haired Carol weighs in from her spot next to my mom. "Now, now. This is getting personal. It's only reasonable that the woman who brought home the total hottie should keep all the juicy, wonderful, delicious details to herself."

My eyes nearly pop out of my head. "You're a bunch of dirty girls, you know that?" I bring the straw to my lips and down a cold drink of latte.

Katie raises a hand, owning it. "Guilty as charged." She glances at Tess. "Besides, did you see how April looked before the Hula-Hoop event?"

Tess waves her manicured fingers at her hair, then points at me, all while balancing the baby on her leg. "You had that tousled look."

I flash back on my first email with Theo. *Just wink, and leave the bathroom during the reunion with tousled hair. The JBF kind.* I wish that were true. Great, now I'm jealous of my fictional sex life. The same fictional sex life that my family members are envious of. But then again, my hair was messed up from that hot little grind-me-good session on the bed. I nearly squirm just thinking about it.

Katie claps and wolf-whistles. "I knew it. I called it. Inked men for the win!"

"Did ya?" Tess prods me. "Did you have a quickie? A little *Hula-Hooping* before the Hula-Hoop?" Her voice lowers as she mutters, "I haven't had that in ages."

I roll my eyes, sidestepping my sister's admission for the moment, since defending myself is more vital. "Just so you know, 'Hula-Hooping' isn't a euphemism for sex."

"So you did have sex? Or did you have a euphemism?"

I hold up a palm. "Not going to answer."

"Did you do it in your mom's golf cart?" Katie calls out.

"No, we did it in Tess's car," I tease.

Tess's eyes light up. "Hey, don't give me ideas. That's where we used to—"

"Katie, Tess," my mother chides; then she turns to me, crisply rerouting the conversation. She's undeterred by the naughty brigade. "What I meant was simply that you seemed under the weather, and perhaps a bit nauseated. I experienced early morning sickness when I was pregnant with Mitch and Tess and you. And that's why I asked if you might be in the family way. There's nothing wrong with being unmarried and pregnant. We'd be thrilled for you. You could even come home and raise the baby here." My mother waves her fingertips in front of the fan, waiting for my answer.

My jaw clangs to the floor. I stare at her. She can't really be serious? But judging from the expectant look on her face, she is. She wants me to move home so badly that she'll happily slide from setting me up with local dudes to building out the nursery for the baby I'm not having?

I'm floored. I barely know what to say, so I go with a sort of truth. "Mom, I'm not in the least bit pregnant," I say, indignant. "Now, if you'll excuse me, I'd like a break from the Inquisition."

"So, that's a no? Just to confirm. Not pregnant?"

I slash a hand through the air. "So not pregnant."

She sighs dejectedly. "Consider it, though. It's not a bad idea." She stage-whispers, pointing at herself, "Free day care here in Wistful."

And that's it. My mom is off her rocker. She's now resorted to suggesting I get knocked up so I can move back home.

"I assure you, I wouldn't mind at all," she says, trying one last time. "I'd be delighted to help you raise the baby."

"Mom. There's no baby." I slide my purse up my shoulder and march to the door. Grabbing the handle, I yank it open. Then I turn my head back and leave them with this thought: "By the way, I'm off to find my hottie boyfriend. And hopefully, we'll have hot public sex somewhere and you'll all be jealous." I wave. "Toodle-oo."

The sound of their laughter follows me out the door, and I know we're all good, even though I still can't quite believe I just had a conversation with my mother and the other ladies about sex with Theo. It's a wildly inappropriate topic.

But sex with Theo is also something I can't get out of my mind. What would he be like in bed? Slow and tender at first, then hard and rough? Would he take his time exploring my body, as he did with my mouth?

Kissing you everywhere. Wondering how you taste. What you sound like.

He'd luxuriate in it. He'd drive me wild. My skin sizzles as my mind wanders, picturing everything.

Will I find out what he's like in bed? Will I give myself permission to take a taste? If I do give in, will I return to my regularly scheduled man diet when I'm back in the city? I tell myself that, yes, I can handle a little indulgence. Yes, I can get real for a couple days with the man I'm sharing a bed with. A few days at a family reunion doesn't mean we'd become an item back in New York.

But a part of me wants more than these few days. My mind is painting vivid images of wandering around Brooklyn with him, a strong arm of his draped possessively over my shoulder. Maybe he'd even meet me after a gig, grab my paints, and carry the bag for me. Some nights, we'd go bowling; other times we'd play retro arcade games. We'd do all the things we said we did as a fictional couple.

Only it'd be real.

So damn real, like the sweet ache in my heart that tugs toward him right now.

That's because the fantasy is so vibrant, so potent, I tell myself. And since it's my fantasy, I decide the realness wouldn't ruin my work focus, wouldn't distract me. I'd win the gig, and win the guy.

But relationships and work are opposing forces in my

life. You can't stay fit and eat cake at the same time. That's why it's best for me to remember that breaking a dating diet is fine for a vacation, but not so wise for a long-term plan.

With that in mind, I walk down the street. My phone rewards me with a text from him.

> **Theo:** If you're taking me to your drawbridge, that must mean I've been good.

> **April:** I guess you'll find out if you've been good when you get there.

> **Theo:** I'll be there. Just because.

And I'll find out if I can have just one bite.

Chapter Twenty-seven *Theo*

The drawbridge cranks open, its metal halves widening like a big jaw ready to snap. From the nearby railing, April gazes at the dinner cruise boat that floats under it. I wrap my hands around the railing as we stare at the placid water, the vessel leaving choppy waves in its wake.

"Are you going to tell me if I've been good?" I ask, turning to her.

"Do you think you have been?" Her green eyes glint with mischief, the brown flecks in them dancing a jig.

I'm dying to know what's on her mind. "What are you thinking, cupcake?"

Her lips twitch in an *I've got a secret* kind of look. The early evening breeze lifts the ends of her curly blond hair, and I want to touch those strands.

"I'm thinking that I have something for you," she says, a little coy, a little playful.

For one dirty lust-filled second, my mind runs through bridge-sex scenarios. I've never done it on a drawbridge, and honestly, I'm not even sure drawbridge-sex is a thing.

I wait for her to say more. She doesn't speak, though. She raises her right hand and dips it into her shirt. Holy shit. We *are* going to have drawbridge sex.

Her hand dips farther into the V-neck of her shirt, down to her bra. But she doesn't take off her peach-colored T-shirt, much to my disappointment. She pulls out a white envelope from one cup, then another one from the other. "I put one on each side for balance," she says sheepishly, explaining, "I didn't want to have a lopsided boob on account of all the Franklins."

I knit my brow. "Franklins? Lopsided boobs? What are you talking about?"

She hands me both envelopes. "Half your fee is in one. Half is in the other."

I straighten, and cold dread races through me. She's done with me? The job is over? "You're through? I thought you were happy with the job I'm doing."

She laughs and clasps my biceps. "God yes, I am. That's not what this is about."

"I don't get it. Why are you paying me now? It's a satisfaction-guaranteed kind of job. That's how I work. It's fair to you that way."

"I know," she says, her expression turning serious, but still soft. "And I'm satisfied."

"And you want me to stay?" I scratch my head, trying to understand what she wants.

"I do. But I can't let you think there's still a satisfaction-guaranteed clause."

I hold the envelopes limply. I've never been paid early. No one has ever handed me the money before the job was through. "But there is a clause. It's a guarantee."

"You've met it. Take the money," she says, firmer this time, as she places her hands on mine and curls my fingers around the envelope. "After you kissed me outside the hardware store, and after you kissed me again on the street, and then especially after we kissed each other senseless in the room, I would feel wrong not paying you till the end. I would feel like a liar. I'm more than satisfied already, and I don't want you to have the pressure of thinking you have to deliver perfectly to earn what you already deserve. You've done so much."

I shake my head, still processing this decision. "What have I done?"

The breeze rustles a strand of her hair again as the drawbridge creaks. Out of the corner of my eye, I see it's closing.

She runs her hand down my arm. That small touch sends a spark over my skin. "You talk to me," she says. "You talk to me about anything. About everything. About silly things. Serious things. Odd things. Anything."

"I like talking to you. I love talking to you. It's becoming a favorite thing. And remember, we don't do companionable silence."

"I just like you, and I don't have to pretend to like you."

Her admission is like a shot of pure pleasure. It charges through me, spreading into my veins. Those simple words—she likes me—mean so damn much. I want to embrace what they mean, and what the money means, too. It means the job is secure. It means I have nearly all I need for Addison. A little more here and there from bartending, and I can cover the rest. Hell, maybe I can still win that crazy all-around prize and be in the clear and then some. But at the same time, an ancient hurt rises up. The old fear that I'm no good for her. Money's not the only issue at play between us.

"You shouldn't like me," I mutter.

"Why?"

I swallow thickly. "There are things I've done you won't like."

She tenses, but then says softly, "Like what? Have you killed someone? Maimed someone? Assaulted someone?"

I give her a look. "I'm not *that* bad a bad boy."

"Then, what is it? Are you a drug dealer? An animal abuser?"

I laugh and shake my head. "No. And God no."

"Then?"

"Let's just say I was a very fucked-up teen."

She breathes a sigh of relief. "What teen wasn't a little messed up?"

I appreciate the way she's trying to make things easy for me, even softening my words, but I can't let her believe my life was on par with the average disgruntled teen.

"In what ways were you messed up?" April asks, but then she holds up her hand as a stop sign. "Forget I asked. You don't have to tell me."

I lift my own hand, run a finger down her cheek. "Maybe someday."

"If you're going to say things like 'maybe someday,' don't say things like 'you shouldn't like me.' Because I already do. I do like you, Theo."

My heart jumps, and I want to warn it to settle down. But hearts don't listen to heads. When have they ever? My father's broken, ransacked heart guided him to his final choice. My brother's heart was given to Lacey long ago, and he thought he needed to con again to win her over. Instead he wound up behind bars.

My situation isn't the same as either of theirs—it's not so tragic, and in this moment, it's not so desperate.

But that doesn't mean I'm any wiser. It takes a better man than me to listen to his head. Especially when the heart has a way of convincing the head that it knows best. "That ship has sailed for me, too, cupcake. I like you."

I drop a kiss to her forehead, catching a faint whiff of her hair, and that raspberry scent. I can feel her smiling as my lips press to her skin.

"Then let's just have a good time for the next few days," she says as I pull back and put the money in my pocket at last.

"Don't you know, we always have a good time?"

Screw it. I do want her more than I want to resist her. And I want to enjoy the hell out of the rest of this reunion with my fake girlfriend, who feels more like a real one every second.

"We always have the best time. By the way," she says breezily, "how was the boat ride this afternoon?"

"It was very manly. Very macho. We took off our shirts, beat our chests, and spoke in cave grunts as we hauled in fish with our bare hands."

"So, a typical day on the boat."

"Your dad spent plenty of time saying, 'Isn't this great?' 'Don't you love fishing?' 'What's better than a day on the water?'"

She laughs. "He's really working this new angle hard, isn't he?"

I nod. "He definitely is. But I do like his new tactic better than the one where he tried to keep me away from you."

She lowers her eyes.

"I missed you on the boat," I say, and the words taste awkward on my tongue. But they also feel right. Because they're true.

"You did?"

"Seems I like spending time with you." I press a kiss to her lips.

I can feel her smile as she says, "You should go for a boat ride with me."

"Count on it," I say—then an idea knocks me upside the head. Something that isn't about me or what I want. "Hey, I just thought of something we should do first."

"Tell me."

I share my plan, and she quirks up a corner of her lips. "That'll take some convincing."

"I know. But you seem to have some sort of magic effect on your sister, and I suspect you've noticed her husband has a man crush on me."

She laughs. "I have absolutely noticed. And she said something at the nail salon that gives me an idea for how to pull it off." She drops her voice to a whisper. "Apparently, my sister and her husband used to do it in cars."

I laugh. "Let's make sure they can go for a ride, then."

When we return to the inn, April pulls her sister aside. Tess furrows her brow at first, but as April keeps talking, Tess's expression shifts, perhaps to interest. I turn away from them, clap Cory on the shoulder, and say, "Give me your kids. April and I are going to watch them for an hour. We won't take no for an answer, and if I were you, I'd make sure you make good use of that hour."

"Thanks, man. I owe you," he says, relief and excitement in his voice.

April and I don't do anything the others in her family couldn't do. We simply plop the kids in their strollers and wander around the neighborhood while Cory drives off somewhere with his wife.

"It's odd that Tess and Cory didn't do this sooner. My mom loves to help with the kids," April says as we push Davey and Andi. "Why not let my mom watch the kids and go park somewhere?"

But I think I know the answer to that. Sometimes you

don't realize what you need until you see what you don't have. "Maybe they needed to *see* what they were missing, you know? Maybe they didn't even know it until they saw us."

She arches an eyebrow. "We're what they're missing?"

I shrug, not wanting to say too much more at the moment. "Maybe. Maybe they needed to see a guy and a girl who really seem to dig each other's company. Maybe that was the spark they needed."

"I do dig your company."

"And I bet Cory and Tess are digging each other's company right now."

April laughs, and that sound dives down deep into my heart and insists on burrowing there.

When we return and meet them at the curb outside the inn, April points to Tess's messy hair. "Talk about tousled."

Tess grins, then her face turns serious. "Thank you. We needed that."

"I'm glad you could have it."

Cory extends a hand to me in a big-ass thank-you shake. "Boy, am I ever glad April brought you to the reunion."

"I'm a good luck charm for getting lucky, I guess," I say with a smile.

A minute later, Tess is clutching the baby again and cooing at her little girl, and Cory links his fingers with his son's as they head into the Sunnyside. It's back to business as usual. We didn't change their life, but maybe we changed one night.

Chapter Twenty-eight *April*

"We need to escape now."

I grab his biceps and squeeze, to emphasize how critical the matter at hand is. Admittedly, I may also have ulterior motives when it comes to touching his arm. But right now, I'm conveying the seriousness of the issue. It's eight thirty, and we're in the room post-dinner and pre–evening Scrabble tournament.

Ergo—we must vacate the premises stat.

"I love a good escape, but tell me why," he asks.

"You know how my mom loves to ask questions? Well, that same drive that pushes her to ask one million questions also leads her to want to absolutely dominate any game of Scrabble."

"Sounds like she's a fierce competitor."

"That's the understatement of the century. But it also means one game will turn into five, and the night will never end."

"You're saying you need me to spring you, cupcake?"

I point from him to me and back. "We need to spring both of us, and we need to do it now."

"Do you want to tell them we're going for a walk?"

I shake my head. "They'll try to rope us into it. I want a sure thing."

His brow knits as he surveys the room, as if he's hunting for the pod or hatch that'll shoot us free. "Do you trust me?" he asks when he swings his gaze to me.

The question tugs at my heart. I've spent the last forty-eight hours with him, nonstop. I slept in the same bed with him. I've woken curled up around him. I've kissed him. I've laughed with him. We've talked and fought and talked and made up. That's why I can say with 100 percent certainty, "Yes, I trust you."

"Then here's the plan."

His strategy is simple but risky, and the danger primarily lies in the possibility of broken bones. Shattered tibias are not my favorite outcome, but I can't deny that my speeding heart and pulsing adrenaline say *go for it*. I grab the DO NOT DISTURB sign from the wooden writing desk, open our door, scan the hallway, and since it's all clear, I hang the sign on the doorknob.

I close the door. "Now they'll just think we're doing what they pretty much quizzed me on in the salon. Our sex life."

Theo arches a brow. "They quizzed you on our fictional sex life?"

"You have no idea what nosy perverts women can be when you get them all together in a salon. I didn't even say a word about it, but they'd all decided you're a god in bed."

He puffs his chest, squares his shoulders, and gives me the most smoldering eyes a man has ever given a woman. "Do you think they're right?"

The way he asks sends a shiver down my spine. Like

it's an invitation for me to find out. He says it like he's confident but not cocky. Like he has a mystery for me to unravel.

"It's not really that I think they're right," I say, taking my time as I answer him, keeping my eyes locked to his. My voice sounds smoky to my own ears. "It's more that I hope they are."

I leave it at that. Because I love his reaction. The soft subtle groan. The darkening of his eyes. And, yes, because maybe I'm a pervert, too, I can't help but note the thickening in his jeans.

"Then let's let them think we're doing something they shouldn't disturb." He turns around, sets his hands on the window, and pushes it all the way open. He hoists his leg over the windowpane, scoots out, and stands on the slanted roof outside our room. Anxiety flies through me, but then I tell myself this is fun, this is daring. I climb out the window and onto the roof. I close the window most of the way. Theo sets his finger on his lips. We do our best to pad as noiselessly as we can, but the roof creaks and groans a few times. I say a silent prayer that the Scrabble-heads won't hear.

At the edge of the inn stands a tall oak tree, with a thick branch dangling over the roof. Theo bends and test its strength with his hand, shaking it.

"Seems solid enough." He raises his arms, holding on to the branch above it, then steps across on the solid one, like a tightrope walker.

I hold my breath. The stairs seem a hell of a lot wiser now. But as I regard his wicked smile, the stairs seem like a hell of a lot less fun.

With a few steps, he moves across.

It's my turn. I follow him, keenly aware than I'm twenty or more feet above the ground and climbing a tree to escape with a guy. This is what happens when you're twenty-eight and come home. You can do things you would've done at seventeen, but you're doing them for completely different reasons.

We reach the trunk, and like jungle gym monkeys, we climb down, branch to branch, until we reach the lowest one, about ten feet from the grass.

Theo sits on it, then hangs, then drops down. He lifts his arms as if to catch me.

But I've got this.

I sit, swivel, and jump. My knees buckle, but my feet absorb the landing. I grin with glee. We did it. We made our great escape. We look at each other with utter delight. For a moment, neither one of us moves, we just hold the other's gaze. I feel like we're coconspirators, partners in arms. Like *this* is something we could do. Take off on adventures together, big and small.

Like this is who we are together.

He holds out a hand.

I take it.

Chapter Twenty-nine *Theo*

We don't go on the sidewalk or the main road.

"I know all the paths in the woods," she whispers, and hell if there's anything sexier right now than following this gorgeous girl to the trees, then a path that runs behind the homes. We cut across a hard dirt trail. With each step to wherever she's taking me, my heart beats faster. Fifteen minutes later, she forks left, and I follow her down the hill.

At the bottom is a blue glassy lake. It's quiet and placid, and moonlight streams across the water.

"My backyard."

I rub my finger against my ear. "I'm sorry, but did you say that was your backyard?"

"Something like that," she says with a sly smile. She raises her arm and points. Several hundred feet away is a home. Big and stately and white, it presides over the land and the lake.

"That's where I grew up, right on the water."

I whistle my appreciation. "Damn, that's gorgeous."

"Isn't it?" she says with a happy sigh. She tugs the shoulder of my shirt. "Let's go."

She leads me through her yard, if you can call it a yard. It's more like acres and acres of soft grass and fireflies, of summer air and crickets. We weave through tall trees, and I squint because the farthest one looks like it holds a tree house up high. "Is that what I think it is?" I ask, pointing.

She nods. "Perks of being the youngest of three to a dad who's good at building. I batted my eyes, asked him for a tree house, and he built it for me for my sixth birthday. It even has a sign that says 'April's Tree House' on it."

I laugh. "Bet that didn't keep your brother and sister out of it."

"Not in the least. But I loved that sign."

We reach a small dock. A boat bobs on each side. She steps onto the wooden dock, and I'm right behind her. After untying one of the boats, she says in a singsong tone, "Want to go out on the lake?"

"Hell yeah."

"This is the smallest model. It doesn't have an engine."

I flex a biceps. "I've got these engines."

She hands me the oars.

That's how I find myself doing something I've never done before. Rowing a boat. Correction: rowing a hand-crafted, fifty-two-thousand-dollar boat under the moon-light, across the water, into the middle of a lake in the summer.

This is not my life.

This is not the bar in Brooklyn.

This is not the businesswoman collecting the debt.

This isn't soggy nachos.

This is how the other half lives.

They hop into their parents' boats and glide across the

water, and the funny thing is I don't resent her for all she has. I'm not angry with her. The privilege she was born into doesn't feel like a dividing line between us.

Maybe that's crazy.

Or maybe that's because of her.

When we reach the middle of the lake, April dips her hand into the pocket of her shorts, wiggles her eyebrows, and removes a flask. I laugh loudly, and the sound echoes across the water.

"You are my kind of woman," I say as I pull the oars into the boat and set them down.

"Do you like tequila?"

"Does a panda like bamboo?"

She smiles, and her nose crinkles. She opens the flask and takes the first drink. She winces, then wipes her hand across her mouth. "It's strong. Beware, panda."

I knock back a gulp. It burns, but it's a good burn. April stares at the water. "My dad taught me how to sail. How to row a boat. How to fish," she says, raising her face to the night sky. It's rich with stars. They twinkle brightly across the midnight blue blanket. She sets her hands behind her on the bench she's seated on. "I know this lake so well. I grew up on this lake. My friends and I used to sneak out here at night."

"Did you all bring a flask?"

"Sometimes, yeah."

"You've been a troublemaker for a long time," I tease.

"Sometimes I was. We thought we were so clandestine."

"Do you think your parents knew that you sneaked out here?"

"Not at first, but the one night my friends and I jumped off the boat and into the water and splashed around might have been the tip-off."

"Were your parents pissed?"

She shakes her head. "We were all sober that time, so no one was too mad."

"Is this your way of telling me they'll come looking for us?"

"That 'Do Not Disturb' sign is foolproof," she says with a wink. We're quiet for a minute as we glide across the water. "Tell me about your parents, Theo."

I tense. A knee-jerk reaction. I'm ready to erect walls, but I remind myself that April deserves as much honesty as I can give her. She's been open with me, up front and direct. "They were both teachers. They loved grammar. My mom was a word person, and she loved to correct our grammar, too."

I watch April's face as I talk. Her expression is soft, welcoming. She waits for me to say more.

"She had a T-shirt that said 'Good Grammar Is Sexy.' It was embarrassing to us because when she wore it, everyone commented. We'd go to the library, and the librarian would say something. We'd go to the hardware store, and the cashier would comment. Women would always say how much they loved it."

"Long live good grammar, evidently. Was your dad like that, too?"

"Not so much. He was quieter, more introspective. A thoughtful guy. He liked to write. I think he was working on the—" I sketch air quotes. "—'Great American Novel' before he died."

"Do you know what it was about?"

I shake my head. "It was probably your average guy-meets-girl story. He was mad about my mom. She was his heart."

April smiles ruefully. "That's beautiful and sad at the same time." She lifts the flask and takes a sip. She shudders from the drink, then hands it to me.

"That describes him perfectly," I say. Then it's my turn to drink, and I let the alcohol course through me, warming me up.

I close the flask and slouch back on my bench. My eyes drift to the sky above. To all those stars. "So you grew up under the stars."

"That's why I started painting faces."

I look up, meet her gaze. "How does one follow the other?"

"I loved looking at the stars, and I wanted to paint them. Stars were literally the first thing I ever tried painting."

"That explains your tattoo," I say.

"Well done, Detective Theo."

"How was your first star painting?"

She shrugs and takes another drink. "It wasn't bad, but I don't think I made anything truly good until I painted on my arm. That's when I fell in love with the art, and I think it fell in love with me, too."

Her passion for her work is yet another thing that's insanely attractive about her. "So skin really is your medium."

She nods. "I can definitely paint on canvas, but I vastly prefer flesh. It's weird, isn't it?"

I remember the other night when I stared into the mirror as I looked at the lips she painted on me. "When you painted me, it was unusual. It was sensual. It was clever. But it wasn't weird. Not in the least."

"What about you? When you were younger, did you know you wanted to act?"

A bolt of tension shoots down my spine. I'm not an actor. I'm good at it only because I *can* act. "No," I say, telling the truth.

She furrows her brow. "You never wanted to be one when you were younger?"

I shake my head. "Nope." At least I'm not lying.

"That's so odd. I always think with creative professions that we usually feel that calling from when we're young."

I swallow. "It wasn't that way for me." I hate that I can't be truthful with her. But now isn't the moment to reveal my past to her, so my present has to remain shrouded.

"What did you want to do?"

"I wanted to be an English teacher. Like my parents. It was all I knew. I wanted to be that guy in the front of the room. Be the teacher who truly entertained. Maybe do some funny voices as I read Shakespeare."

She smiles. "You like Shakespeare?"

"You say that like it's the strangest thing you've ever heard."

She nibbles on a corner of her lips. "It's not strange. It's intriguing. What lines did you like?"

I slide into my best stage orator impression. " 'All the world's a stage, / And all the men and women merely players; / They have their exits and their entrances, / And one man in his time plays many parts.' *As You Like It*," I add, since everyone thinks that line's from *Hamlet*. "Or this one from *Othello*: 'Speak of me as I am. . . . Then must you speak / Of one that loved not wisely, but too well.' "

"Do you believe that?" she asks.

"I believe Othello was a jealous bastard who was vulnerable to a man that Disney turned into a parrot in *Aladdin*," I say, and she laughs. "My mom taught that play, using the *Aladdin* movie as a modern-day example. One of her last classes before she was too sick to teach was that play. She was my English teacher in eighth grade."

Her eyes widen. "You had your mother as a teacher."

"I was that guy." I slap my thumb and forefinger onto my forehead in an L.

"Did you think you'd teach Shakespeare?"

"Honestly, I never really understood the finer meanings of his works. But the quotes sounded totally badass to me. I would record them in this little portable recorder. I would mess around with different voices. They were just cool words to say, and I liked the way I could play with them. Make it sound like a cowboy or a truck driver or a swamp creature."

She leans forward, sets her chin in her hand. "It's like you were a DJ mixing your voice."

I nod, digging that comparison. "Yeah, maybe I was."

"Do you want to teach? To tend bar? Act? Record snippets of Shakespeare into a phone?"

I laugh, and lean my head back, staring into the abyss of the night. I'm so far derailed from my childhood dreams. I can't really think about them anymore. Or maybe the issue is that I haven't been able to. "I want to do all of the above and none of the above." I return my gaze to her. "Right now, though, I'm not thinking of any of those things."

"What are you thinking of?"

"You," I say, and it feels like the most honest thing I've ever said. "Why you brought me here. How I'm hardly your fake date anymore." I grab the flask and knock back a slug. My reward for speaking my mind. The liquor warms me all over, and I'm heading into a slight buzz.

"What am I now?"

A firefly races past, flickering against the night. Water slips against the wood of the boat.

I set down the container on the floor of the boat and stare into her dark green eyes. Heat seems to radiate between us. The air crackles.

"You're the woman who's going to tell me what you'd paint on me."

She screws up the corner of her lips. "What?"

I laugh, since I can hear the subtext of her question: *Why are you ruining a romantic moment with talk of paint?* I am making a rolling motion with my hand, like I'm reminding her. "On the train, I asked what you'd paint on me. You said to ask in a few days and you'd have a better answer."

She nods, remembering.

"Tell me," I say, since I'm fascinated by her job. I've been fascinated since she told me about it, and my interest has only intensified since she painted lips on me.

Her eyes seem to twinkle even in the dark. She speaks softly. "*Starry Night.*"

"The painting? By Van Gogh."

She nods.

"You can paint a painting?"

"I can."

"That's what you'd paint on me?"

She lifts her hand toward my shoulder. "There. I'd start there."

The mood shifts inexorably away from childhood dreams, and on to the present. Only the present. Energy thrums between us. Was there ever a doubt in my mind that something would happen tonight? I don't know what, how much, or how far. But my skin heats all over with the aching desire to touch her.

And to be touched.

"Show me," I say, and I grab the hem of my T-shirt and tug it off.

Her breath hitches. She licks her lips. I fight off a smile. Yeah, she's seen me shirtless before, but I can't deny her reaction now feels like every reason I've ever been motivated to lift weights or hit the gym early in the morning.

"I would paint your shoulder a midnight blue, and then

add in the first bright swirly star. Right there." A spark tears through me as she touches me.

"I'd layer in more blue swirls all across your chest, making it my canvas. And then, I'd color in all the yellow and gold lights from the stars," she says, her finger mimicking a brush. She draws an outline on my pec in the manner of Van Gogh. A groan works its way through me. "There are eleven stars in the painting, and I'd paint them all on you." She spreads her fingers across my pecs to my abs.

I breathe heavily, as though I've run a race. Jesus, I'm not sure I've ever been this turned on in my life.

"I'd finish here." She runs the pads of her fingers softly over the hard planes of my abs, down to my jeans. Her eyes follow her hands. She's not looking at me. She's looking at what she's creating in her mind's eye. She's mesmerized by what she's imagining. I stare at her fingers, at the way she's lost in her own world as she traces a sketch of a painting on me. I burn. With lust. With desire. With a deep and potent need. I want to feel connected to her.

"I've never wanted to kiss someone as much as I want to kiss you now."

She raises her face and blinks, like she's coming out of her artistic haze. "Are you drunk?"

"God no." Then a dangerous idea plants itself in my head. "Are you?"

Please say no.

She shakes her head. "No. A little tipsy, but that's okay."

"Why'd you ask?"

She licks her lips. "I wanted to make sure you meant what you said."

"I'll show you how much I mean it."

I place my hands on her knees, stretching across to kiss her. She parts her lips for me, opening her sweet mouth, and we sigh. We moan. We kiss.

As our lips come together, we find a rhythm that fits us. It's both tender and rough. Intense and sensual. Dirty and romantic.

She threads her hands in my hair, roping her fingers through the strands, and when she lets out a sexy little sigh, my temperature soars.

I break the kiss and grab her hips. "Come closer," I whisper roughly. "There's a space between us, and I don't like it. Come onto me."

The sturdy boat bobs only slightly as she rises, moving up and off her bench so she can straddle me, a knee on either side of my thighs. Her hands trail down my arms, stopping at the compass tattoo. She kisses my neck as she asks, "Why a compass?"

I push against her. "I felt lost. I needed to know some things were constant."

"Like the stars?"

"Yeah, like the stars," I echo as I grip her hips and move her against me. She ropes her fingers in my hair. "April?"

"Yes?" Her voice sounds dreamy.

"All the stories we tell feel true to me."

"They've always felt true to me, too."

I nip her collarbone. "From the start. From the second I met you. Don't ever forget that, okay?"

She curls her hands tighter around my head. "I won't. It's that way for me, too."

I grind up against her. I want to take off all her clothes. I want to experience her—flesh to flesh, skin to skin. But it's too soon. I know once we do that, it'll be even harder for me to let her go. It'll be harder for me to move on when she leaves me. I push between her thighs. "I thought about you the first night I met you," I say, blurting it out.

She rocks her hips against my hard-on, seeking more pressure, more friction. "How? How did you think of me?"

I run my finger over her bottom lip. "Your mouth, I love your mouth. Your lips. I imagined you taking me deep."

She grins wickedly. "You dirty man. I love that you went straight for the money shot."

I laugh. "I love your mouth. It's not just because these lips are so pretty," I say, and slam my mouth to hers. She gasps in surprise as I kiss her hard. Rough. Matching each consuming kiss with a punch of my hips. "I love all the things you say with these lips."

"But I bet I wasn't talking in your fantasy," she says in a silky purr. "I bet I was sucking."

"Ah fuck," I say as my dick thickens even more and desire shoots down my spine. "You were sucking me deep, and that's the first time I came thinking of you."

She blinks. "You've gotten off to me more than once?"

I rock my hips against her. "Yes. Shower. B and B. You in my imagination."

"Oh God," she says, throwing her head back, exposing her neck, and unleashing a long sexy moan. The moonlight streaks across her pale skin. "Me, too. The first night here. I touched myself. I came under the water thinking of you."

I rock harder, faster, kissing her, and my kisses turn wetter, deeper because my mind is a white-hot blur. I picture her in the shower, fucking her fingers. Then I zoom in on her now, fucking me with clothes on. She moans and pants, and her breath comes in faster, more erratic bursts. She tugs on my hair, arches her back, and cries out. "Don't stop! Please don't stop."

"Never," I say, and I keep the pace. She's riding the edge of pleasure like this, chasing her bliss. Her cheeks flush, and her mouth turns into the loveliest O. She squeezes her eyes shut.

Ohhh.

Yes.

Please.

She's so sensual. She's so beautiful. And I'm so screwed because I don't want to stop with her. She shatters, in a mind-blowing gasp, as a shudder unfurls down her body. It's gorgeous, watching her fall apart riding me, under the stars, floating on the lake.

Saying my name.

Chapter Thirty *April*

We stop.

Immediately.

But I don't want to stop.

I want him to feel just as good as I do. He grits his teeth and sucks in a tight breath. Gently but firmly, he pushes me off him. He looks me in the eyes. "It's not that I don't want you rubbing against me. I do. But I'm dangerously close to coming."

"But coming is fun."

Coming courtesy of another person is even better, and I've just had a refresher course on how infinitely better orgasms are when someone else delivers them to you.

My body is glowing. My head is a lovely haze of endorphins and giddy lust. All my guidelines, all my boundaries have been smashed to pieces—and in this moment, I don't care. Maybe I don't even care beyond this moment. Perhaps nights like this could keep unfurling? My heart pounds harder, giving me its answer to the question in my head.

Silly heart.

"Coming is great fun, but—call me crazy—I don't want to come in my pants and then walk to the inn like that," he says.

"There are other ways I can make you come," I say, feeling bold, feeling reckless.

He laughs, rolling his eyes. "Wait, cupcake. Just wait with me. Enjoy the moment. I just want to be with you right now."

That sounds damn fine, too. I want to gobble up every second with him. I want to savor these times. A warm flush spreads down my chest as we settle in on the floor of the boat, snuggled together, his arm around me. He leans to the side and retrieves the flask, then hands it to me. We drink, and we lie on the floor of the boat, and we talk about summer nights and growing up and dreams we had. We gaze at the stars. It's so achingly romantic, I want it to never end.

I show him Orion's Belt and the Big Dipper, but that's as much as I know about constellations, so we make up names for others. A twinkling star far to the south becomes the Southern Flask, while a jagged line of stars right above us is dubbed the Little Puppy Lights. Theo cracks up over that one, as if he's achieved the height of humor; then he nuzzles me, kissing my neck. Our kisses are wetter, longer, a little drunker than before.

Emboldened by tequila and the Little Puppy Lights, I fumble at his zipper, tugging it down. "Let me touch you."

He laughs and shakes his head, zipping up his jeans. "I have to take a piss now."

I roll my eyes. "So much for romance." He rises, and I stare at him for a second. "Are you going to pee in the lake?"

A scoffing sound bursts from his mouth. "That's gross."

I shrug. "Mitch used to do that."

"That's even grosser. And that's why I'm not going to piss in the lake. It's your parents' lake. I'm not going to urinate in it."

He grabs the oars and rows us to shore. Once we tie up the boat, I gesture to the house in the distance. "I'd let you in to use the little boys' room, but I don't have a key, and they actually keep the doors locked."

"That's wise, keeping doors locked," he says. Then he winks and dips his head close to me, whispering. "Crime is everywhere."

I swat him. "Always best to be safe."

"Always, cupcake," he says, then drops a kiss to the end of my nose. I grab his waist, and kiss him back harder. I'm not sure if I'm more buzzed on the tequila or on him. But as his lips slide across mine, I decide he wins. I'm definitely intoxicated by Theo, and I want another drink, then another, then one for the road.

He's like a potato chip. I tell him that as we walk toward the woods. "You're Lay's."

"Like the chips?"

I nod. "You can't eat just one."

He laughs. "You want the whole bag of me? Is that what you're saying?"

"Yes, I'm going to keep dipping my hand in and going back for more."

He looks down, reaches for my hands, and threads his fingers through mine. "I won't stop you." It sounds like a whispered promise. My heart thumps as I look at our joined hands.

He gives my fingers a gentle squeeze, and it reverberates in my body, like a vibration all the way to the center of my heart. Then his phone rings, and we break the hand-hold. His face lights up as he looks at the screen. "It's Heath."

"Hey, man," he says. His voice—I've never heard it like this. It sounds like pure joy.

He listens as we amble across the grass. "You called me to discuss superpowers?" he asks, laughing. "Dude, you know how I feel about this one. It's the only time I ever pick the mind."

I arch a brow, and Theo shakes his head as he chuckles.

"Time control is far too dangerous, and mind control would be the ultimate superpower." He sounds happier than he ever has before.

Another pause.

"Lacey picked time control? Hold on one sec. I gotta take a leak. Talk to April for a minute. She's fucking awesome." He thrusts the phone at me, and I blink. He wants me to chat with his brother?

Theo walks off to a bush in the shadows.

I stare at his phone in my hand, and his brother's number blinking up at me. He's in Boston, I register from the area code. I bring it to my ear. "Hi. I'm April, and evidently, I'm effing awesome."

I'm greeted by a hearty laugh. "Hey, Effing Awesome April," he says, and I smile when he goes with my word choice, since it says he listens. "Tell me something. Is my brother behaving?"

I laugh at how seamlessly Heath has slipped into a conversation with me. "Yes, he's fantastic. We're at my family's reunion in Wistful."

"That so?"

"Yes, and for the record, I'd pick time control, too.

Everyone worries about the fabric of the universe, and fate, and the butterfly effect of one thing changing a million things when you pick time control as your superpower. But I say you never know till you try."

Heath whistles his appreciation. "Damn, I like your spirit." He hums. "Wistful? That fancy town in Connecticut?"

"Yes. I grew up here. It's the best town ever. Home of the Wild ThunderCoaster, beluga whales, the Maritime Museum," I say, reciting our town motto.

"I love roller coasters, and so does my brother, but do not take him on a Ferris wheel. He hates them. They terrify him."

My heart twists. That tidbit makes him seem so human. "Thanks for the heads-up." Out of the corner of my eye, I see Theo step out of the shadows and crunch across the grass.

"He's on his way back. It was nice chatting with you." I glance at the screen one more time, then hand the mobile to Theo.

He drops a kiss to my forehead. It feels like a thank-you for talking to his brother. I'm not sure why that earned me a kiss, but I'll take it.

"Hey, man. I need to go. Say hi to Lacey. Oh, wait. I just did it with my mind control. Anyway, I'm going to hang out with April for a while longer."

There's a pause.

His smile spreads. "She's my girlfriend."

My heart thumps harder as I meet his eyes. They say he means it in a whole new way.

It's a summer miracle. When we return, the inn is mostly quiet. Only Katie is awake, reading a book in the living room, her red hair twisted into a messy bun. Mo, the orange cat, is curled on her lap, purring.

She smirks. "How was your night sneaking out?"

I give her a blank look, playing dumb.

She rolls her blue eyes. "I was sent to find you for Scrabble, and I saw the Do Not Disturb sign. But your room was quiet, so I figured you gave us the slip."

I eye her suspiciously. My bawdy, dirty cousin. "Did you actually put your ear on the door and listen in to see what you weren't supposed to disturb?"

She nods, owning it. "Absolutely." She brandishes the paperback in the air. "I'm reading a filthy sex scene. You think I'd have a problem putting my ear to your door and seeing what you were up to? Not one bit."

I crinkle my nose. "If you want to listen to me, I feel like that might make you ridiculously naughty."

"If the shoe fits . . ." Katie sticks out her foot, her slipper dangling off the end of her toes as Theo laughs at her antics.

"What did you tell everyone after your search and rescue mission proved fruitless?"

"I told them the truth. That there was, effectively, a sock on your door, and far be it from me to violate the sanctity of that."

"You're such an excellent self-appointed wing woman," I say.

She blows on her fingernails. "Now, tell me. Where'd you go?"

I shrug evasively. "Around."

Katie points at me, like she's caught me even more red-handed. "You didn't do it in your mom's golf cart, did you?"

"Why don't you go take it for a spin and find out?" I toss back at her.

Theo grins wildly, clearly impressed.

Katie slaps her thigh. "You are a dirty girl, indeed. I knew the poodle walker was all wrong for you. When your mom and my mom said we should find you nice guys from here, we all offered up our suggestions, but I've always known you're a better fit for a Hottie McTottie with tats," she says, wiggling her eyebrows at Theo in a deliberately salacious manner.

He drapes an arm around me. "She's a perfect fit for me." He dusts a kiss on my cheek. Everything he does to me feels like magic.

"Honestly, I think Jeanie's been trying to set you up because she's bored since I haven't produced grandkids for her yet," Katie says.

"Do you and Joe want to?"

"Someday. When we're ready. But not yet. So my mom gets together with your mom, and they start plotting to find a man for you."

"And it's a damn good thing you didn't set her up with anyone," Theo says, a note of possession in his tone. "Otherwise, I'd have had to go full alpha in front of everyone."

Katie makes an appreciative groan. "That's what I want Joe to do to me when he returns from his assignment. Go full alpha. I like the sound of that."

"Of course you do," I say.

"Oh, don't pretend you don't love a good throw-down on the couch."

My cheeks flush red.

Katie raises her chin to Theo. "Go do something about our blushing April."

He gives a shrug that seems to say, *Why the heck not?* He turns to face me, lowers his shoulders, and loops his arms around my waist. In an instant, he lifts me up, and I squeak out a surprised "Oh!" as he raises me to his right shoulder, drops me over it, and gives a tip of the imaginary hat to Katie with his free hand. "It's time for me to go full caveman and take my woman upstairs."

Katie raises a victorious fist in the air. "Woohoo! You go give it to her good."

"Katie, remind me to take you to a strip club next time you're in the city. You would be in your element," I say dryly.

"I'll break into my special billfold and grab all my one-dollar bills," she says as Theo takes the first steps up the staircase.

Like the ad. Just like one of his à la carte options. My life is imitating a GigsForHire ad, and as I laugh while Theo carries me to the second floor, I couldn't be happier.

When we reach the room, the DO NOT DISTURB sign still dangles from the knob.

He sets me down.

"You're strong," I say, stating the obvious.

He smiles. "You're light."

"That is the absolute sweetest thing you can say to a woman."

He laughs and unlocks the door.

Once inside, I grab a fresh pair of panties, a tank top, and sleep shorts. I head to the bathroom to change. Even though I climaxed while dry-humping him like a teen at prom, I'm not ready for the intimacy of changing in front of him. After I brush my teeth and wash my face, I return to the room, and he's in those low-hung sleep pants. He takes his turn in the bathroom while I grab some lotion for my hands, rubbing it in. I dim the lights, slide under the covers, and wait for whatever comes next.

I've no clue what we do now. How we act. What we say. If we make out like bunnies all night long. I have no clue about so many things, but that's what throwing out my rules for dating has done to me.

The bathroom door creaks open, and he joins me in bed. "I'm glad your parents didn't catch you on the lake tonight."

"Me, too. Especially since I've never taken a guy onto the lake before."

Silence descends, and his voice is laced with surprise but also wonder. "Really?"

"True that."

"Why'd you take me?"

I stick my tongue out. "You're special."

He rolls his eyes. "Seriously."

"Fine," I say, like it costs me something. "I wanted to get you naked under the stars. It was all a plot."

He tickles my waist, and I squirm. "You can't be serious, can you?"

"It's difficult for me, admittedly." I adopt a stern expression. "But I am quite serious. I did *want* to get you naked. And you denied me. You wouldn't let me touch you."

"We've been over this," he says in a deliberately serious tone, like he's a professor admonishing me.

"You're so practical," I say with a mock sigh; then I run a hand through his soft hair. *JBF* hair. "I took you on the lake because I like you, and because I wanted to be kissed by you under the stars."

His eyes float closed. "You say those things. . . ."

My heart skips a beat. "And . . . ?"

He opens his eyes. "And it does something to me."

Tingles spread into every single molecule in my body. I float. "What are we doing?"

"I don't know."

I face him and run my nails over his ink. "I want you to find your constant."

He shudders, and runs a finger over my bottom lip. "I want you to be kissed under the stars."

"I want to paint *Starry Night* on you for real," I say, nerves threading my voice as I lay bare these confessions. They aren't just sexual. They speak of so much more. "Then I want you to kiss me all night long till the paint bleeds onto me. Onto my chest. All over my body."

His eyes blaze, and he stares at me like he wants to devour me. "That's what I mean. You say these things, April," he says, and drags a hand roughly through his hair.

"What's wrong with saying that?"

He breathes out hard. "It's the sexiest thing anyone's ever said to me."

I brush my hand down his arm. "We'd be covered in midnight blue and bright gold."

"I want to be covered in paint with you," he murmurs as he threads his hands in my hair.

I drag my nails over his abdomen, dancing them along the waistband of his pants. "I want you to whisper sweet dirty things to me. And then do them."

"Like kiss you everywhere?" he says, and I tremble, whispering yes. He slides a hand between my legs, pressing a palm against me through the cotton of my shorts. "Lick you," he murmurs. "Kiss and suck and consume until you're all over my face."

"Oh God," I gasp.

"Let me. Let me now," he says, and it's a dirty, dangerous plea.

I find the will to push his hand away. "If you did that to me, I wouldn't be able to be quiet. I'd scream in pleasure. They'll all hear."

He smiles so damn wide and proud.

"Besides, it's my turn to touch you." My hand darts out to cover his erection. I press a palm against him, thrilling at how hard he is, how thick he is. He groans so sexily, I think I might come again just from the sound he makes. "I've been checking out your package since I met you." I run my hand over his hard length.

"I know," he says, thrusting into me.

"It's that obvious?"

"Yes," he says with a rasp. "Your eyes drift down constantly."

I laugh. "I've been busted for looking."

"I won't bust you for touching."

"Can I? Touch you?"

"God, please."

He sounds so needy, and so desperate, and I'm dying to do everything with him. But I don't want to sleep with him here. I don't care if everyone is slumbering. I want to be alone, truly alone, when that happens.

I mean *if* it happens.

I slide my hand down the elastic waistband of his pants, inside his boxer briefs, and I touch him.

I shiver. He shudders.

His lips part, and he moans, and words tumble free from his lips as I stroke him.

Oh God.

Fuck.

Feels so good.

More. Keep doing it.

He makes the sexiest sounds, and I nearly melt. He feels amazing. The skin is so soft, and he's so hard. He's pulsing. I stroke and touch, and he thrusts into my hand. His eyes squeeze closed.

"Can you do it faster? Just a little faster," he says, and the desperation in his voice slinks through me, settling between my legs like a heavy ache.

I speed up, tightening and shuttling my palm faster. My

hands are still slick from the lotion. I think it helps. I think it's all he needs.

"I'm going to come embarrassingly quickly," he whispers on a broken pant.

I smile like a happy fool. "I want to watch you fall apart."

He groans, and wraps one hand around my skull, wincing as he rocks into my hand. His breath comes quick, his speech is choppy. "It's perfect. Keep doing that."

I've no desire to stop. I want him to fall to pieces. I want to watch him when he comes. Soon he groans as quietly as I suspect he can, and my name chases it. It sounds filthy the way he says it.

April. Coming.

And then he's on my hand, thick and hot, and his breath is in my ear, and his mouth is on my neck. He utters a string of appreciative curse words. His body jerks. His moans don't stop. His lips spread into a naughty grin. He looks so damn satisfied, and I gloat inside.

He whispers, "You're getting to be addictive."

I want him addicted. I want him mine.

I slip out of bed, wash my hands, and return to him, sliding under the cool covers.

A ping zips through the air, startling me. "What was that?"

I turn toward the sound. It comes again, a plink against the windowpane. Theo laughs softly. "Sounds like a squirrel is chucking acorns at the window."

"Maybe he's trying to get our attention."

"Remember that time I threw acorns at the window to get your attention?" he says, tugging me closer, draping an arm around my waist.

"Yes. We had a fight. You wanted to climb through the window and make up with me."

He presses a kiss on the back of my neck, making me shiver. "I don't like going to bed angry," he says in a whisper; then his lips roam across my skin, and the conversation ceases. We don't talk about what any of this means. I'm not sure I even want to know. In fact, we don't talk at all. Instead, he spoons me, and I assume this is when we snuggle and doze off. But he runs his hand over my belly. He travels down my skin, slides his fingers between my legs, and finds how much he turned me on.

"So wet and soft and slick."

I arch against him as his fingers glide over me.

His sounds fill my ear. His moans, his breath, his desire for me. "I can't stop touching you, April."

"Don't stop."

My breath hitches as he slides his fingers over me. He takes his time, whispering sweet, dirty words as he promised, using his voice. No characters. No pretend. Only Theo.

Love touching you.

You're so close, aren't you?

Want you to come again.

I do as he asks, and it's like an explosion.

A quiet, gorgeous, blissful explosion that I think I could become addicted to as well.

Or maybe I already am, and that's why I don't want the family reunion to end. This slice of time with him is like a vacation, but the end is speeding toward us, and time feels like it's moving even faster.

I want to delay the end of these days here. I want to experience every moment with him before I return to regular life in New York, lugging my paints, waiting and hoping for the big gig.

Now I want so much more than that. That's the trouble

with feeling this way for another person. His happiness matters to me.

For now, though, I want him to have the time of his life while he's here.

The only question is—how can I make that happen?

Chapter Thirty-one *Theo*

The fourth day

As April tends to a few work calls, I head downstairs to see if I can help her family with any prep. I find her father in the kitchen, fighting with a blender as morning sun streams through the large window. He's mixing up yogurt and fruit, and the damn machine is rattling way too fast for the job.

"Try the frappé setting," I say.

"That silly one?"

I nod. "It works."

He switches from blend to frappé, then eyes the glass container. It's mixing smoothly now. "Thanks. Are you a blender expert?"

"Bartender. Close enough. Can I help you with the rest?" I survey the assortment of fruit on the counter. Peaches, strawberries, raspberries, and blueberries.

"I'm making breakfast smoothies," he says, shaking his head. "Whatever happened to good old eggs and bacon? But Emma begged me for a smoothie before we all go to the amusement park, and far be it from me to resist my granddaughter."

I laugh. "She's pretty irresistible."

As I slice a peach, he pours more yogurt into the machine. After clearing his throat, he says, "My daughter likes you."

"I like your daughter."

He narrows his eyes at me. "I can tell. That's why I'm going to say this: Don't hurt her."

I straighten my shoulders. "I don't intend to, sir."

"I'm sure you don't plan to." His deep voice is gruff and intense as he doles out his warning. "But young people today don't always think about what they're doing. They bounce from job to job, town to town, without any stability. They don't think about the people in their lives."

I have no problem speaking the truth when I say, "I think about April a lot. I care deeply for her."

He turns to face me, one big paw parked on the top of the vibrating blender. "She has the biggest heart of anyone I've ever known."

My chest warms. I'm not sure if it's from the sun, or from the girl I'm thinking of. "She's amazing," I say, smiling.

"I can tell she's happy with you. I'd like to see that happiness more," he says as he gestures for more fruit. "I still wish she'd come back and do her painting here. She could open a painting studio. That would be perfect in downtown Wistful."

I'm not really sure this town needs a painting studio, or if there's even a market for one anywhere, to be frank. I'm reminded once again that April's parents don't entirely *get* what she does for a living, but she wishes they would. "I understand wanting to keep her close, sir. But the work for someone of her skills is around the city. She's so talented. Her portfolio blows my mind," I say as I scoop the peaches into the blender.

"It makes no sense to me how anyone could earn a living like that."

"It might not be a traditional job, but it's a real one, and she's incredibly successful." *So successful, she hired me to play her fake boyfriend to get her family off her back.* "When you have that much talent, you rise to the top," I say, and though I once flared hot with jealousy over April's ease with money, now I want to make sure her parents understand that she's not simply the cute, quirky, artsy one. She's the wildly talented one who's carved out one hell of a career. I've known April for only a few days, but I already know she's the best at what she does. "Her work is truly epic, and I'm sure you're proud of her."

Or you should be.

He screws up a corner of his mouth. "Epic?"

"Epic," I repeat. "You should see the cheetah she painted on an athlete's leg. She showed me a picture. I swear, you'd be hard-pressed to tell where the person ended and the cheetah began. She's that good."

His lips curve into a small smile.

"Have you seen it?"

He shakes his head.

"Let me show you."

He stops the blender as I grab my phone from my back pocket, clicking over to the picture April sent me on the train. I asked for it then because I thought it was cool, but also because it said something about her talent.

I show him the picture and walk him through everything April told me about the job. He nods, listening attentively. I'm not saying anything April couldn't say herself. That fierce, strong woman doesn't need me or anyone else to be her megaphone. But I *want* to tell the world she's fantastic, and sometimes the world, or just your family, needs to hear it from an outsider.

"Wow." When her father raises his face, he claps my shoulder. "Thanks. I appreciate that." His comment is pithy, but I hear what's underneath those words—gratitude. He sees something in his daughter that perhaps he didn't appreciate before. "I guess that's why she didn't go into the family boat business," he says a bit wistfully.

I smile and nod. "You make beautiful boats. April makes beautiful paintings on the human body."

His grin is as wide as the lake now. "You're a proud boyfriend."

That's exactly what I want to be for her. "I am. I'm proud of her."

April's dad pours a few smoothies into glasses, presumably to take them to his grandchildren. He walks past me on his way out of the kitchen and tips his chin at me. "Thanks for the help with the frappé blender deelio smoothie, and with the cheetah. You know, all I want is for April to be happy."

"I know. I want the same thing, too."

I head outside, and I see April at the edge of the porch, her hair swept up in a messy bun, the back of her neck exposed, talking to Libby and Emma as they drink smoothies.

My heart stutters.

It slams against my ribs.

When April turns around and spots me at the open door, her smile spreads across her face. That look, that sweet and carefree smile, makes my heart leap toward her.

Oh hell.

I know why I want her to be happy.

I'm falling for her.

Chapter Thirty-two *Theo*

We ride a huge log on the Water Twister, massive waves splashing our T-shirts. Naturally, this becomes my favorite part of the day because . . . boobs.

April looks fantastic in her now-wet T-shirt. God bless water's ability to cling to cotton and reveal swells.

Forget the life-sustaining features of H_2O. *This* is my favorite thing about water.

As we weave through the exit of the ride, my eyes roam over her shirt. "Remember the time I said your arms were distracting?" She nods, and I bend close to her ear. "They have nothing on your tits. They're a world-class distraction."

She nudges my side with her elbow.

I hold my hands out wide, like I'm immune to any accusations of ogling. "You admitted you were checking out my goods. I'm just doing the same."

She squares her shoulders, making her breasts look even more majestic; then she smirks.

Damn, I could keep her around.

We join up with some of the younger ones, spinning on the Tilt-A-Whirl with Emma and smashing around in the bumper boats with Libby. After we leave the boats, April makes a pit stop at the nearest water fountain for a drink. Libby points her thumb to the looming air devil behind us. "I love the Ferris wheel. Want to ride with me?"

My stomach churns. "The line looks long," I say, squinting at the short queue and lying.

Emma jumps into the fray, pleading with her doe eyes that nearly make it impossible to resist. "Please! We love the Ferris wheel because you can rock this one when you're at the tippy top."

My stomach plummets. I can handle spiders, snakes, any sort of cleanup work, but Ferris wheels make me want to curl into a ball and rock myself to sleep.

"Wow," I say, trying to keep my voice even as I call upon my onetime skills. The number one rule of conning is never to reveal your true intent. "Rocking at the top. That just sounds—"

"It sounds amazing!" Emma presses her palms together as if in prayer.

Yes, pray for me to live through the Ferris wheel.

"It's awesome," Libby seconds. "You just hover there at the top for a while as the final people get on. Isn't that the best part, April?" Libby gestures to April as she rejoins us.

"Hell yeah," she says, and I'm officially screwed. But then, she grabs my hand, squeezes hard, and raises her chin to meet my eyes. "The thing is, I'm pretty sure Theo promised me a roller coaster ride? In fact, I think we have a few roller coaster rides planned."

I want to marry her. I want to get down on my knees and kiss her feet. "Of course, I promised you some roller coaster rides, cupcake. And I intend to deliver."

Emma nearly stomps her foot. "But the Ferris wheel is fun."

April leans in close to her. "I know, missy. But I've been on it a million times, and I like coasters more. So I'm claiming dibs on a seat partner." She clasps her hand on my shoulder, a move that feels thoroughly possessive. And I'm completely okay with her owning me right now. "You girls go ride," she says, shooing them away.

They head to amusement park hell, and I breathe a sigh of relief. "I hate Ferris wheels," I admit.

She smiles softly. "I know."

I raise an eyebrow. "How do you know?"

"Heath told me last night. So I didn't want you to go on one," she says as we walk toward the Wild ThunderCoaster.

"You did that for me?" I ask, something like wonder in my tone.

"Of course."

It's so small, but so big, and I stop in the middle of the park to drop a kiss to her lips. I press my forehead to hers, and I sigh. It's hot and sticky, and the scent of cotton candy and fried dough wafts through the summer air. Nearby all the members of April's family and the Moores, too, are spinning in the sky, or shooting down hills, or riding on swings, mirroring the cascade of emotions inside me. It's only been a few days with her, and I should not feel this way, but my heart pounds harder, my bones hum, and I can't get enough of her.

She wraps her arms around my neck and tilts her face up at me. "How about a 'just because'?" she asks.

I kiss her in the park, just because. It lasts longer than an amusement park kiss should, but it's not long enough, because I want more of her.

We pull apart when a deep male voice lands on my ears. "You guys want to ride the roller coaster with us?"

I turn to see Dean with his triplet brothers.

"Sure," April says, and all things considered, riding a roller coaster with four dudes versus hovering midair above the park in a Ferris wheel is a no-brainer. We join them, chatting about rides and sports and the weather as we queue for the Wild ThunderCoaster, waiting near the station where the ride begins. Once the cars arrive, April and I hop in next to each other near the back. The two-hundred-foot climb under the hot noon sun and the groaning of metal against metal give me something to focus on besides this gnawing desire to have more of her. Not just more physically, but emotionally, too.

Because I do want her. More than I've ever wanted anyone.

And I don't know what to do about that.

But then we reach the apex, and I don't care about anything but the sheer exhilaration of raising my arms high in the air and shouting as we scream downhill at rocket speed. April's shrieks burst through the air, and as we rattle up another hill, I'm reminded yet again of sounds I want to hear her make. Trouble is, there's the little problem of our cozy room tucked amidst rooms full of family members. How the hell do guests at a B and B get it on? There's no more time to linger on possibilities, since we zip into a loop-the-loop and the ride corkscrews upside down. We whip around another curve, race up a short hill, then slalom down one final descent before we pull back into the station, breath coming fast, eyes wide.

April's hair is a wild mess. It's a look she wears well. "Want to go again?"

There's no other answer but yes. As we wait in the line, the sun baking us, we chat with Dean and his brothers to pass the time. I learn the names of the big boys.

They're Steve, Paul, and Henry, but I still prefer to think of them as Huey, Louie, and Dewey. I get to know Dean and his work a little better. He mentions a few commercials he's worked on, including one with a talking toaster. "It was good, but we wanted the toaster to go deeper," he says, sounding a bit bummed.

"Toasters can be notoriously shallow," I say, deadpan.

We chat some more, and I decide to let go of my jealousy. After all, I'm the guy who had his hands all over April last night. Sure, a part of me still thinks she's better off with a guy like him. Someone wildly successful in his job. She probably deserves a man who has his act together like Dean.

But even so, that's not enough for me to back away.

Soon, we reboard the Wild ThunderCoaster.

As we chug up the first climb, I survey the hills in the distance, lush with trees. A wickedly brilliant idea pops in front of me, fully formed. I smile to myself.

April's shrieks sound like foreshadowing as I put my plan together.

We ride again and again, and I'm more sure than ever of what needs to happen when we leave this park.

After the fourth time, we weave through the exits and circle around to the front of the ride. April stops in her tracks, peering in the distance to see Emma and Libby leaning over a trash bin, revisiting their smoothies again as they heave them up and out of their bodies.

"I was right. Those Ferris wheels are the devil," I say to April.

Back at the inn, as parents tend to temporarily sick kids, I grab a few supplies, stuff them into my backpack, and tell April I have an afternoon activity for us. She wiggles her eyebrows. "Will I like this activity?"

My voice goes low and smoky. "If I'm doing it right, you'll love it."

We head downstairs, and I take her hand in mine.

I didn't hope for the girls to be sick, but the lull in the action is just what I was looking for. We let her mom know that we're going for a walk into town.

"See you for supper," Pamela says from the kitchen as she and her husband prep for the meal. "Can you bring me a pepper on the way back?"

"Consider it done."

That's enough to avoid an inquisition.

When we reach the sidewalk and our stride places us several feet away, April doesn't even ask where we're headed. I'm not sure if she knows, or if she trusts me. I like to think it's the latter, especially since she says, "Remember that time you whisked me away and took me someplace wild and unexpected?"

"That was a fun afternoon. Do you think this one will compare?"

"Guess we'll find out."

Fifteen minutes later, we're at the base of a tree in her family's eerily quiet backyard.

There's an afternoon hush in the air. The sense that we're well and truly alone. No one's around. Only the birds can hear us. We climb the built-in ladder to April's Tree House.

Chapter Thirty-three *April*

The tree house has been baking for days. Inside this ten-by-ten-foot childhood paradise of mine, it's hot and, unfortunately, stuffy. I've no idea when anyone was last in here. It has that creaky, unoccupied-in-ages feel to it. But it boasts two fantastic windows, so I open the shutters to the outside, letting a warm breeze inside to get some air moving. The fading afternoon sun casts long shadows across the trees and the yard as I peer into my one-time stomping grounds.

As a kid, I spent hours upon hours in this little tree house. I painted here; drew reams upon reams of creatures, animals, and humans; dragged dog-eared paperbacks and sandwiches up with me; and ate lunch by myself.

I did everything here.

Except one thing.

That's about to change. I shiver, even though it's not cold. Nerves shimmy over my skin. As I stare out the open window, I will them to go away. I've had sex before, plenty of times, but something feels vastly different about sleeping with Theo. My heart thumps with a wild ache to get closer to him.

I inhale sharply, imagining the oxygen calming my fears. I'm not afraid of him. I'm afraid of how good it will be to take him inside me, and of how much harder it will be to pretend that what's happening between us isn't huge.

I turn around. Theo spreads a thin blanket over the wood floor.

I'm on my knees, and I tug at my peach tank top, sticking to my skin in the heat. He pushes a floppy mess of hair off his forehead.

I giggle. "It's really hot up here."

He laughs. "It sure is. Want to leave?"

He's on his knees, too, and I grab the neck of his shirt, yanking him close. "Not a chance."

I kiss him, and the nerves vanish entirely. This kiss is electric. It's like a storm cloud hovering on the horizon, gray and swollen, ready to burst with rain and drench us all. I want to get caught in a downpour with him. To kiss in a way that's beyond urgent, that disregards the weather, the world, everything.

That's how he kisses me.

Then he slows down, and the kiss takes on a new tempo. It feels important. Like this kiss is the start of something. In the way his lips slide over mine, in how he threads his hands into my hair, curling them around my skull, it feels like a new beginning.

At some point, I know we should talk about what's happening between us. Give voice to the way our fiction has spun into a bizarre and wonderful reality. We've vaulted over all the lines, and we're crossing the final one now, but in some ways, we were never truly playing pretend. We were real from the start.

I kiss him deeper, trying to convey all these strange and new thoughts in the press of my mouth. In this kiss, I try to tell him that I want more than this weekend. My lips press harder, and I turn more demanding, saying *be mine, be mine, be mine*.

I want him to know that there can be so much more to us.

Gently, he falls back on the blanket, pulling me down with him. His hands slide over my sides, along my hips, down to my short skirt. He pushes it up, his hands grabbing my ass.

He plucks at the hem of my tank. "What do you say we take this off?"

I rise back up and pinch the fabric of his shirt. "Ditto."

Then we kneel, because standing up is near impossible in a tree house. He tugs off his shirt, and I pull off my tank, and soon we're down to boxers and panties, and my entire body is a live wire. One touch, and I'll spark. He grabs me by the hips and maneuvers me. "Lie down, cupcake." He presses a palm to my naked belly and pushes me down. "I want to look at you."

I lie on the blanket, resting on my elbows, watching him watching me. He runs his palms down my body, stopping at my breasts, cupping them. A burst of heat flares inside me, and my back bows.

He moves down, his fingers mapping my body, and his lips follow as he brushes kisses in the valley between my breasts, down to my navel. My skin sizzles, and my bones hum. A pulse beats between my legs. He hasn't even touched me there yet, and I long for him—his fingers, his mouth, his hands. His touch.

He presses a kiss to the cotton panel of my panties, and I ignite.

I moan. I gasp. I writhe.

"I think it's safe to say I'm a little turned on," I whisper, since my panties are soaked.

"A lot," he corrects. He brings my panties down, revealing me, and he groans as he takes them off. He drops them at the edge of the blanket and returns to me, pressing his hands on the inside of my thighs.

"So pretty naked," he murmurs, then settles between my legs, staring at me like he's ravenous. "God, I've wanted to go down on you for days. You smell so incredibly good all over, and every time I got near you, I thought about how you'd taste. Right here." He drags a finger through my wetness, and I arch into him, unleashing a moan that sounds feral even to my own ears.

"How did you think I'd taste?"

"Delicious," he murmurs, whispering kisses on the soft inside of my thighs, teasing me with how close he is. "I bet you'll taste delicious all over my tongue." He moves to my other leg, driving me wild with whispery little kisses on my thigh, until I'm practically bucking against him, begging him to touch me.

"Please," I whisper, my voice jagged with need. I spread my legs wider.

The sight of me opening to him destroys his need to tease, because he presses his lips to me, and I cry out. Loud like I promised.

I sound anguished. I feel amazing. He wraps his arms around my thighs, and he covers me with his tongue. I push my hands through his thick hair, and he moans against me as he licks and sucks and kisses. I open my legs wider, letting them fall apart at the knees, giving him complete and utter access to me. I lift my hips, finding a perfect rhythm against his tongue.

Pressure builds in my body, climbing up my legs.

I know I'll come soon, but I know, too, what I need. "I

want your fingers," I whisper, and he flashes me a smile that says, *Thanks for telling me what you want, because I'm about to give it to you.*

He rubs one finger across all that slick wetness as he sucks on me; then he pushes in.

The sounds I make are criminal. They're the only noises echoing across the hot afternoon air, and they're pornographic. But I don't care. I am free here. Free to let go. Free to let him have me.

He adds another finger, twisting them inside me, and I reach the point of inevitability. Pressure builds low in my belly, radiates to my legs, and nearly swallows me whole. I ache for him to make me come. It's an exquisite ache, hovering on the precipice of torment and bliss as it builds and builds and then I shatter. I rock into him, grabbing at his hair, calling his name, letting the pure bliss obliterate my hold on the world.

I'm white hot and bursting with pleasure so deep, it spreads to my toes, it ripples all through my bones, like an earthquake.

A minute later—maybe it's an hour, who knows since I lose track of time—Theo's above me. He runs a finger down my cheek, and I lean into him. I smile dopily. Is there any other way to smile after an orgasm like that?

"I think you just wrecked me with the greatest orgasm ever," I murmur.

He grins. He looks pleased, and he looks like a hungry wolf, too. "So the tree house was a good choice, then."

"I can't believe I'm naked and sweaty and you just made me scream high up in a tree," I say, covering my face with my hand as if I'm truly mortified.

But I'm not. I'm amazed that this is my life. That I went on a dating diet to focus on work, and I hired a guy from an ad to play a platonic part of my buffer, and now this man—this actor—just gave me the best orgasm of my life in a tree house.

Maybe it's because I'm bathing in endorphins, but I'm pretty sure I'm falling for him.

The thought floors me. It rattles my foundation. I blink, trying to process what this means. Where we go from here. How the hell I fit this unexpected twist into my crazy career-centric days and nights in New York.

But even though this new awareness should scare the living hell out of me, it doesn't knock me down. Yes, somewhere in the far corners of my mind, I'm terrified. I've worked so hard to get to a place where work is solid and steady.

I don't want to mess *that* up.

But I don't want to mess *this* up either.

I cup his cheeks and meet his eyes. "Get inside me."

Chapter Thirty-four *Theo*

There are no better words than those. *Get inside me.*

I push off my boxer briefs and grab a condom from the packet I brought. She pushes up to her elbows. "Can I put it on you?" Her green eyes are wide and eager.

I grow harder just from her question. "Hell yeah."

I hand her the condom, and she tears open the wrapper. "Just curious. Did you bring these along for the trip?"

"You want to know when I procured them?"

Her lips quirk into a smile. "I do."

"I picked them up at the drugstore after fishing yesterday."

Her eyes sparkle. "Presumptuous."

I lower my gaze to her hands, removing the condom from the packet. "And yet, you're about to put one on my dick. So perhaps I'm both presumptuous and right."

"Cocky, too," she says, a flirty tone to her voice.

"Says the woman who just called my name to the heavens."

She rolls her eyes. "You love teasing me, don't you."

I nod. "I do."

She wraps her hand around my length and strokes down, head to base. I shudder.

"Are you sure you want this?" she goads, running her hand back up, gliding it over the tip so perfectly that I swear I could come if she does that just a little more, a little longer.

"Please." My voice is hoarse. "Put. It. On. Me."

Her eyes twinkle with satisfaction. She sits up higher and rolls the condom down my length. I watch her every move. It's erotic. It's intense. It makes me feel even more connected to her as she readies me to be inside her. I swallow as she finishes, pinching the tip of the condom. Once she's done, she raises her face and meets my gaze.

"Hi," she whispers.

Heat crackles down my spine. I'm not sure I can withstand the wanting much longer.

"Hi," I say as she lies back down. I lower one hand to the blanket, palm flat on the floor of the tree house. With my other hand, I position my erection between her legs. I try not to invest the moment with too much significance. It's just sex.

But hell, it's not just sex.

I'm crazy for her.

I ease the tip in, and she gasps, wrapping her arms around my neck. "Oh God," she murmurs.

She trembles as I push in more. She's so soft and wet, and so ready, and she feels unbelievable. I can't believe I'm doing this, that I've broken this golden rule of my side business, but with the way she feels beneath me, I'd break it a thousand times over.

We fit.

"You feel amazing," I whisper as I lower my chest to hers. Her lush body is pressed to mine. I can't get enough of her. I want to feel her everywhere. I want her softness against me. I want her wetness gripping me. I slide in more, and I'm rewarded with a sweet little hiss of her breath.

"It's okay? Doesn't hurt?"

She shakes her head. "It's so good." She licks her lips, her eyes pinned to mine. *"More."*

I move in her, taking my time, letting her adjust, letting myself adjust to the extraordinary feel of being inside this woman I can't resist. I move my hips, stroking deeper.

She leans her head back, stretching her neck. It's so inviting. I dip my face to her neck, grazing my teeth across the delicate skin. Her breath catches.

"I feel like I'm on fire," she says in a feathery voice.

"Yeah?"

"Everywhere. My skin. My heart. Just everywhere."

I push deeper, with longer thrusts. Electricity crackles in my body, sparking down my spine.

We move like that for several deliciously intense minutes, her sounds echoing in the summer air, our bodies sweat-slicked and hot, our breath in each other's ears. Her hands travel all over me, exploring my shoulders, traveling down my back, stopping at my ass. She grabs me, pulling me deeper.

"More," she groans. "Harder."

The last word is a shot of lust straight to my groin. Burying myself in her, I fuck her with long, rough strokes.

"Oh God, oh God, oh God."

Then I slow the pace, so I can torture her, and let it build again. She moans, a tiny sound of frustration. I bring my lips to her earlobe and nibble. "I'll get you there."

"I know."

"Do you trust me?"

She nods. "I do."

"I'll make it so good for you."

"I know you will."

I want it more than good. I want to shatter her world. I want to see how she looks beneath me, falling apart into a thousand beautiful pieces.

I punch my hips into her. She matches me thrust for thrust, moving fast and hard with me. I ease back, slowing, and she whimpers. Such a needy gorgeous sound. Picking up the pace again, I reach down, running my hand along her thigh, grab her foot, and hike up her leg.

I bring her knee up to her shoulder and marvel at how sensual she looks beneath me. Under me, trusting me to take her there. "You like it like this?"

I ask because I want to know everything. I want to record all her likes, I want to learn where my touch drives her most wild, I want to catalog every beautiful response from her. She arches her back, and a low, sexy cry comes from her lips. *"Yes."*

Tension builds in me; it tightens and intensifies with each stroke. Her warm body grips me, her hips rocking up like she can pull me deeper with each roll.

I go as deep as I can, needing this closeness.

And when she threads her fingers through my hair, whispering my name, I feel something unlock inside me. *"Theo."*

It feels as though all the secrets I've been keeping are bubbling up, threatening to spill over, and I know I will tell her. I know I will share everything. I want her to know me. Want her to understand who I am. Because I want her to feel the same damn way I do.

I want her to fall in love with me, too. The real me.

"Are you almost there?"

She nods and pants, a flush spreading up her skin, traveling to her neck. "Yes, keep doing it," she says; then her sounds grow hoarse, turning into incoherent pleas.

"Not stopping. Never stopping."

She shudders, and her eyes squeeze closed. I watch her face, watch the start of an orgasm bloom on her expression as her mouth twists, then falls open, and she's noiseless at first. Just the tiniest gasp, then a long, lingering, gorgeous groan. Like a bomb, she detonates. She rocks up into me, grabbing at me, kissing me, pulling me closer.

I grit my teeth, holding off my own orgasm because I won't miss a second of this explosion. She's panting now and moaning, those aftershock sounds as she bathes in her pleasure.

"You're beautiful when you come," I grunt. Then I pound into her, wilder, harder, letting loose, letting go until my own orgasm powers through my body, lighting me up, making my bones shake with pleasure. My body jerks as I come hard, filling the condom.

I pant and breathe hard, as if I've run a race.

When I open my eyes, the sight before me is heaven. April is blissed out, high on her second orgasm. Her face glows, dewy with a sheen of sweat, and her smile is all natural and naughty.

The words she says next make my heart leap. "I want to keep you around."

I bury my face in her neck, kiss her skin, nibble on her ear. "Keep me."

Chapter Thirty-five *Theo*

On the return to the inn, I can't keep my hands off her. We stroll past a white colonial with orange tulips bursting in the front yard, and I kiss her cheek.

We stop at the market to grab a pepper, and I run my hand down her arm.

After we cross the next street, I inhale her neck. "You smell like me."

"So I'm sexy and manly and edgy?"

I snort. "Correction. You smell like you've been well fucked."

"It's the JBF look you promised, I believe." She loops her arm around my waist. "And, yes, I've been quite well screwed, thank you very much."

Pride surges in me. There's nothing so good as pleasing your woman.

My woman.

Hell, she's my woman, and I have to find a way to keep her. We stop under the canopy of a tree, and once again, my hands dive into her hair. "Can I have you again to-night?"

She arches one brow. "Maybe I'm presumptuous, but I figured that was a given."

"Even at the inn? You'll have to be quiet."

"I can be quiet." She places her hands together as if in prayer. "I promise I can be quiet."

I move in closer to her. "Then I'll sleep with you in the dark," I tell her, trailing kisses on her neck. She trembles. "Under the covers. The sheets slipping down to our hips. I'll tell you to be quiet, or I won't let you come."

"Will I? Be quiet?"

I run my index finger along her cheekbone. "It'll be tough, but you'll want it so bad, knowing how good it can be."

"How good will it be tonight?"

"Even better than this afternoon."

Her breath hitches. "Why? Tell me why," she says, and I know she loves that we talk like this. We tell stories of our desire, and those stories are coming true.

"Because it'll be the middle of the night, and we'll take our time, we'll linger on each other, as if we have hours. I'll pull you on top of my body, you'll slide down on me, and you'll fuck me like that," I rasp out, and she sways closer. I whisper in her ear. "You can ride me tonight. Get on me and ride me, nice and slow and easy, in the dark, shadows falling across us. I want it like that. Do you?"

She swallows, and her eyes flutter. She shakes her head. "Who are you?"

I blink, taken aback. "What do you mean?"

"Who are you to just fall into my life like this and say these things? You say these things, and I want to climb you again now."

I smirk. "Tonight, cupcake. Climb me tonight."

"Like there's a chance I won't." We resume our pace on the tree-lined street toward the inn, and I take a deep breath, figuring now is as good a time as any to tell her the truth. I don't know exactly how I'll do it, but I want her to know who I am.

Hey, I used to be a con artist and I scammed people out of tons of money to pay for college, and I'm not really an actor, but I did kind of once want to teach Shakespeare, but that shit is hard to understand, and I hope you'll be cool with the fact that I spent two weeks in County for selling fake IDs, but that's nothing on my brother, since he did a stint in prison for fraud. Aren't we the most adorable family?

But before *hey* can fall from my lips, I notice April looks at her watch, a clever little grin tripping across her face.

"What's that smile for?" I ask, figuring I'll get to my confessional soon enough.

"I have a surprise for you!"

Color me intrigued. "You do?"

"Something you'll like."

"Something?"

"Actually, *someone*."

I furrow my brow. "Who?"

"You'll see."

A minute later, we reach the inn and a familiar shape appears on the wooden swing on the porch. A broad set of shoulders I'd recognize anywhere, a mess of brown hair, a jaw like mine.

My heart freezes. Heath rises, an easy, loping gait to his stride as my past crashes into my present well before I'm ready.

Chapter Thirty-six *April*

Heath wraps his brother in a hug, and I want to jump up and down. I want to kiss the sky. Instead, I stand on the stone walkway in front of the inn, practically bouncing on my sandals.

"So good to see you," Heath says, his big voice booming with warmth and happiness. He's tall like Theo, but broader. Bigger chest, bigger shoulders, more ink. His hair is a touch darker, and he has blue eyes. I wonder if he gets his eyes from their mom or their dad.

"Yeah." That's all Theo says, and his tone is strained, his voice dry. Maybe he's too overcome to speak.

The woman who must be Lacey is bursting with excitement, too. Her long brown hair is cinched back in a neat French braid, and silver bracelets adorn her tan wrists. Both ears are brimming with small silver earrings. I count seven on each. A dangly bracelet with charms circles one ankle.

"I'm Lacey," she says, extending a hand to me. We shake, then she pulls me in for a hug. "That was so cool of you to do this. Heath is so excited to see Theo. It's been too long. He misses him."

"They should get together more," I say, and I can't stop smiling. I'm thrilled I pulled this off. It seemed silly to be so close to Heath and not invite him to the reunion. Boston's only two hours away, and since I have a crazy good memory for numbers, I didn't even need to look at Theo's phone again. I remembered Heath's number from the first time I saw it flash on the screen. When Theo left the room this morning, I called Heath, told him my idea, and he drove down after I sent him the address. My mom said she had an extra room. Easy peasy.

"I couldn't agree more," Lacey says. "But Heath hasn't been able to leave until now, and Theo's been so busy."

"Right, of course. Heath must be so busy, too," I say, though as the words come out of my mouth, I realize I don't know what Heath does for a living that keeps him so busy, so I shift gears to Theo. "And with Theo, he has so much going on, balancing auditions and the bar and whatnot."

Lacey furrows her brow momentarily. Confusion seems to cross her pretty brown eyes, but then she smiles again. "I'm so excited to meet the woman that has our Theo so happy. We didn't even know he had a girlfriend."

I wave a hand dismissively. "It all started quickly between us," I say, and that's true. The last few days have been a whirlwind of falling into each other. Who cares if it's been only a few days—or a month, as we told my family? The fact is, it sure seems like we're together now for real, and that's all that matters. A day or two ago, I would never have done this. But last night on the phone, Theo introduced me to Heath as his girlfriend. He could have told his brother the truth. He could have said I was a friend, or a client, or anyone. He didn't need to keep up the act with his brother, of all people, and that admission was permission enough for me to invite the person he loves most to join us.

A jingle sounds in the air, and it's Lacey adjusting the shoulder strap on her purse.

"I love all your jewelry," I say.

"Thank you. I make them. I've started selling it at fairs and such. It's turning into a nice business. And it's great, since Heath is building up his brand-new business, too."

I'm about to ask what Heath does, but then Theo breaks the long embrace, and turns to us. "So . . ."

His tone is flat. For a moment, I worry that I've made a mistake by inviting Heath and Lacey. "So here we all are," I say with a cheery smile. "My parents are making dinner, and we have the scavenger hunt this evening, and if you want to be part of the games, that would be great. But no obligation. You can wander around town instead. Whatever you like. I have a room for both of you."

"We'd love to be part of the games," Heath says, his arm still around Theo, squeezing his shoulder. Heath steps closer and extends a hand to me. "And you rock. Thanks for doing this."

Theo shoots a bright smile, but it seems forced. "And now you've seen me."

Heath arches a brow. "You giving me a hard time?"

"Never," Theo replies.

"You better not." Heath drops his knuckles to Theo's head and gives him a noogie. Theo slips out of his grip.

"You should arm wrestle him," I tease.

Heath glances at Theo, a look in his eyes that seems to say something, that feels almost challenging to Theo, like he's correcting his younger brother. But I can't figure out why.

"Anyway, do you want to head inside and put your

things in your room? Or did you already? Were you waiting long?"

"We had just arrived before you did, and we were enjoying the swing," Lacey says, setting a hand on Heath's
arm.

They head up the stone path. I hang back and give Theo
a curious look. "Isn't this cool? I thought it would be good."

He mutters something I can't understand, and the worry
sets back in.

"I called him this morning. I had his number from when
we talked last night. It seemed like you really wanted to
see him," I say, my pitch rising as my throat closes up from
nerves. Did I read everything wrong? I thought for sure
he'd want his brother here.

"Sure." His voice is monotone still.

"*Are* you sure?" I ask, and now all I can think is I've
misstepped badly, and at the worst possible time.

He closes his eyes, then opens then. "I just wish . . ."

"Wish what?"

"I wish you'd asked first." He doesn't sound like the
man I know.

My heart sinks. My voice wobbles. "I'm sorry. I thought
you wanted to see him. I thought this could be fun for you."

He blinks, then shakes his head like a dog shaking off
water. It's as if he's trying to collect his thoughts. "It'll be
great," he says with another forced smile. "Family is just
hard."

Awareness smacks me upside the head. This must be
difficult because family is difficult for him. I should have
known better. "I'm sorry. I didn't even think of it like that.
I honestly just thought it would be nice to have everyone
together. But that was foolish of me."

"Don't worry, April. It's okay."

But it hardly sounds okay. He makes a move to head

into the inn, and I grab his arm. "Please. I wanted to do something nice for you because you've done so much for me. I thought it was brilliant and clever, but now I can see that I was looking at it only from my side of things."

"Hey," he says, his voice soft, and he finally sounds like himself again. He drops a kiss to my forehead. "You're not foolish. You're amazing, and I really want this to work between us."

I blink.

Did he just say what I think he said? That we're definitely an "us"? That what's been happening is going to keep happening? My heart skips, and I'm ready to burst into song.

"You do?" I ask tentatively.

He nods vigorously. "Is that not patently obvious?" He waves animatedly in the general direction of the tree house. "After this afternoon, you think I could want anything but that? I want that. I want you. And right now, I honestly just want to find a way to be back in New York with you."

His eyes gaze into mine, and my stomach flips. My heart hammers. The last thing I expected when he seemed to shut down was for him to come back like this.

I want to throw my arms around him and kiss his face. So I do. I tackle-hug him, and kiss his fabulous lips. "I want that."

I head inside to take a shower, knowing everything will work out fine.

Chapter Thirty-seven *Theo*

Keep cool.

Keep calm.

Stay confident.

Those were the skills I had in spades.

I might be done with the racket, but I still know how to navigate an uncomfortable situation.

Did I lie to April outside the inn a little while ago? As I raise a fork to my mouth and take a bite of the red pepper salad April's father made, I can say with certainty that I did not.

I desperately want us to work. I want to be back in New York, carving out time with her, figuring out how we're going to make a real go of being together.

That's the solid gold truth.

But I lied about why I don't want my brother here. It's not because family's hard. It's because I don't want to have to keep playing the angles, and now I must.

There are things Heath doesn't know. Things I've kept from him. I didn't want to weigh him down with my troubles while he was serving time, so I dealt with my life on my own terms. He's been free for only a few months, and I saw him once, when I was able to get away. He had to receive permission to travel outside the state, and even though he could have obtained it, it was easier for me to see him.

His parole ended a few days ago.

I almost wish it had lasted a few days longer, because then he wouldn't have been able to pull off the trip from Massachusetts to Connecticut so easily.

The way I see it, I have one more night to make everything work. If I win the scavenger hunt, I have a chance at winning the big prize. I can get in, get out, and get the girl. All I have to do is make sure the two pieces of my life don't bump up against each other before I'm ready.

That's why tonight I'm going to tell April the truth about my past. I'll tell her in bed. This girl is the real deal, and I feel confident that she's not going to pull a Richelle on me and kick me out of her heart simply because I'm not a squeaky clean guy. But I haven't had a moment alone with her since, well, since the tree house, and I was all set to tell her on the street before she pulled the rug, the flooring, and the earth out from under me with her *surprise*.

I squared the situation with my brother when we hugged, whispering to him in a ridiculously prolonged brotherly embrace that he simply needed to go along with things if April mentioned to him that I was an actor. He'd given me a *that's not cool* look, but he nodded, letting me know he'd have my back.

That's really the only issue. April's family thinks I'm simply a bartender, April thinks I'm an actor and a bartender, and my brother doesn't entirely know about my boyfriend-for-hire work.

All I have to do is keep juggling until I can sort out everything.

For now, Heath has slipped seamlessly into the family, telling a tale of how he nearly caught a home run ball at Fenway Park last week. He's in his element. Heath can fit in anywhere. "I swear it was landing in the palm of my hand," he says, one arm raised. "Then the young girl next to me reached up and nabbed it before I did." He shakes his head and sighs heavily. "But hey, it all works out in the end. She probably needed it more than I did."

As April's father serves grilled chicken, April's mother fires off questions at Heath, just as she did to me when we met. He survives every single one, including when she asks what he's doing for a living. "I started a consulting business. I do ethical hacking," he explains. She asked him where he learned the skills, and he says he studied computer science at school.

That's not the whole truth, but it's true enough. He learned how to hack ethically because he did the opposite. Breaking into online sites was part of his stock scam. He's learned how to share only the necessary bits and pieces of his life.

When the meal is done, April's father rises.

"As you know, the scavenger hunt is the final event of our summer reunion games," he says, like he's giving a speech. "We will begin tonight and finish it tomorrow morning. You will go in teams, and you can earn points for the individual and team competition. Don't forget the individual competition for the five-thousand-dollar prize is a particularly tight race, with Emma, Theo, and Katie all strong contenders." My brother shoots me an *isn't that interesting* look. "And as for the team competition, since we have two newcomers, I've decided that any points the newcomers win, will be awarded to me." Everyone laughs at his joke. "In all seriousness, Bob and I convened and we decided that if Heath and Lacey wish to join Theo and April as a team, that each person will win points on a half-point level. That way the four of you will work together as a team, but you'll earn points as if you were two. Does that sound fair to everyone?"

Heath and Lacey nod. The rest of the family chimes in with their yeses.

"We'd love to be a part of it," Lacey says.

I say a private thank-you, since this approach means we can kick ass in this game, with double the mind power. The sooner we finish tonight, the sooner I can be alone with April. I can tell her everything, and I can tell her my past is behind me, too. She'll understand. I know she will.

Besides, my brother would never rat me out.

An hour later, the four of us crowd into a stall inside the restroom at the ice cream shop in town and shoot a selfie. April makes a duck face, Lacey pouts, and Heath gives his best psychotic look with one eye closed. I adopt a stony expression as I click the camera on my phone.

"There you go," I announce as we check out our mugs on my screen. One of the items on the scavenger hunt list is a digital photo of the entire team standing in a bathroom. We've already snagged a receipt for fifty cents' worth of gas—none of us has a car, so we bought fuel for someone in line—a takeout menu from the restaurant next to the ice cream shop, and a photo of an out-of-state license plate when we spotted a Vermonter cruising by in a yellow Honda.

I squeeze out of the stall first, followed by Heath. Then April shoos us out of the bathroom. "Time to pee. See you later."

"Me, too," Lacey says.

I look at Heath. "Let's order some ice cream."

We leave the ladies behind and wait in line to order. It's the first time I've had a moment with him.

He claps me on the shoulder. "All right, little dipshit. What's the deal?"

"What do you mean?"

He holds out his hands. "Don't mess with me. You told me to go along with the whole 'you're an actor' thing. Want to tell me why she thinks you're an actor?"

I scrub a hand over my jaw. "She hired me to play her boyfriend. Her family is always trying to set her up, and she didn't want to come alone and be subjected to dates with local dudes she's not into. So she hired me. I told her I was an actor because I've done a few of these boyfriend-for-hire gigs. Don't laugh, but it pays well, and it's helping me with some bills. I never mentioned them to you, because you were in the joint and I knew what you'd say."

He laughs in disbelief. "What would I say, O Oracle?"

I sigh heavily. "You'd tell me to focus on one thing."

"And isn't that good advice?"

Yeah, but then your ex came calling, demanding payment. I did it for you so you could have this life you want now.

"Maybe. But I'm quitting the biz," I say, and as soon as I voice it, it feels completely right. That's exactly what I need to do. I need to focus on April, concentrate on what kind of work I want long-term, and shut down all my GigsForHire ads. I have a girlfriend now, for all intents and purposes, so I can't pretend to be someone else's arm candy anymore.

"Jesus. You make it sound like you're a gigolo," he says, as he eyes the ice cream case, surveying the mint chip, the triple chocolate, and the coconut almond fudge.

"Nope. Definitely not a hooker."

"Are your feelings for her even real? You said she was your girlfriend when we talked on the phone. What the hell is even true?"

"Of course they're real," I say indignantly.

He scratches his chin, as though he's trying to process this news. "She hired you to play her boyfriend, and you became a real thing? Sounds like a romance novel."

I smirk. "Crazy, right?"

He fixes me with a serious stare. "You sure that's all that's going on?"

I cock my head to the side. "What do you mean?"

He shakes his head. "I don't know. You scored a nice, rich girl. I saw that inn. They're rolling in it. She's loaded and she's crazy for you. You sure you aren't scamming her?"

I recoil. "What?"

"C'mon. Level with me. You told me to *pretend* you're an actor." He stabs my chest with a finger. "But she *believes* that you truly are. Why not tell her the truth? You didn't, though, because she said to Lacey that you were auditioning for roles. You're letting her believe this line of bullshit."

"I'll tell her the truth later. It wasn't important at the time. Besides, who are you to talk?"

He shoves my shoulder. "I got clean, man. I'm on the up and up. My woman knows the deal. She knows my shit. She loves me no matter what. But you? You're playing a part, and you've let her believe you're falling for her." He narrows his blue eyes. He has our mom's eyes, and it always gets to me. "But are you really just scamming her? Are you working the angles to get her money?"

"That's ridiculous!"

"Is it? There's a five-thousand-dollar prize on the table. How on earth are you *not* doing this for the money?"

"One, I don't even know if I'll win. And two, so what if I win?"

He shakes his head. "I expected more from you."

"Enough of the holier-than-thou attitude. I have bills to pay, okay?" I say, nearly snapping. Some of those bills are because of him.

He drops a hand on my shoulder. "Yeah, and from where I stand, it sure as hell looks like you're pulling some kind of big con on her and her family."

"How can you even say that?"

"You're going to look me in the eye and tell me you're not angling for her money? Are you honestly telling me she's not your mark?"

I'm about to say, *Are you out of your goddamn mind?* when I hear another voice. A softer one, but it's full of fire.

"Am I your mark, Theo?"

My heart crashes to the floor when I turn around to see April, her green eyes like frost. Her lips form a ruler-thin line.

"No. You're not," I say quickly, reaching for her, desperately trying to right this ship. "I can explain."

She steps away, holds up her hands. "I've been there. I've done that. I have the T-shirt." She gestures wildly to the ice cream case. "Enjoy your ice cream. The mint chip leaves a great aftertaste." She pauses, raises her chin, and fires. "Unlike some other things."

Chapter Thirty-eight *Theo*

I'd rather be riding a Ferris wheel than be rushing out the door, chasing April down the street, my heart cratering.

That feeling that everything is crashing into you, that your chest has been hollowed out, and you can't hold on? That's it. Right now. My skin prickles as I call out her name.

"April!"

She shakes her head and jams her hand behind her, like a receiver with the football trying to ward off the defense. She's not running, though, and fortunately, I'm taller and determined. With my long stride, I catch up to her at the end of the block, reaching for her arm. She shakes me off.

"What?"

"Let me explain."

She cackles, lifting her chin like she's challenging me to tell her something amazing. "Let me get my popcorn. This is going to be good if you want to explain. Oh, and in case you were wondering, yes, I heard everything from the prize to the bills to the con."

"April," I say, and then I fumble on what to say next. Because this is *not* how I wanted to tell her. This is not how things were supposed to go.

"Ah, I thought it was something like that." The sarcasm drips from her voice.

"I'm not a scammer. Everything I've told you is true, but I'm not an actor. Not really."

She laughs, like she just can't believe me. "Maybe you want to try that again. Because you kind of contradicted yourself right in the middle of your—" She raises her arms and draws exaggerated air quotes. "—'explanation.'"

I rub my hand over the back of my neck. I try again, exhaling heavily. "I'm a bartender. Xavier can vouch for me. The only acting I do is this stuff. The boyfriend-for-hire jobs."

A cough bursts from her mouth. She crosses her arms over her breasts. "And you're awesome at it. Hell, it should be your full-time gig. You don't need any other work, since you do this so well."

Her tone is harsh, and I deserve every angry word.

"This isn't what I want," I spit out.

"Then what do you want? To swindle money from well-off women?" She stares at me, like I'm a math problem. Like she can't even conceive someone like me exists. She holds up her hand. "I don't even want to know."

"I'm not trying to take your money. I'm trying to earn enough to pay off a debt. Okay? Life hasn't always been easy for me. My brother and I had to do everything on our own. We had nothing. Absolutely nothing. I told you that. It's true."

"So you con women? Is that why you took me to the tree house? Wear down my defenses, tell me you want to be with me in the city, and then drain my accounts?" She says all this as if it's incredulous, and it is. "News flash. I'm not rich. I just have a job that pays well."

"I don't want your money. I just wanted to earn a living to pay off the debt that my brother's ex is chasing around. When he went to prison for stock fraud, his ex came to collect on a big fat debt, and I didn't want him to know. I didn't want Heath to have one more thing hanging over him and keeping him from going straight," I say, laying it all on the line as I tell her. "So I started the boyfriend-for-hire gigs to earn money on the side to pay off his debt to Addison. The only reason I'm remotely good at acting is that my brother and I are former con artists. We paid our way through college working cons on the Jersey Shore."

Her laughter turns into the coldest sound I've ever heard. "Are you kidding me? Are you seriously saying this? Are these words coming out of your mouth?"

"Yes," I say, biting out the word. "Yes, it's all true. You can ask my brother."

"Your brother who went to prison? He's your character witness?"

"Yeah," I say, digging my heels in. "Does that make him less of a person because he went to prison?"

For the first time, she balks. She opens her mouth, but only says, "Um . . ."

"Don't judge me and don't judge us, unless you've lived my life and faced our choices. I'm not saying I made the best choices. But I made the ones that worked for me, and for us. We didn't have what you have. So we made our own way. We played the angles, we conned frat guys in arm wrestling, we swindled clerks to make bigger change, and we tricked people into thinking we had an apartment to rent them. Oh yeah, we also told men who were easy prey that Heath's girlfriend was jailbait after she picked them up, so we got money out of assholes that way by promising we wouldn't tell on them. So there you go. That's who I am. The guy who put himself through school thanks to grifting. While we're at it, here's one more thing," I say, my voice hardening as I spill all to her on the street corner near an ice cream shop. "I made fake IDs when I was nineteen and got tagged and went to jail for two weeks. That was fun. I had to spend my days in a jail cell with no shoelaces, so I wouldn't turn shoelaces into a weapon. I know I told you I never went to prison, and that's true. Prison is long-term, so I went to jail instead. But go ahead and judge me. Because I'm sure you know exactly what you'd do if you were left with nothing."

April's hand covers her mouth, and a tear slips down her cheek. I feel like a bigger asshole now that she's crying.

"I'm sorry. I'm sorry you went through all that," she says, her tone the soft one I've heard many times already, the one I've come to love. She drops her hand. "But you can't just dump that all on me like this and expect me not to be surprised. I need a little time to process all this."

"Yeah, most people do. The last girlfriend I had walked away when she learned."

Her voice hardens again. "Don't lump me with other people. I'm not her."

I stab my index finger against my sternum. "And I'm not the married asshole who lied about being with someone. I've been as honest as I possibly could be with you. The only thing I lied to you about was being an actor, but everything else I've told you has been the truth. There are things I've held back, but I was going to tell you tonight. Because I'm crazy for you. And I want you to know who I am and what I've done."

She takes a deep breath, straightens her shoulders, and nods. I dare to breathe a small sigh of relief, because it feels as though we might be making progress. "I might not have the moral high ground. After all, I basically hired you to lie to everybody, so I'm not pure. But the thing is," she says, her voice calm and certain, "I didn't lie to *you* about anything, especially my feelings for you. And I asked you to be straight with me when it was just the two of us. We agreed to pretend with others, but be honest when it was only us."

"I have been honest with you."

"But you haven't," she says insistently. "We've talked repeatedly about your career. I asked you so many questions about being an actor, and everything you said was untrue."

"It's just one thing," I say, desperation thick in my voice. "Can't you see that it didn't make any sense for me to tell you? It's just not something I've shared?"

Her eyes float closed for a brief moment, and when she opens them, they shine with the threat of tears. "But see, I thought we were different. I thought you could tell me the truth. I thought you could be honest with me in a way that you weren't able to with others, because I thought we were real. But now I feel like I have been played."

"I didn't play you."

She holds up a hand. "I need to clear my head. I'm going to take a walk, and I don't want you coming after me."

I swallow and stuff my hands into my pockets. The least I can do is respect her wishes. "Okay."

She turns on her heel and walks down the street toward the water.

A minute later, Heath's hand is on my shoulder. Instinct kicks in. I turn around and shove him. "Thanks a lot."

He stumbles. "What the hell?"

"You ruined it for me."

"You messed it up yourself."

I shove him again. This is how we communicate. We've always been physical. Lacey licks her ice cream cone as she watches us lazily.

Heath lunges for me, wrapping his arm around my neck, getting me in a headlock. "You stupid idiot!" he barks. "Just tell a woman the truth. Watch this: Hey, Lacey. I love you."

"Love you, too, babe."

"Now, say it to me, dipshit."

"Never."

"I'll let you hit me if you do."

He taught me how to throw a punch. He taught me how to win a fight. It was a necessary skill in our line of work. From this position, I have access to his belly, so I swing my fist into his stomach.

"Oof," he says. But then he straightens. "Love you."

"Love you."

He lets go of my head and fixes me with a serious stare. "But I believe you need to do some explaining to me now."

I roll my eyes. "Is there anyone who doesn't want an explanation from me?"

He drops his big hand on my shoulder once more, ignoring my sarcasm. "Why did I hear the name Addison when you were talking to April?"

The first rule of conning is to have an answer for everything.

When my lips part and no sound comes, Heath nods. "That's what I thought. Now, fess up."

Chapter Thirty-nine *April*

When the noise hits my ears, I glance behind me. What the hell? I squint. Theo is shoving his brother, and now Heath has Theo in a headlock, and then Theo slams his fist into his brother's gut.

I flinch. That must hurt.

Meanwhile, Lacey's licking an ice cream cone.

"I can't believe this," I mutter, and I flash back to the ad.

> 5. Start a fistfight with any of the other guests,
> including but not limited to your mom, your dad, your
> sister, your brother, and/or any of the guys. (Don't
> worry about me, sweetheart. That stint at County
> taught me excellent fight skills.)

I fling up my hands. I can't even deal with this anymore. It doesn't matter that the à la carte options in his ad are coming true once more. None of this matters.

All that matters is that I can get out before I'm in too deep.

I don't head home right away. As twilight wraps its navy blue arms around this sleepy town, I walk to the water's edge. Boats bob and sway in low tide, and I lean against the wooden railing of the dock. I stare at the dusky sky. I tell myself it's good that it worked out this way. That I figured out his jam before I was too far gone.

A drop of water falls onto the wood by my hands.

Oh.

That's not water.

That's a stupid tear having the audacity to spill from my eyes. I swipe at my cheek, wiping away the evidence. I won't cry anymore. Yes, I might feel unbelievably foolish. But I need to remember that I learned the truth before it could hurt.

Another salty tear falls.

Who made all these dumb tears leak from my eyes? Stop. Just stop.

I draw a deep breath, telling myself to stay strong. After hunting around in my purse, I find a tissue and I dab at my eyes. There.

I try to distract myself, so I check my phone and scroll through email. I squeak. "Oh!"

There's a note from *Sporting World*. With everything happening at the reunion, I'd nearly forgotten about the job. The subject line is vague. It's simply "Hello." My fingers shake as I open the email.

> I hope this note finds you well. My team and I are suitably impressed with your portfolio, and we hope you're available in two months for our shoot. Along those lines, would you be able to join us for a lunch meeting next week to discuss details?

I shriek. "Oh my God, oh my God, oh my God!"

A sob wrenches through me, tumbling out my mouth. My emotions apparently work on only one setting tonight—*through the roof.* I'm crying happy tears at the dock, but soon enough, they turn sad when I stupidly realize there's one person I want to share this good news with.

I return to the moment on the train when we were just getting to know each other. I can still hear his voice when he said, *You have to tell me when you land that gig. Promise me you'll tell me.*

I promised him I'd tell him.

But people say things they don't always mean. I shove that promise aside, collect myself, and walk to the inn. On the way, I call Claire, tell her the news, then update her on nearly everything—the good, the bad, and the ugly.

"Wow," Claire says. "That's a hell of a backstory, and Xavier never knew any of this?"

I shake my head. "I doubt it. You know Xavier. He doesn't keep secrets, and Theo obviously does, so he kept it all from him, and I suppose since being an actor means you don't always work as an actor, you often work more as a bartender or a waiter, it seemed plausible that he was doing the boyfriend-for-hire work to supposedly work on his acting."

"He *was* acting, in a way. Playing all sorts of parts for clients. Just in an unconventional way, rather than on Broadway."

I manage a small laugh. "True. I suppose Theo is making a living as an actor. He was just doing live-action role playing."

"More power to you if you can make a living LARP-ing," Claire says. Then she takes a beat. "So what happens with you two now?"

I scoff as I reach the block with the Sunnyside. "Well, it's a damn good thing I found out now."

Claire's quiet at first. "Is it?"

"Yes. Before I'm in too deep with him."

"Oh."

I sigh. "What's the 'oh' for?"

"The 'oh' is for 'Oh my, but does this change how you feel about him?'"

I answer swiftly. "Of course. He deceived me."

"About *actually* being an actor, April," she says, taking her time with each word. "That's really all he deceived you about."

I huff. She's wrong. She's so wrong. "Not entirely. It's all wrapped up together. It's not just one thing."

"But it kind of is," she says pragmatically. "He's done stuff in his past, he's learned, he's moved on. He told you. Maybe it wasn't the ideal time or place, but he did tell you. Not everybody has a perfect background."

I thread my fingers through my hair, frustration coursing through my veins. "I know that. I'm not some judgy person who will only be involved with pristine, perfect men. Honestly, it's not even that he was a con artist that bothers me. It's that he lied about what he does, and he did it repeatedly. We talked about him being an actor so many times, and every time it was a lie."

"I can see how that would bother you," she says calmly. "It would bother me, too. But is it so terrible that it's unforgivable?"

The frustration bubbles over. "Why do I need to forgive him?"

"Because you're falling in love with him, and he's not sticking his dick in another woman or living in his parents' basement or lying to you about a million more vital things," she says, her tone rising, too. "Plus, he *does* act. It's just a little different than usual."

I breathe in through my nostrils. I'm a dragon right now, and I don't like it, so I try to let go of my anger.

"Look," she continues, "I know you think he might be conning you, but was he? Did he steal from you? Take your phone, your wallet, your money?"

"No," I grumble. "I even paid him yesterday."

"And yet he stayed. He could have left in the middle of the night, but he stayed."

"Stop trying to be reasonable."

Claire laughs. "Look, just think about things. It sounds like he's been through some tough times, and I understand you want honesty from the start, but then again, you didn't tell him you invited his brother to the reunion. You didn't ask him if that was okay."

I swallow harshly as the truth hits me hard in the gut. Are the situations parallel? I'm not entirely sure. My voice softens as I ask Claire, "Do you think they're the same?"

She sighs as I walk up the steps to the inn. "There are things he didn't fully disclose. There are things you didn't fully disclose. Are they lies? Or are they truths that weren't ready to see the light of day yet?"

I open the door. My mom and dad are parked on the couch, surveying their scavenger hunt loot. My father holds up a small cocktail umbrella, an item from the list. He smiles, pleased with the booty.

I smile back, then point to the phone against my ear. Somehow, this exonerates me from any conversation or questions. I must remember this trick anytime I want to excuse myself from potentially awkward conversations.

"What would you do?" I ask as I walk up the stairs to

my room, bracing myself to see him again. I have no clue what to do when I see his pretty face again.

"I don't have any answers, but he did seem to open his heart to you, and you did to him, in a way, so don't discount all that yet."

When I reach the room, I unlock the door and walk inside. I nearly stumble as I stop in my tracks, pointing to the bed even though I'm the only one here. I whisper, "There's an envelope on the bed with my name on it."

"What does it say?" Claire asks curiously.

I take cautious steps, like the envelope is a ticking bomb. When I reach it, my nerves have hit sky-high level. My name is written on the front. My body hums with anticipation.

"I'm opening it now," I say to Claire as I give her the play-by-play.

All my breath rushes from my lungs when I see what's inside.

It's all the cash I paid him.

Chapter Forty *Theo*

It's late when we arrive in Manhattan. It's even later when we make it to Addison's block in Chelsea, and Heath hits the buzzer for her apartment.

Silence.

He turns to me and huffs. "Still pissed at you."

"Still pissed at you, too," I echo.

Lacey rolls her eyes. "Neither one of you is pissed at the other."

Heath jabs the button again. "I'm intensely mad at him."

"You're so not mad at him. You ridiculous man, you," she says affectionately, patting his cheek. Her bracelets jingle. "The two of you had the entire ride to sort it out, and you did."

It went something like this:

"Why the hell didn't you tell me about this? You're not responsible for that money."

"I wanted you to be able to get out and start over without that hanging over you."

"I'm starting over just fine, and I'm paying my own way."

"I didn't think you'd have the money for it."

"And you're wrong again. I told you I started a new business, and I have a retainer from my first client. So don't ever do that again."

"Okay."

"Now, take me to Addison so I can pay it off, dipshit."

I suppose, if I had to do it all over again, I'd have done it the same way. I did it for him. I did it because I love him. I did it because I well and truly did not want him to fall back into old habits. Sometimes you don't know how a man will handle a situation until he's pushed to the limits. I've seen Heath pushed before. He hasn't always made the best choices. Nor have I. So I made the one that made sense to me at the time—taking on the debt.

Now, he's making the choice that makes sense to him—paying it off. Because he's making better choices in his life these days. He's making choices our mom might even be proud of at last. The only trouble is—it looks like little Miss Southern Loan Shark isn't home.

"C'mon," he mutters, stalking across the stoop.

He presses the button one more time when a voice floats from a window above. "Well, look what the cat dragged back into Manhattan."

Heath sighs heavily and cranes his neck. Addison's brown hair is yanked into a messy bun, and she stares coldly at the three of us. Even from two stories high, her eyes are ice. "Good evening, Miss Addison. I've dragged something you want." He reaches into his pocket and waves a check. "Now, let me give it to you so you can leave my brother the fuck alone."

Her eyes narrow. "Is it everything?"

"Everything and then some." He stuffs the check back into his jeans pocket.

She casts her gaze to Lacey, then steps away from the window and slams it shut.

"Maybe I should take a walk," Lacey suggests, pointing her thumb down the block.

Heath shakes his head. "Nope. We're settling this, and there's no need to take off."

Or maybe we're not settling it. Because one minute passes. Two minutes. Three. Four. Five. Heath paces on the stoop, Lacey fiddles with her bracelet, and I stare at the glass window on the door. What I don't do is check my phone. I need to finish this before I even see if April has responded to the letter I left her with the money.

My fingers itch to grab my phone from my pocket.

Slide my thumb across the screen.

And look for her name.

My heart aches with the wish that I'll find her words on the other end of the line. She doesn't seem like a woman who takes kindly to being hoodwinked, and I can't say I blame her. But I'm hoping she'll give me a chance when she reads what I wrote. I want to get to the next phase of my life, and I'm dying for her to be a part of it, but I need to finish this chapter first.

Six minutes later, footsteps sound in the foyer, and Addison appears at the door, unlocking it. She's freshened up, I suspect. Her hair is looped into a ponytail, and her lips are slicked with peach gloss. Her eyelashes are long, mascara combed through them.

"Good evening," Heath says.

"It's almost midnight."

"Huh," he says, acting surprised as he checks his watch. It's only ten. We made it here in one hour and forty-five minutes. Heath doesn't exactly honor the speed limit. "Hope you don't mind taking a big fat check at this late hour."

She crosses her arms and stares at Lacey. "Will it even cash?"

"Yeah, it'll cash." He reaches into his pocket and hands her the check he wrote on the drive.

She unfolds it, eyes it like it's something dirty. She stuffs it into her bra.

Next, Heath removes a sheet of paper from his pocket. Lacey jimmied up the contract on her phone on the way in, sent it to a copy shop, and picked it up during a four-minute pit stop. "And these are the terms saying the personal loan between you and me is paid, free and clear. Sign it, and we'll be done."

He pats his pocket for a pen.

Lacey laughs softly, dips her hand into her purse, and fishes out a pen. "Here you go."

"She speaks," Addison says cruelly.

Lacey smiles at Addison. "Yes, I do speak. And I believe I speak for all women when I say, you have very lovely hair. It's quite pretty."

I wrench back and stare at Lacey. What the hell was that? Then it dawns on me. She's not using the same weapons as Addison. She's not fighting fire with fire. She's disarming her with kindness. And I'm reminded once more why Lacey is the one my brother has always loved.

Because she loves.

Addison's jaw hangs open. She has no clue how to respond to someone like Lacey. Instead, she huffs, grabs the pen, scrawls her name, and thrusts the paper back at Heath.

He holds it up in the air, and Lacey shines the flashlight from her phone on it. I snap a photo of it.

"I'll send this to you, Addison. So we'll all have a copy," I say. Then I extend a hand. I'm dying to say something biting, like *Wish I could say it's been nice doing business with you.* Instead, I take a page from Lacey's playbook and say, "Thanks for the help when we needed it, and best of luck in all your ventures."

We leave, and the debt is paid.

Sometimes things are easy when you stop hiding the truth. I wish I'd known sooner how easy it would be like this. But I suppose we don't really learn until we're ready.

Or maybe until we meet the one person worth telling all your truths to.

As we walk to the car, I take a deep inhalation of the New York night. This is what I want. New York. With her. This life.

"So tell me, O Oracle, what do I do now to get the girl back?"

Heath cracks up. "Are you talking to me or are you talking to the expert on all things lady-related?" He tugs Lacey in and gives her a NSFW kiss.

I groan. "No PDA, please."

He breaks the kiss. "More? You said you wanted more?"

Lacey laughs and drops a kiss to his lips. When she breaks apart, she says, "You need to try again."

"And what exactly does that entail?" I ask, dropping my hand into my pocket, eager to check my phone.

Heath says three words, and I know that's what I need to do.

Chapter Forty-one *April*

I imagine he wrote this note on the Sunnyside notepad while I was down at the docks, swiping tears from my face. I picture him leaning over the bureau, writing it standing up, concentration etched in his brow.

Trying to find just the right words.

I still can't believe he returned the money.

Maybe that's why I'm still in shock a couple hours later as I sit curled up on the red couch, running my hand over the note.

In my defense, I haven't been sitting here staring at the paper for two hours. I did manage another shower. Showers have a wonderful way of resetting your mind, and I needed that. I needed to feel the water streaming hot down my body, as I thought about what to do.

Now here with my damp hair, sleep shorts, and T-shirt, I know what to do.

I read the note one more time.

April,
When I first met you in the park, I knew I was screwed.

You were the toughest client I ever worked for. Not because you're hard to get along with, but because I was attracted to you from the second I saw you.

It was instant, sort of like how you felt for my T-shirt.

But even though we started as a made-up couple, concocting fables and telling tales, that spark between us was always real. And then, as I got to know you, it turned into something more. It turned into the real deal. That's what you are to me, and that's what I want to be for you.

Maybe that's why this job has been the hardest one of all—because I had to pretend the whole time that I wasn't falling in love with you.

I am completely in love with you, and that's why all the stories I've told you about us feel true. They're true to what I want with you. I want a real future. I want to keep creating stories to tell. Real stories of us. I want you to know who I am, and I want to know who you are. I have a past, yes. But I have a future, too, and I want you in it. You know how to find me.

Theo

I'm dying to call him. I'm longing to reach out to him. But I have to take care of something else first. Something that's stood in the way since we started. Time to knock it down.

I stand, leave my phone behind, and exit the room.

The door clicks shut, and I raise my chin up high. It's nearly midnight, and I suspect my father is asleep. I don't relish waking him up, but I need to talk to both my parents. I pad quietly down the stairs, then through the quiet living room. Sounds of laughter and clinking glasses drift from the back porch. I'm pleasantly surprised to find him there, parked in an Adirondack chair, my mom cuddled on his lap, the two of them staring at the stars. He tells her something I can't hear, and she laughs.

I push the door open wider, so they hear me. "Hi."

They turn their heads to me. "Hey, little puppy," my father says.

"You're up late, Dad," I say as I grab a chair across from them.

He shows me an empty glass of wine. "Your mother lured me out here with wine. I was powerless to resist her charms."

She smiles at him. "You always have been."

He dots a kiss on her forehead. "I always will be."

I could gag if it weren't completely sweet.

"But how are *you*?" my mother asks. "Do you still have a headache?" She popped by when I first returned, and I waved her off, claiming a malady I didn't have since I couldn't deal then. "Do you need anything? What happened to Theo? He rushed out in a flurry with his brother and that woman."

A flock of nerves descends on me, but I tell it to scatter. I am strong. I am tough. I am confident.

"I hired him, Mom."

She knits her brow. "Hired? What?"

I steel myself to tell the truth. "He's not my boyfriend. I found him on GigsForHire."

My father blinks. "You can find men on GigsForHire?"

My mother gives him a look, chiding. "Joshua. You can find anything on GigsForHire. Especially men."

"Have *you* been looking on GigsForHire for men?"

She laughs. "Never." She snaps her gaze to me, undeterred. "Is he an escort?"

My mouth tastes metallic as I manage the uncomfortable

words. "No. But yes. He's not a sex worker. If that's what you're asking."

They cringe in unison.

My mother's eyes narrow. "You're going to need to explain better. What is he, then?"

"He's a bartender. That's true. But he also owed some money for something that happened to someone he loved, and he has been making a side living as a boyfriend-for-hire. That's how I found him. My friend Xavier knows him, and told me he's done this before. He picks up side work as a platonic date for women who need a buffer at events. There's actually a decent market and he's good at it."

My father holds up a finger, his brow furrowed. "This morning he said he cared about you. He seemed legitimate. He showed me pictures of your cheetah."

"He did?" I ask, a smile tickling at my lips.

"He seemed quite proud of you. This makes no sense," he says, leaning closer, as though he needs to get a better read on this heaping dose of absurdity I'm serving up.

"He showed you my work?"

My father nods. "He bragged about you. Frankly, he helped me better understand what you do, and I'm afraid to say I don't think I've always quite gotten it until then."

I beam inside, and my smile is full wattage. "That's the thing. He meant it. Because even though I hired him, we fell in love with each other," I say, knowing with my whole heart that those words are wholly true.

My mom's eyes widen. "So you hired him, and then you fell for him?"

I nod. "Yes, but that's not what I came out here to tell you."

"There's more?" she asks, as if she can't believe there could possibly be anything else to add to this insanity.

"Yes," I say as calmly as I can, drawing a deep breath. This is when I speak the truth, when I stop hiding behind the easier path of hiring a shield. I need to tell them how I truly feel, even if it hurts them. "I want you to know the reason *why* I hired him. And it's because I don't want to be set up on dates. I specifically don't want to be set up on dates with men from Wistful." I meet their eyes. "And that's because I don't want to move back home."

My mother frowns. Sadness flickers in my father's eyes.

I press my hands together, like I'm making a plea. "I know you want me to. That's why everyone is always trying to set me up. You're hoping I'll fall in love with the hardware store owner. Or maybe if Aunt Jeanie connects me with the mortgage broker, I'll be so besotted, I'll move into a cottage a mile away with him. I do understand you come at it with the best of intentions, but it's not what I want," I say, feeling as though a weight is sliding off my shoulders. A heavy, brutal weight. It's freeing to speak the truth, even if it's scary.

"I just worry about you," my mother says softly, her voice vulnerable.

"I can't ever stop worrying about you. You're my youngest," my father says, seconding her.

"But sometimes you treat me like I can't make my own decisions about work or men."

"Well, you did hire someone from GigsForHire," my mom points out.

I nod, taking this one on the chin. "Maybe that was a crazy decision. But at the time I made it, it was easier for me to have a shield here at the reunion in the form of a boyfriend. You've all been so concerned after what happened with Landon that anyone I date from New York will be a charlatan. But Landon was simply a mistake. It happens. I'm young. I'm supposed to make mistakes." I bring my hand to my heart. "But I love my life in New York and I love my job and I love my friends and I love my choices, and I want you to respect them, even if you don't understand them." I lean closer and ask honestly. "Can you?"

Crickets chirp, and an owl hoots. A squirrel scurries along the porch railing, perhaps in hot pursuit of acorns. My mom appears deep in thought, her worry lines more prominent. "I don't entirely understand why you'd hire someone. I don't understand why you didn't just tell me."

Her question is valid, and it deserves an honest answer. "Because it was easier to pretend. It was easier to hire a buffer than to deal with the dates, or to disappoint you with the truth. But in retrospect, maybe I should have just told you." I take a beat. "But would you have relented?"

My father shakes his head, casting a soft glance at my mom as he answers for her. "You wouldn't have, Pamela. You're a determined monkey, and you've been fixated on setting her up."

"I know," she admits.

"I want to make you both happy because I love you so much," I say, a sob climbing up my throat. I swallow it down. "And it was easier for me to avoid the truth. But I want you to believe in me, and I want you to trust that I can make my own choices, and I want you to know that my choice is to live in the city and pursue my career there."

My mom raises her chin. "We do believe in you. We are proud of you. All we want is for you to be happy. We're so happy here, and when you've had setbacks, our natural instinct was to try to get you to come back home. But I understand that New York calls to your heart."

I smile softly. "It is my heart. I do plan to live there, and work there, and, I hope, to love there. But," I say, bouncing in my chair, "I have amazing news. I just found out I won a huge contract to paint the models for the *Sporting World* swimsuit issue."

My dad's eyes turn to saucers. "The swimsuit issue?" His voice rises an octave.

My mom swats him. "Try not to get too excited, Joshua."

"I don't even know what the swimsuit issue is," he says, feigning innocence. "It was a question. I was asking her a question."

She rolls her eyes at him, then turns back to me. "So where does this leave you with Theo?"

"I want him back. Are you going to be okay with me being with a guy I hired off GigsForHire to trick you into thinking he was my boyfriend and then we fell for each other for real?"

My mother's lips curve into a smile. "I might be a hard-ass, but I'm a romantic at heart. That actually sounds incredibly, nontraditionally, bizarrely romantic."

And I laugh. "Yes. Yes, it does."

I say good night, and as I leave, I see them both shrug and give each other that *kids today* look. Then they kiss. As soon as I shut the door to my room, I grab my phone and send the guy I hired off GigsForHire a text.

Chapter Forty-two *April*

> **April:** Do you remember the time you threw acorns at the window? We'd just had a fight, and all we wanted to do was stop fighting and make up.

I stare at the text for another minute. My phone is quiet. But for the first time this evening since I heard the word *scam* at the ice cream shop, it doesn't hurt when I breathe. I set down my phone on the covers. I brush my teeth and wash my face. After I finish, I hear a ping. I nearly trip on the carpet, running back to the bed. When I grab my mobile, my smile is the biggest in recorded history.

> **Theo:** I remember it well. Like it's about to happen in an hour or so.

I flash back to what he said last night—just twenty-four hours ago—*I don't like going to bed angry*. I slide under the covers and tap a reply, repeating his words, using them as my own.

> **April:** I don't like going to bed angry.

> **Theo:** I don't like going to bed without you. But I need to put my phone away. See you soon. I promise.

I wait. I read a book. I play with apps on my phone. I rewind the day. But it's well past midnight, and this day has wrung me dry. I'm not sure when I stop holding my phone, but the next thing I know, a plink interrupts a dream that I'm painting a tree like a silver frog. Tugging at the corners of my sleepy mind, the next plink pulls me out of the frog-art tree. I blink, sitting up. I rub the heel of my hand over my eyes; then my gaze lands on the window.

He's there, crouched outside the pane. His hair is a mess, wild and windswept. His eyes shine with happiness. My heart hammers, and I fling off the covers. I shove up the window, and before he can climb in, his hands are on my face, and he's kissing me.

Like he doesn't want to stop. Like he missed me with the same heavy, raw ache inside him. Like it hasn't been merely six hours. He's kissing me as though being without me has been hell. I kiss him back the same way.

I've always been the daring one. The one who takes chances. Right now, every chance I've ever wanted to take, every risk I've been tempted to try points in one direction. Jump in headfirst with Theo. I want this man in my life with a bone-deep certainty. This man who came back to me, climbed a tree, and threw acorns at the window.

We kiss more, soft and hard and greedy and full of a profound need for each other. I know we should talk, but I want to do other things with mouths right now.

Eventually, we stop, and he climbs inside, then shuts the window. We sit on the couch. "There's a snarling leopard outside."

My brow pinches and my brain tries to grab on to what he might mean. Then I remember. "Your bike?"

He nods, looking pleased. "I rode it back from New York. We had to go there to settle the debt. I asked my brother what to do next, and he said, 'Go to her.' I was going to wait to hear from you, but I couldn't wait. I had to come to you."

I can't stop grinning. "I'm glad you couldn't wait. I'm glad you came before you were even called."

"I don't usually fire early," he says with a knowing wink.

I curl my hand around his shoulder. "I'm glad you were already on your way, but please tell me you didn't text and ride."

He laughs. "I had to stop for gas, and that's when I saw your note. It made me so happy."

I breathe a sigh of relief. Then I run my hands through his hair. "I'm so sorry."

"I'm the one who's sorry, April. I'm sorry I didn't say something earlier. I'm sorry I didn't know how to broach it. I'm sorry you ever thought I was scamming you. I'm not," he says, running the backs of his fingers along my cheek. His lips curve into a grin. "But you know, I think you pulled the big con on me."

I wrench back, shooting him a *what are you talking about?* look. "What does that even mean?"

"Do you know what a long con is? Or a big con?"

"Not really."

He takes my hand and draws lazy lines on my palm. "It's a con that unfolds over several days or weeks. You have to lay the foundation. Maybe on a train ride. Then there's a buildup, like late-night, hushed conversations that bring you closer. Often, there's a small payoff along the way—a kiss, a touch, more." He closes his eyes and presses the softest kiss to my forehead. It ignites fireworks inside me. "Then there's a sudden crisis. Something unexpected. Everything moves quickly. People are frantic. Worry sets in that this new love will all go belly-up." My chest pinches, remembering our fight. His eyes stay on me, and he swallows. "Then the mark goes home to get his dough. Time to go all in."

I'm breathless, waiting for the rest of the story. "And?"

"He bets it all on the girl. He doesn't look back. Because he was never conning her. She pulled one over on him, and she didn't even know it. She didn't even have to try. Just by being herself, she got him to fall madly in love with her. That's the big con."

My eyes float closed for a moment, and my skin warms everywhere. This is what it feels like to fall in love. This is what it feels like to break your dating diet in spectacular fashion. No more carrot sticks, no more celery. I dig into a rich, decadent piece of chocolate cake.

When I open my eyes, Theo's still looking at me. I point at him. "So you're my mark, then? And I pulled a fast one on you?"

He smiles and nods. "I'm the mark, and you pulled it off, cupcake. I'm in mad, crazy love with you."

I run my thumb over his top lip. "I'm madly in love with you, too. But you need to know something," I say, taking a breath.

"What?"

"It's not a trick. It's not a con. It's real."

"I know." He scoops me up, drops me on the bed, and strips off his jacket.

I sit up and hold up a hand as a stop sign. There's something else I need to say. "I want you to know I don't care about your past. I'm not afraid of it. I'm not ashamed of it. I admire your drive. I truly do. The only thing that bothered me was whether you were honest with me. If we're doing this for real, I need you to be honest."

He nods, a contrite look in his eyes. "I know. I will. I promise. And I want you to know where I was tonight. I went into the city with Heath. He paid off Addison, and we had a heart-to-heart. He told me I didn't have to take it on for him, but I was worried he'd fall back into old habits. He says he's on the straight and narrow now, and I choose to believe him. And I want you to know that I'm done being a boyfriend-for-hire."

"You are?"

"Duh. I have a girlfriend. That's so not cool to keep it up."

I smile like a crazy person. "What will you do? Just tend bar?"

"It's not a bad living. It's an honest living. I know I'm not as established as you are. But I'll figure something out."

"I always thought you'd sound sexy just reading the phone book. Let's find you a job doing that."

He smiles. "The only thing I know for certain is I don't want to do any of it without you."

"Then don't be without me," I say, reaching forward to tug off his shirt. I tap my chin. "Now, if memory serves, wasn't there some climbing that needed to happen tonight?"

Soon, we're naked under the covers.

I explore his torso, running my hands over his sunburst ink. "Do you remember that time we met and fell in love in just four days?"

His hands find their way to my back, and he runs his fingertips down my spine. "It seemed crazy that we could fall in love so fast."

My entire body longs for him. Gooseflesh climbs up my limbs, and I am bursting with lust and want and desire. "But that's exactly how it all went down. The funny thing is, it was kind of inevitable."

He reaches for my hip, pulls me on top of him. "How so?"

"Everything came true. Don't you think that's bizarre? Even the last part." I recite from his ad. " 'Break up with you and then engage in a huge makeup lovefest involving (a) a ladder, (b) a megaphone, or (c) an announcement during a parade in your hometown. (Note: Public scenes aren't new to me. I know the drill.)' "

"I didn't use a megaphone or announce it during a parade. But I must confess, I did break out a ladder to climb the tree. Turns out it's easier to jump down from a ten-foot-high branch than to jump up into it."

I laugh—then my laughter fades as he slides his hands up my sides, over my ribs, to my breasts.

I draw a sharp breath. He cups my breasts, and I tremble. My breathing turns ragged. "Please," I beg, and he stretches his arm to the side, reaching into the pocket of his jeans.

Quickly, he opens a condom and covers himself.

He positions me over his erection. "Get on me and ride me," he says, his voice husky, smoky. "Do it nice and slow and quiet."

I slide onto him, taking him deep inside me. We both

groan. It feels so good. It feels so right. I drop my lips to his, kissing him so we can swallow all the sounds we want to make.

Then, under the covers, with shadows falling over the bed, I take my time. I roll my hips, moving up and down. I let every second linger. The expression on his face is delicious. His lips are parted; his eyes stay on me. His hands squeeze my ass, and he clutches my flesh as I move.

I lower myself, my breasts brushing against his strong chest, my hands sliding up into his hair. We lose track of time. I bury my face in his neck. I kiss his ear, and he runs his hands down my spine. Every sound I make is tiny, as quiet as can be. At one point, I take him so deep, and stay like that, that he nearly growls. I bite his lip, and he moans into my mouth.

His hands thread into my hair, and he murmurs, "Let me make you come."

I fall onto him, letting him guide me, letting him move me up and down as he makes sure he hits me where I need his touch most. Pressure builds low in my belly. Then it tightens, and tightens, and climbs higher up my thighs. The tension is exquisite, and it centers between my legs, an ache that bursts forward, like an explosion of pleasure. I crash over the edge, falling to pieces. Melting into him. I bring my mouth to his neck, biting and kissing and burying all my sounds in his skin.

In a second, he flips me over to my back, rises up on his knees, and pounds me wildly, hard and deep and fast until he collapses on me with a beautiful groan in my ear. "Amazing," he whispers.

I run my hands down his sweat-slicked back. "Well, you do come with the promise of Satisfaction Guaranteed."

Chapter Forty-three *Theo*

The fifth day

The sun streams through the kitchen window the next morning as I stride up to her father. He's whisking eggs in a skillet.

"Mr. Hamilton," I begin, since I need to set things right with her dad. April told me that her parents know how we began. I want him to know what we've become. "I meant everything I said yesterday morning." He looks up from the pan, waiting for me to continue. "I do care deeply for your daughter. I love her, and her happiness means the world to me. And I will also do everything to bring her back here as often as I can steal her away from the city."

He nods several times as he cooks. "I meant everything I said, too. Look out for her, don't hurt her, and make her happy."

"That's a promise."

He gives a crisp nod, a sign that we're all good for now. I start to leave, but he calls out. "Theo."

"Yes, sir?"

He laughs. "You don't need to call me sir. Mr. Hamilton or Josh is fine."

"I'm not sure I can do Josh, but I'll try for Mr. Hamilton, sir." I laugh, realizing my faux pas.

He laughs, too. "We made a few small tweaks to the final round of the scavenger hunt. There's a new item on your list." He lowers his voice. "I'd appreciate it if you can make sure April finds it."

He reaches into his back pocket with his free hand, gives me the new sheet of paper, and then tells me where the item is hidden. I smile when I see what it is.

"I can do that, sir." I correct myself. "Mr. Hamilton."

"You have time. You'll get there. Oh, and I've been meaning to ask if the rest of your team from last night is still joining you."

That's a good question. I took off so quickly, I never gleaned a clear answer from Heath and Lacey. That might also have been on account of them face-sucking most of the evening.

"You looking for us?"

The question comes from Heath, who strolls into the kitchen freshly shaven and with wet combed hair.

"You made it back last night," I say, stating the obvious.

"Of course I did. Your woman was nice enough to book a room for us at this fantastic inn. I wasn't letting it go to waste. Slept like a baby. Besides, we have a scavenger hunt to win."

I tell Heath and Lacey to wait on the street outside April's parents' empty home. They listen, since they have more face-sucking to do, it seems.

"I can't believe you're seriously trying to sneak off for

more tree house nookie," April says to me as we walk through her backyard toward the lake.

"Trust me, I'd like nothing more. But that's not why we're here."

She snaps her fingers in an *aw shucks* gesture. "We could try," she suggests.

"I've turned you into an addict."

"You have. You should give me my fix."

I gesture to the steps leading onto the dock. "Patience, cupcake."

She steps onto the dock. "Okay. What are we looking for here?"

"Right behind you." I point to the wooden slats on the dock, and she turns around.

"That's odd." She kneels and picks up a small wooden object. A cutout of a cat. But not just any cat. It's a cheetah cutout. She gasps. "Oh my God."

She shows it to me. It's simple, carved quickly overnight by her father. But it gets the point across. Especially the words on the bottom, written out. She reads, " 'We are so proud of you. Congrats on the gig! Love, Mom and Dad.' "

She looks at me, blinks, trying to process this small gift from her parents, a gesture to show they *get* her. But there's one thing I don't quite understand.

"What gig are they talking about? Is it the *Sporting World* one?" I ask, crossing my fingers in hope for her.

"Yes, isn't that crazy?" she says, her voice full of awe. "I found out last night. I forgot to tell you when you returned, since I was so busy kissing you."

"And other things with me," I add.

Her eyes drift to the cheetah again. "I guess my dad made this for me."

I wrap her in a huge hug, picking her up so her feet don't touch the ground. "I knew you'd land the job."

"Thank you for believing in me." Her arms circle around me, and she holds on tight. "I love this cheetah. I love that they did this."

"They wanted me to make sure you found it."

"I don't think I would have without you."

"Pretty sure that's safe to say."

When I set her down, I kiss her again. It's hard not to.

I take her hand and we leave the yard to rejoin my brother, Lacey, and the rest of the crew back at the inn for the end of the events.

It occurs to me as we walk onto the lawn at the Sunnyside that I haven't thought about winning it all since last night. It occurs to me, too, that I don't actually care.

That's a good thing.

Heath hauls a wooden box to the middle of the lawn while I carry a crown made of paper boats. I set the crown on a picnic table as my brother positions the box at the edge of the lawn.

"How's this look?" Heath calls out.

April's dad gives a big thumbs-up. "Nice work, Heath," he says, then turns to the beefy triplets to ask for their help in rearranging the chairs.

He's enlisting everyone now, not just calling on me. I didn't mind helping, but I'm glad he's no longer testing me. I have a feeling I've passed his test, and I'm so damn grateful.

Heath joins me and drapes an arm around me. "Family is crazy."

I nod, laughing. "Sure is."

"But I kind of like it."

"Yeah, I kind of like it a lot."

A few minutes later, April's mom marches to the wooden box, Carol by her side.

Carol brings the megaphone to her mouth. "Ladies and gentlemen of the Quadrennial Hamilton and Moore Summer Lawn Olympics and Games. The moment you've all been waiting for is here. You've played valiantly. You've competed intrepidly. And most of all, you've had a blazing good time. Right?"

Arms rise in the air. Voices whoop. Kids shimmy. And April winks at me, mouthing *the best time*.

"And it is with great honor and pride that this year I pass the statue from my family to my good friend Pamela's," Carol says, reaching to the grass for the team trophy and handing it to April's mom. "Oh, wait. I'm sorry. Did you think your husband might want to pet it instead?" she deadpans, and Pamela laughs, clutching the trophy.

"That's what he'll do with it. Maybe even sleep with it under his covers until next year," Pamela says.

I raise an eyebrow at April. "Is this yearly?"

"It used to be every four years. Looks like we have some eager beavers."

Out of the corner of my eye, I notice April's dad standing on the grass a few feet away, squinting as the sun shines overhead, bouncing on his toes. The dude is eager to claim his prize. "Go get it, Mr. Hamilton," I say. "You've earned it."

He meets my gaze. "Theo?"

"Yeah?"

"Thanks for taking care of my daughter."

"Anytime."

As he strides to his wife, an odd sensation courses through me. One that I can't quite name at first. Then it settles into my chest, as I realize it's belonging. Like I'm part of this crazy group of family and friends.

It's a damn good feeling to belong.

April's dad holds the trophy high over his head and says,

"This means so much to me only because it means you're all here. With all of us. And that's all I want."

He takes a few steps away from the wooden box-turned-podium, stops, and says, "Oh, should I announce the individual winner?"

"Yes!"

The shouts come from Emma and Libby, and Huey, Louie, and Dewey. For a brief moment, a flicker of hope ignites in me. Maybe I'll win.

But ten seconds later, Josh's voice booms. "And thanks to amazing work in Junk in the Trunk, lawn bowling, and watermelon eating, I hereby pronounce Emma the victor."

The teen shrieks and dances for joy.

That flicker of hope in me morphs into happiness for her as I watch the sixteen-year-old dance a victory jig. Josh and Carol place the paper boat crown on her head. Everyone cheers for her, including April, Heath, Lacey, and Dean.

As I watch April's prom date clap, an idea occurs to me. I excuse myself, swallow my pride, and head over to Dean.

"Hey, man. I was hoping I could chat with you about something."

"Sure, have at it," he says with a cheery smile.

We walk away from the crowd as I say, "You mentioned a talking toaster that needed to go deeper, and that got me to thinking. . . ."

Chapter Forty-four *April*

Saying goodbye is harder than I expect.

Maybe I do like being home.

Maybe a part of me will always be in Wistful. That evening I hug everyone a million times, it seems, before Aunt Jeanie pulls me aside on the back deck.

She takes a deep breath, as though she's about to say something big. "I was a little pushy when I first saw you the other morning. Pushy about Linus, and I'm sorry about that."

"Aunt Jeanie, it's totally fine. Don't even think twice."

She raises a hand to silence me. "But I have thought twice about it, and about a lot of other things, too. And I hope this isn't too pushy either, but it might be fun for me to come into the city, maybe take you out to lunch, go to a museum, see more of what you do."

I blink. I wasn't expecting that. But then, maybe this offer does jibe with Katie's observation the other evening that Aunt Jeanie wants a little more excitement now and then. More than her chicken ladies are giving her on the egg farm. And if she's not getting the action yet in a grandkid either, perhaps she'll take it by venturing into the strange metropolis of *the city*.

That more than works for me.

"I would love to be your host," I say.

"It's a date, then."

As we make our way to the snarling leopard so Theo can drive me to the train station—hello, I'm not riding two hours on the back of a bike—Tess throws her arms around me one more time.

"I'll miss you," she says softly.

"Oh, stop it. You have no time for missing."

"I will absolutely miss you," she says, her tone serious.

"Hey, are you okay?" I ask, pulling apart to roam my eyes over her. "Also, where's your koala baby? Is she in your pouch?"

"Cory and I are going to counseling," she blurts out.

My jaw drops. "What?"

She nods, her expression both sad and hopeful at the same time.

"But I thought," I begin, furrowing my brow. "I thought things were better after the car."

"They were. They are," Tess says reassuringly. "That's why we're going. To keep them that way. We've both been so overwhelmed with the kids, but especially me. And it wasn't until we sneaked away for an hour that we realized we were drifting apart. We need more than one hour now and then to make things better. So, Mom is going to watch the kids while we go to counseling on a regular basis."

"This is a good thing?" I ask, just to make sure.

She nods and smiles. "It's a good thing. It'll take work for us to find that spark again. We found it that night in the car, and now we want to make sure we don't lose it again."

A lump rises in my throat. "I love you."

"I love you, and I'm still annoyed that you turned out to be so awesome, since I'm stuck being the middle child and you're the cool baby of the family."

I laugh. "I am pretty cool."

Epilogue

One year later

"We're going to be late," I call out to April, who's stuffing a bikini in her black suitcase.

"We'll catch the next train," she says, as carefree as she's always been about travel.

I shake my head. "No. We're catching *this* train."

"I've barely been home. I've hardly had any time to breathe." She recently returned from an assignment in Los Angeles, working on a movie, painting space creatures gold.

"You can breathe in Connecticut," I say, since we're on our way to Wistful for the weekend. I promised her parents I'd take her there as much as I could, and I've honored that commitment. I kneel down to help her zip her suitcase.

We've been back to see her parents more than a half dozen times since the reunion. There was Thanksgiving, Christmas, a few long weekends, and my birthday. Heath and Lacey met us there for that occasion, and Lacey gave

April's mom a hostess gift—a new necklace she made herself. April's mom even wore it the next time I saw her. On that visit, Cory wore a T-shirt I gave him for Christmas—it had the word FOR above an illustration of a fox, above the word SAKE. I'd picked it up at the hipster T-shirt shop in Brooklyn, and that was all it took for him to think it was the height of cool. Fortunately, Cory doesn't seem so enamored of my single life anymore, and that's not only because I have a girlfriend. It's also because he and Tess are happier now.

April and I live together, since I moved out of the tiny studio in Brooklyn and into her bigger pad. We split all the bills. Yes, my girlfriend does quite well for herself, and the *Sporting World* swimsuit edition was such a hit that she was invited back for the next one. But I'm not doing too badly myself. I still tend bar, since you just never know when the work will come in as an actor.

That's the funny thing. I wasn't an actor, but now I am. That recent network commercial featuring a new pickup truck that speaks in a Southern drawl? That was me. The box of Tiger Puffs breakfast cereal with a talking tiger that roars? Yours truly. I also have picked up a voice-over gig as a recurring character on a late-night naughty cartoon about a superhero who delivers orgasms to women deeply in need. That's a fine show. My character is a talking vibrator. Look, all things considered, there are worse gigs than giving voice to a pleasure device for the ladies.

A lot worse things.

Dean helped me break into the voice-over business, since his agency cast me in my first commercial doing a French accent for a French roast coffee brand. But it was April who deserves the credit for planting the seed. Little did she know that her comment about me reading the phone book was the flame that lit the match. I suppose I've had a special talent all along, right in plain sight. I just needed someone to hear it, and to give me a nudge. I don't miss the boyfriend-for-hire gig. Being her real boyfriend pays much better, and I don't mean money.

As for April's fee for my services, she tried to pay me again. She tried many, many times. I refused every single time. She said she was never going to use the money, and she dug her little heels in. Until I figured out how to get her to stop asking. I took the fee and donated it to the arts program where she volunteers, the one she said she'd donate to if she won the all-around at the reunion.

When she found out, she wrapped her arms around me, smothered me in kisses, and said, "I knew you weren't a doucheberry."

But I will be if we miss the train, so I scurry her out of our apartment, down to the waiting Lyft, and off to the train station. We rush through the terminal and make our way to the train. She heads onto the first car she sees, a coach cabin.

I tsk her. "First class, cupcake."

She arches a brow. "La-di-da."

I take her hand, and we head to our cabin, where we're seated in cushy, luxurious seats. "You are the best talking vibrator I've ever known," she says as she settles in, then gives me a kiss. As the train chugs out of the station, she inches closer to me, turning her head so our eyes meet. "Remember our first train ride?"

"I remember every detail. And I remember everything you told me then, too."

She lifts an eyebrow in question.

A few minutes later, we go to the dining cabin, and we're the only ones there. We sit down at a table with a linen tablecloth and champagne flutes already filled.

She gives me a curious look.

"Train travel is so romantic, don't you think?"

She laughs. "You said it wasn't at all!"

I shrug as I hand her a glass of champagne. "I don't recall that."

"You mocked me for wanting caviar."

"Well, I do stand by that. Caviar is revolting. But champagne is not. Let's toast."

She raises her glass. "What are we toasting to?"

"To train rides being romantic."

She clinks her glass to mine. "I can drink to that."

She takes a sip of her bubbly, and I do the same. When I set down the flute, I reach into my pocket and grab my phone, sliding my thumb across the screen.

She raises an eyebrow, asking what the hell I'm doing interrupting a moment with a mobile phone.

"I saw something earlier I think you'll get a kick out of," I say, hitting Send on an email draft.

"And you're showing me now?"

"Open your email."

She shrugs and heaves a *this better be good* sigh as she grabs her phone. "It's a GigsForHire link," she says, raising her face.

"Huh. How interesting."

Her brow furrows. "Are you looking for a hamster wheel?"

"Open it."

She clicks on the link, then says softly, "It's an ad."

I watch the reaction in her green eyes as she reads the screen.

☆ Going Anywhere and Need a Permadate?
   I'm Your Man

I'm a good-looking, 29-year-old ex-con-turned-actor. My most valuable possession looks best when you ride it with me, your arms wrapped around my waist on the snarling leopard. As a talking vibrator, I work odd hours, but so do you. If you'd like to have me as your date for a wedding, reunion, party, dinner, airplane flight, work soirée, or even the gym, I'm game. In fact, if you'd like to have me as your date for pretty much everything, just say yes.

I can do the following things at your request:

1. Share amusing stories that make you laugh, like the one about the trip we'll take to the California gold country town, where I'll tell you spooky ghost stories that make you jump into my arms.

2. Build a tree house or a home for you.

3. Adopt an emu together if you want. We can name him Bart, but only if we call him by his full name— Bart the Emu.

4. Be by your side through life's ups and downs.

5. Hula-Hoop. Yes, that's a euphemism.

6. Play foosball, arcade games, and go bowling with you since we've established I regularly beat you at those games, but I'll let you win since you're so adorably pretty, sexy, and beautiful when you get excited about a game.

7. Make sure you visit your family often, even if it
    involves lifting dozens of chairs, sleeping in a tent, or
    lugging charcoal, since they love you so much, and I
    love them now, too.

8. Love you for the rest of my life.

If any of these skills meet your needs, please respond and
book me for the lifelong event. A wide range of accents
remains available. My services are strictly non-platonic, and
ideally I hope you'll exercise the horizontal option nightly.
There is no fee, except if you choose to opt for all menu
items, please give your yes in the form of a kiss. If you're
completely happy with my work, let's prepare for a black-tie
and white-dress affair on the weekend of your choosing in
the near future. I come with a 100% Satisfaction Guaranteed
commitment to making our life together amazing.

When she looks up, I'm already down on one knee.

"Theo," she whispers in wonder.

I take her hand in mine and ignore the wild stampede
of nerves galloping through me. "Do you remember the
time I asked you to marry me?"

She gasps and makes a surprised coughing sound.
"Yes," she blurts out. "I said yes."

Her enthusiasm is another reason why I love her so
much. I take the diamond solitaire from the box in my
pocket, flip it open, and say, "Will you marry me?"

She laughs, tugs me up so I'm sitting next to her, and
says, "My answer is still yes. Always yes. Only yes. You're
the real deal for me. You always have been. You always
will be."

I slide the ring on her finger. "It's beautiful," she says.

"So are you. Inside and out. Thank you for loving me even when I was a guy with a past. I'm still that guy, but I'm a better man now because you're in my present."

A tear slips down her cheek, and she presses her forehead to mine. "And your future. Don't forget that."

"I would never." I tuck a strand of hair behind her ear. "Oh, and that's the last thing from the original à la carte list that came true. 'Propose to you in front of everyone.' I modified it a little. I proposed in front of you."

"And that's how I wanted you to do it."

Then I slide into my best after-dark voice, the one that really gets her going. "But I believe you had another train fantasy, cupcake."

Her lips curve into a naughty grin. "I did. Is that one coming true, too?"

"Have I told you why we had to catch *this* train? It was only recently added to the train schedule, and it has something no other trains have that run in this area."

She shakes her head. "No, you haven't."

I lean closer to her, brush her hair off her shoulder, and whisper in her ear. "It has a sleeper car."

And we make excellent use of it the rest of the way to Wistful.

Acknowledgments

Thank you to Eileen for making this incredible opportunity possible, for giving me the chance to let the story shine, and the insight to make it better. I am grateful to the whole team at SMP, including Jennifer for her eagerness in bringing me on board, and Tiffany for managing the process. Deep gratitude to KP Simmon for all her strategy and guidance, to Helen Williams for her fine talent every day, and to Kelley, Keyanna, and Candi for their daily work. Thank you to Lynn for eagle eyes. Most of all, thanks to Michelle Wolfson, the wizard behind the curtain and the woman who understands the care and feeding of an author, and who always has my best interests at heart.

Amazingly, my family still manages to put up with me every day and I am grateful for their love and support, both from the two-legged and the four-legged ones.

Always and with every book, my deepest gratitude goes to those who make this possible—to my readers. I love you madly.